DRINK WE DEEP

Arthur Leo Zagat

Alias the Night Wind

BY VARICK VANARDY

*The Blue Fire Pearl: The Complete Adventures
of Singapore Sammy, Volume 1*

BY GEORGE F. WORTS

Clovelly

BY MAX BRAND

The Gun-Brand

BY JAMES B. HENDRYX

Jan of the Jungle

BY OTIS ADELBERT KLINE

Minions of the Moon

BY WILLIAM GREY BEYER

The Moon Pool & The Conquest of the Moon Pool

BY ABRAHAM MERRITT

Tarzan and the Jewels of Opar

BY EDGAR RICE BURROUGHS

*War Lord of Many Swordsmen:
The Adventures of Norcross, Volume 1*

BY W. WIRT

DRINK WE DEEP

ARTHUR LEO ZAGAT

INTRODUCTION BY

WILL MURRAY

COVER BY

EMMETT WATSON

ILLUSTRATIONS BY

VIRGIL FINLAY AND SAMUEL CAHAN

ALTUS PRESS

2017

EDITED AND DESIGNED BY
Matthew Moring

PUBLISHING HISTORY
"Drink We Deep" originally appeared in the July 31, August 7, 14, 21, & 28, and
    Septmeber 4, 1937 issues of *Argosy* magazine (Vol. 274, No. 6–Vol. 275, No. 5).
    Copyright © 1937 by The Frank A. Munsey Company and assigned to Steeger
    Properties, LLC. All rights reserved.
Cover and additional illustrations originally appeared in the January 1951 issue of
    Fantastic Novels magazine (Vol. 4, No. 5). Copyright © 1951 by Popular
    Publications, Inc., and assigned to Steeger Properties, LLC. All rights reserved.

THANKS TO
Will Murray and Rob Preston

ISBN
978-1-61827-302-4

Visit *altuspress.com* for more books like this.
Printed in the United States of America.

TABLE OF CONTENTS

INTRODUCTION

LIKE FELLOW WRITER Erle Stanley Gardner, Arthur
Leo Zagat (1895–1949), was a lawyer who forsook his profession in favor of the uncertain life of a pulp magazine writer.

A veteran of the First World War who attended City College
of New York and Bordeaux University, Zagat graduated from
Fordham University Law School in 1929 with the intent of
practicing law. But it was the beginning of the Great Depression, and so he turned instead to writing with his fellow lawyer,
Nathaniel Schachner.

Their first collaboration, "The Tower of Evil," appeared in
Wonder Stories Quarterly, Summer 1930. Ten others followed,
all appearing in the top Science Fiction titles of the era, *Amazing
Stores, Wonder Stories* and *Astounding Stories of Super-Science.*
They also sold to *Weird Tales.* In 1934, Zagat struck out on his
own, branching out to write for Popular Publications magazines,
where he made a name for himself writing detective stories and
contributing to Popular's trio of weird menace magazines, *Dime
Mystery Stories, Horror Stories* and *Terror Tales.* Thus he became
known as "The Horror Story Man." He was also prolific in
Detective Tales, Ace G-Man and *Strange Detective Mysteries.*

When he had more than one story in a magazine, Zagat used
the pseudonym of Grendon Alzee—the last name a play on
his initials. He was James F. Henderson in horror titles produced
by Martin Goodman's Red Circle line, as well as Popular Publications. For Culture Publications' sole entry in the weird

menace sub-genre, *Spicy Mystery Stories,* Zagat passed as as Morgan Lafay. He is said to have written as Anton York, which was the name of the hero of Eando Binder's famous story about an immortal. Curiously, Arthur Leo Zagat was known to some of his colleagues as Leo, but to intimates as "Bob."

Few series emerged from his typewriter over a 20-year writing career comprising an estimated 500 published stories. His longest and most famous, Doc Turner of Morris Street, ran for nearly a decade in the back pages of *The Spider.* It was one of the most popular backup series in any similar pulp magazine. Featuring the ministrations of kindly old Bronx pharmacist Andrew "Doc" Turner, it was inspired by Zagat's period of working at his father's pharmacy while attending Fordham. Mendel Zagat had been president of the Bronx Pharmaceutical Association. Nearly 70 Doc Turner short stories were published between 1934 and 1942.

The counterspy Red Finger had a much shorter run in the back pages of *Secret Service Operator #5.* The character was the closest to a pulp superhero that Zagat ever produced. Zagat's series starring Steven "Tiger" Carlin appeared in Street & Smith's *Detective Story Magazine* in the early 1940s. Carlin was assisted by an elderly neighborhood druggist, Richard Frost.

Reflecting on the pros and cons of authoring a popular pulp series in his 1943 *Writer's Year Book* article, "To Writers With Love," Zagat confessed:

> … the series character, or the series bound together by some other device, is an eminently desirable class of merchandise for any writer to have on his shelves. Once established, it has an easy market. Occasional lapses from the author's best style and plot are not nearly as damning, since the momentum of previous narratives in the series will carry editor's and readers' through an occasional semi-dud. So much of each story is already set before one comes to write it that the tune and thought and labor required to plan the rest are considerably reduced.

There are flaws, however, in the series picture. One may grow careless, familiarity breeding contempt, and thus both kill the series itself and damage one's reputation, one's good will. One may find a series, or a number of them, so easy to write and so profitable that he confines his writing almost wholly to them and thus both lose his ability for fresh creation and sacrifices growth and improvement, becomes caught in a rut that leads sooner or later to frustration.

Or one may find oneself Frankenstein to a monster of one's own creation, doomed forever to write tale after tale about a single character who once dearly beloved, becomes at length anathema.

One wonders if Doc Turner failed to appear in *The Spider's* final year because readers tired of the kindly old dentist—or the beleaguered author had finally exhausted his endurance.

Arthur Leo Zagat was best known for his memorable fantasy serials written for *Argosy,* among them, *Drink We Deep, Seven Out of Time* and the *Tomorrow* stories featuring a teenaged Tarzan named Dikar battling for freedom in a future Japanese-occupied America. Zagat also appeared in *Blue Book.*

The author once frankly admitted to living a relatively color-less life, where he hinted at the origins of *Drink We Deep:*

I have often read with envy the biographical sketches of my fellow writers as they appear in the magazines, of far adventures, of exciting lives, but the envy has been for the adventures themselves, not for the story material which they have supplied their participants. I have had no adventures in far lands. I have worked in a drugstore. I have sold insurance from door to door. I have ridden in the subway and walked the city streets with eyes and ears open. I have read Mother Goose....

"There was an old woman who had three sons, Jerry and James and John. Jerry was hung, James was drowned, John was lost and never found..." and that was where "The Third Son" came from. An American Legion dance became the background for "Taps At Eleven," a school bus on a country road suggested "You Can Only Hang Once." My daughter's summer camp gave me the setting and the inspiration for "Drink Me Deep"; fog on a Long Island beach started me off on "Cops Are Blind In The Fog...."

Drink We Deep originally ran in *Argosy*, in six installments, beginning with the July 31, 1937 issue. It was later reprinted in *Fantastic Novels*, but has been out of print since that 1951 appearance. Undeservingly so. Reminiscent of fantasist A. Merritt's best works, *Drink We Deep* is the uncanny narrative of archeologist and paleontologist Hugh Lambert, and his eerie encounters with mysterious subterranean dwellers in rural upstate New York. The editorial blurb heading *Drink We Deep's Fantastic Novels* reappearance sets the stage:

> Beneath the timeless rocks of the Heiderberg's—slumbering below Lake Wankooka's unfathomed waters—lies the seed of Earth conflict. For their lives the strange and troubled race of other worldlings, waiting, always waiting, for the hour of deliverance.... And on the earth's surface, one man feels in his blood an irresistible summons that calls him to their side...."

Inasmuch as A. Merritt was a slow producer of fiction and Argosy readers constantly clamored for more Merritt, we can safely assume that Munsey editor John L. Byrne commissioned this explicitly Merritt-esque fantasy to satiate that unquenchable thirst. With this novel and *Seven Out of Time*, Zagat arguably produced his most superior work, and demonstrated that he could write on a level above common pulp.

During World War II, Zagat served as Chairman of the Pulp Writers' Section of the Authors' Guild, a branch of the Authors' League of America, where his legal background proved invaluable. Zagat left to join the Office of War Information, dividing his time between his New York apartment and his desk in Washington, while continuing to turn out stories.

One of Zagat's last substantial works, *Slaves of the Lamp*, was written during this period and revised by Theodore Sturgeon for publication in *Astounding Science Fiction* in 1946. Time may have been passing the author by—at least insofar as standards for fantasy and science fiction storytelling were evolving during the World War II era.

A lifelong resident of the Bronx, Arthur Leo Zagat died of a heart attack on April 3 1949, at the age of 53. Later that year, his most acclaimed work, *Seven Out of Time,* was reprinted in a hardcover edition. New short stories continued to pop up in pulp magazines until 1951—a tribute to his prolific popularity.

Of himself, Zagat once wrote: "I do not think of myself as an artist. I am a tradesman, a merchant of tales. It is the way I make my living, and I behave towards it as any man behaves towards his means of livelihood."

FOREWORD

Circumstances, the nature of which I am not at liberty to disclose, have recently released me from a promise to keep the following curious documents secret until the death of certain individuals named therein.

I nevertheless give them to the world with a great deal of hesitation since their publication will be certain to cast upon their authors doubt of their veracity, or their sanity. With this in mind, I have endeavored to substantiate the narratives, in so far as possible, by affidavits of disinterested witnesses, which I transmit herewith.

Unfortunately the greater part of the report of Hugh Lambert cannot *ipso facto* be thus supported, and I can only rest his case for credence on his reputation as a paleontologist and archaeologist of eminence, and on my own simple statement that I believe utterly and absolutely in the truth of his statements.

A.L.Z.

PROLOGUE

I

Extract from the diary of Ann Doring, screen actress:
August 15, 1934

IT IS REALLY the morning of the sixteenth, but this is the first chance I have had to get my diary up to date. Though it's going to take simply hours to write down everything, I'm going to do it, because I don't want to forget the least little bit of what has happened.

Was yesterday a day!

It began, calmly enough, with my driving alone from New York to visit Dick at Camp Wanooka, high in the Helderbergs. It ended with me in a doctor's waiting room, somewhere in the outskirts of Albany, biting my nails and wondering whether the man I love would live through the night.

The man I love. It still seems queer to write that. Yesterday afternoon Hugh Lambert was only a name to me, and not an important one at that. By midnight I knew that if he died, life would have no meaning for me any more.

It was Dick's fault in the first place. That kid brother of mine wasn't satisfied with my paying a thousand dollars for his summer at the ritziest boys camp in the East; he insisted on my coming up here for him to show me off. The brat knew how to wangle me into it, too. About his second or third letter he started raving about the camp director. This Hugh Lambert had everything. Looks. Strength. Personality. Not only had he

2

been all-American halfback in '26, but he'd explored half the blank spaces on the map since graduating from Dartmouth. He was managing the camp this summer only to get funds for another expedition to Cambodia or Patagonia or some place like that.

The camp, Dick wrote, was overrun every week end with the year's most glamorous debs, but Lambert didn't give any sign he knew they existed, though he was the cause of their sudden access of sisterly and cousinly affection.

Leave it to these sophisticated youngsters to get on to that. And they did more than gossip about it. When Dick learned I was making a flying trip to New York between pictures he wired me that he was on the long end of a bet Lambert would break down before the end of the summer, and that he had as good as lost. He begged me as a pal to rush up and save him from going about in rags and tatters all winter.

Now I ask you.

Well, I got to camp just about supper-time. I found Dick brown as a berry, and grown till he was half a head taller than I. I don't think I would have known him if he hadn't pounced on me, yelling like a Comanche.

After the family greeting was over, the young nut didn't even give me a chance to fix up my face but dragged me into the mess hall and right up to the head table where that paragon of his was waiting for the kids to settle down.

I'll swear Hugh Lambert never knew whether the boys ever did get to their places. He took one look at me and he was sunk. Maybe I didn't think that was a compliment, too. Not because of the brother's build-up, either.

That chap knows his women, or I don't know my men. He hasn't got that cleft in his chin, and that slow, crinkly smile around his grey quiet eyes for nothing. I knew, right away, that the reason he hadn't fallen for the society girls was because they just didn't stack up against the other women in his life, the exotic ones on the other side of nowhere.

I was rather in a daze myself, which was something new for me. The tops among the Hollywood glamour boys have made a play for me without raising my blood pressure two points but Hugh Lambert is different.

He's big. I don't mean physically, though he's that, too—wide-shouldered and narrow-waisted; his skin a slinky bronze sheath for flat, slithery muscles. But there's the bigness of all outdoors in him, and a deep, deep strength that comes from matching oneself against savage nature and overcoming it.

Against savage men, too. His blunt chin and one bony cheek are creased by a white scar, Dick tells me was made by a Galla *assegai*.

WELL, IT was Ann and Hugh right away, as if we'd known each other forever, but what we said didn't mean anything, because there were others at the table. The head councillor, Ed Hard; a couple of other men whose names I didn't catch; and the freckle faced, pug-nosed camp nurse, Edith Horne.

After supper Hugh excused himself. Dick begged me to go

to some kind of entertainment in the recreation hall, but I made him carry my bags to my room in the guest house, where he chattered till I chased him out so I could wash up and change to that blue knitted sport suit I had Schiaparelli send over on the *Normandie*. I had a date, you see, to meet Hugh down by the lake after the kids were tucked away for the night.

He was there before me. A bugle sobbed taps behind us, and then the quiet settled around us. Not silence. There was the lapping of the water at our feet, the trees whispering to a gentle breeze, the almost rhythmic shrill of a million crickets, but it was all hushed and dreamy, and somehow melancholy.

Lake Wanooka lies deep in a cup of high, wooded hills whose dark bulk shut it in last night, so that although Albany is only an hour away, civilization seemed as distant as the stars that dusted the soft glow of the sky.

The moon was a great golden half-globe, hammocked in a black fold on the mountains crest. The shimmering silver film spread over the quiet waters was like limpid music magically visible, and all that nostalgic beauty was just for the two of us. There was no one else in the world.

Hugh's voice, when at last he spoke, was a deep, throaty murmur. "They've waited for us since the beginning of Time, the Old Mountains and the ancient lake!"

"The Old Mountains. The Helderbergs." Some imp of the perverse made me matter-of-fact. "Why did the Dutch call them that?"

"Because they are old, the oldest mountains in America next to the Laurentides."

"And the lake?"

"The lake is almost as ancient. It has neither inlet nor outlet, and its bottom has never been plumbed. The geologists say that as the Great Glacier melted, its waters filled an immensely deep valley here. Fifty thousand years ago, that was."

"Fifty thousand years," I repeated, feeling creepy and insignificant as I matched that against the sixty or seventy years I might expect to exist.

"It's a long time Lake Wanooka has been waiting for us to come together on her shore." Hugh's arm crept around my waist. "Five hundred centuries, Ann dear."

He was a fast worker, I thought. Too fast. I'd better put the brakes on.

"Who lived here before the ice melted," I said, laughing. "The Eskimos?"

"No one," he answered. "No human existed in this region until long after the Ice Age." *

Just then the echo of my laugh came back from across the glimmering lake. It must have been an echo, but I had an eerie feeling that it was the mountain itself that laughed.

Hugh must have noticed the little shudder that ran through

---

* Editor's note: Mr. Lambert's statement agrees with the findings published in *Bulletin 33*, Smithsonian Institute, Bureau of Ethnology, q.v. But cf. *Races of Man*, J. Deniker, pp, 510, 511, where are mentioned certain eoliths and early paleoliths as dating back before the end of the Pleistocene.

me, because he shrugged me closer to him and asked, very tenderly, "Cold, Ann?"

"Not any more," I managed, my heart beating against my ribs wildly. "Not…"

His body was suddenly rigid against mine, and I knew he wasn't listening to me. He was staring at the lake, his brow furrowing.

"What—" I gasped. "What's the matter?"

"It's there again." Hugh wasn't answering me; he was thinking aloud. "Queer. Damn queer."

I followed the direction of his eyes. About a hundred feet from the lake's far end there was a disk of greater luminosity on the water; for all the world as if a searchlight were shining up through it from far below. Within the circumference of that pale glow, the surface was strangely smooth, glistening like silk stretched tight over an embroidery hoop.

"It is queer," I whispered, not knowing why I whispered. "I never saw anything like it before."

Just then a tiny black spot marred the silver shimmer, not *in* but right next to the strange radiance. From where it had been (it was gone at once) something darted toward the shore, an invisible something one was aware of only by the long narrow triangle of its wake creasing the water.

Hugh gulped, swallowed.

I whispered. "What makes that light?"

"I don't know," he said slowly. He shook himself; and then he was looking down at me, and his tender smile was crinkling the corners of his eyes, making me warm again, warm all over.

"What does it matter what it is? We're together, and—"

A twig snapped in the woods behind us! Hugh whirled around to stare into the shadows where the moonlight was shut out by the thick foliage. I was terribly frightened. Then I wasn't frightened any more but mad. I'd heard a boyish giggle in there, and the hiss of a whisper, quickly hushed.

"Some of those darn kids, prowling around," Hugh growled. "If I get hold of them…."

"Oh, what's the difference?" My hand on his arm kept him from diving into the brush, as he was about to do. "Let them have their fun. Come on, we'll go for a ride in my car." I had to stop him. I didn't want him to catch Dickie, though my brother'd hear plenty from me tomorrow.

Of course it was Dick—I'd know that giggle anywhere—and probably the kid with whom he had bet. The merry brats had been spying on us to see who'd win.

"Fine." Hugh responded to my suggestion. "Come on."

Then he had my arm and we were running up the long campus hill to the little plateau where the camp buildings clustered.

AS WE were getting near the gate where I had parked my roadster, I asked him a question, the reply to which still has me wondering.

"Why should a fish breaking water and swimming towards shore startle you, Hugh?"

"It shouldn't," he replied. "Except that there *are* no fish in Lake Wanooka."

Hugh insisted on driving. I got in alongside him and we started off. The little clearing around the camp entrance was bright under the moon, but when we had crossed that the road dived into the woods, and we were in darkness.

I heard Hugh's hand fumble at the dashboard, and a click. The headlights didn't come on.

"Oh," I exclaimed. "The bulbs both went last night. I meant to buy new ones on the way up here but I forgot. Now we won't be able to have our ride." I was almost crying with disappointment.

He must have noticed that, for he said, "Yes, we will. I know this trail so well I can drive it blindfolded, and when we get to the main highway we'll get some bulbs."

The road was so narrow the tree boughs met overhead and

the underbrush scraped along both sides of the car. After it got around the spur of the hill it pitched steeply downward. I realized how confidently Hugh drove, and then I was rather glad it was so dark. It brought back that feeling of there being just the two of us, and no one and nothing else in all the world.

After a while the road was smoother. Hugh started going faster. I saw, just ahead, the paleness of the concrete highway. It came swiftly toward us—and was blotched out by the black shape of a man who lurched out of the brush right in front of the roadster.

There was a deep ditch on our left, a telegraph pole on our right. Hugh shouted. His right arm shoved me down in the seat as his left twisted the wheel. There was an awful crash, the smash of splintering glass, a scream. I just had time to think, "We've hit the pole; but we've hit the man too," when the roadster careened over, flinging me out of it.

Half stunned, I shoved my hands against dirt, pushing myself up. I saw Hugh lying terribly still in the road. I saw his leg plainly in the moonlight. A dark pool was spreading around it, and a stream was feeding that pool, a stream of blood that spurted from his leg, where glass from the windshield had gashed it!*

II

Letter from Jethro Parker, farmer

Dear Mr. Zagat:
I have just come home from the Grange meeting and Martha had told me you'd been here and she promised you I would write down what happened the night of August 15th two years ago. I would rather plow fifty acres than do this

---

* Editor's note: In dealing with this material I shall take no liberties with the actual text but will cut and arrange it so as to present its narrative in a coherent, chronological order. In pursuance of this policy I here omit the balance of Miss Doring's entry and present the following letter.—A.L.Z.

chore, but Martha will not leave me send back the ten ($10) you left to pay me for my trouble so I guess I will have to.

Nurse Horne from Camp Wanooka was here that night to massage Martha's leg for the rheumatics and we were in the kitchen having a snack when all of a sudden there was a thundering big crash from way up the road. Miss Horne and I jumped up and ran across my corn lot to where the noise came from.

We got near where the camp road comes out on the high-way and I saw a car on its side, crumpled up against the tele-graph pole that's there. I heard a kind of moan and then I saw a girl in the dirt.

She was on her knees and she was holding on to a man's leg with both hands. Blood, was spraying up between her fingers like it was a busted water pipe she was holding on to. I could not figure out to this day how she had the gumption to do that, specially shaken up as she was and maybe bad hurt for all she knew.

Well, Miss Horne got right down on her knees alongside the girl and first thing I knew she was tearing a piece from her dress and tied it around the man's leg.

I helped the girl stand up and I see that she is not hurt bad. Her dress is all torn and bloody; but she was the prettiest female I ever saw.

"Get a car," she said. "Quick. We've got to get them to a hospital."

I had not seen no one else. "Them?" I asks, puzzled like.

She pointed into the dark farther back. I made out what I thought was a big bundle of rags. It heaved a little and I saw it was a tramp lying there. Except for his arm moving just a little bit I would have thought he was dead, the rest of him was so still.

"Hurry, Jethro," Nurse Borne said.

I ran back through the corn lot to my barn, cranked up my flivver and drove back to the crossroads. When I got there the girl was helping the man with the hurt leg to sit up, and I saw it was Mr. Lambert from Camp Wanooka. Miss Horne was busy over the tramp. I could not see what she was doing because the thick trees made it so dark back there.

Well, sir, between the three of us we made out to get both the hurt men in the back of the flivver. The nurse got in back with them and the other girl got in alongside of me and I started off down the mountain.

I heard Mr. Lambert say, "Where are we going?" and I heard Miss Horne answer him, "To the Albany Hospital."

Mr. Lambert said, "If you take me there they will keep me for weeks and I must get back to camp. How about Doc Stone? You used to work for him. Don't you think he can take care of us at his house?"

"I guess so," Nurse Horne answered. "He has all the equipment and it is lots nearer too. Jethro, it is the big white house on New Scotland Road just before you get to the city line."

"I know," I said. "I used to take my neighbor Elijah Fenton there to have his neck dressed before he got drowned in Lake Wanooka last winter."

"Please go faster," the girl beside me said. "Oh please. He must not die."

I was already going like a drunken bat so I looked around at her and I saw her mouth was blue and trembling. I was scared she was going to have hysterics so I started to talk to her to get her mind off her excitement.

"Elijah was drowned," I said, "the time the ice broke on Lake Wanooka and two score of the Four Corners Church moonlight skating party went through it. It is so deep there we did not get back any of the bodies, but every time I see Jeremiah Fenton I get cold all over. Jeremiah is Elijah's twin and like as two peas from the same pod. When he came walking in to memorial services there was three women fainted. I—"

"Stop!" she screamed. "Oh, stop it!" Now ain't females funny? I never could make them out.

Well, Mr. Zagat, Martha's been reading this over my shoulder and she says that this is all you want me to tell about, so I will stop. Hoping this is satisfactory, I am,

Yours truly,

Jethro Parker.

P.S. There is something been bothering me ever since that night, but I don't know just how to write it down. Next time you are up this way will you please drop in to visit me and I will tell you about it? Come to noon dinner and sample Martha's chicken dumplings.

Parker.

III

Account of Courtney Stone, M.D., Surg. D., F.A.C.S.: Chief Surgeon Albany Post–Graduate Hospital, etc., etc.:

AT ABOUT ELEVEN P.M. on August 15, 1934, I was in my study, too tired to retire. I had that afternoon performed nine operations at the hospital, including the excision of a cerebral carcinoma of which I was a little proud; and had attended a joint consultation by the medical and surgical staffs that had gone on and on, endlessly.

Two days before, a patient in a coma had been brought in from the Helderberg region. The routine tests had revealed no pathologic malfunction, no trauma sufficient to explain his condition; nor did his symptoms correspond to any known disease. In a manner of speaking there were no symptoms except the stupor and, so gradual that it was almost imperceptible, a fading away of vitality that unless checked must inevitably result fatally.

Although surgical intervention was by no means indicated I had been intrigued by the puzzle this case presented and was pondering it when my meditations were interrupted by the furious tingling of my doorbell. I waited an instant for Mrs. Small, my housekeeper, to answer it, recalled that I had given her the night off and shoved myself unwillingly out of my chair.

A nervous, hysterical quality in the bell's pealing told me that the late caller was in search of my professional services. My practice has long ago reached the point where night calls are merely a matter for resentment, and I was prepared to send the fellow to young Adams, down the road, with a flea in his ear.

I changed my mind however when, opening the door with one hand as I clicked on the hall light with the other, I looked straight into Hugh Lambert's face, pallid and dirt-streaked. He was palpably in a state of collapse and would have fallen if he had not been supported on one side by Edith Horne, the nurse I had recommended for his camp, and on the other by a second girl whom I perceived only vaguely.

It was she who had been ringing. "We've had an awful accident," she blurted. "Hugh's terribly hurt."

"Slashed artery, Doctor Stone," Edith interposed, "in the left leg. He's lost a lot of blood."

"Get him into surgery and I'll get right to work. I'm glad you brought him to me instead of the hospital." That was quite true. Anthony Wagner, Wanooka's millionaire owner, is also a financial mainstay of the hospital and so the medical supervision of the camp has devolved upon me. I visit it frequently. Despite the disparity of our ages I have grown extremely fond of Hugh and I should not have wanted some half-baked intern messing around with him. "Here, let me help you."

"I can... hop... along," Hugh muttered between set teeth. "Help... other—"

"That's all right," a nasal twang came from the porch. "I carried him this far an' I can manage to get him the rest of the way." As the others shuffled past me, a gangling gaunt-visaged man in overalls shoved in through the door, his arms cradling a dark form whose limbs dangled flaccidly. I realized that I had another patient.

"Come on in. You know the way."

I had recognized Jethro Parker, a farmer who the winter before had once or twice accompanied a friend here. He grunted acquiescence and I turned to go through the entrance hall to the rear of the house.

"Get Hugh on the examining table, Edith," I called. The nurse elbowed a tumbler switch beside the surgery door and the white blaze of the white-tiled room silhouetted the slowly

moving trio. Hugh's legs caved in. I saw that at the last minute
he'd lost consciousness and I sprang to aid the girls.

PARKER CHOKED out an exclamation behind me, but I
paid no attention other than to throw over my shoulder a direction for him to lay his charge on a leather-covered couch nearby.
Lambert's left trouser leg was a gory sponge. The cloth was
slashed and the flesh beneath it deeply gashed, so that the
anterior tibial artery was laid open for two inches as neatly as
though it had been done with a scalpel.

The lacerated vessel should have been literally fountaining
blood, but there was only a slight seepage. I looked for the
explanation, disentangled from the sopping jumble of cloth
above it a tight bandage of once white fabric, that had been
knotted over the gastrocnemius to make a crude tourniquet, so
expertly applied I knew it was Edith's work.

*I saw a tiny doll-like face, oval
and sharp-chinned and sad....*

"Will he be all right, doctor?" the other girl asked, behind me. "Will he live?"

"Of course," I answered with the gruff curtness I have found to be more reassuring to jittery relatives and friends than a gentler manner. "You can't kill a bull like this with a scratch." But I wasn't as confident as I made myself sound. His exsanguinated pallor told me that Hugh had spilled a devil of a lot of blood. "Just go out in the waiting room, please, and make yourself comfortable while we take care of him." I felt Hugh's pulse. It was damned feeble and twice too rapid.

"Mr. Parker," I continued, "you've been here before. Please show the lady." *Sotto voce* to Edith I murmured, "First thing is to sterilize and suture that artery. Prepare what I'll need while I take a look at the other one. You know where everything is, don't you?"

"Yes, doctor," she answered, crisply; though she was whiter around the gills than a nurse of her experience should be even with her patient as bad a mess as Lambert. "I haven't forgotten."

She moved away and I straightened to examine the other case. Parker was between us. He had slumped into a chair, his head buried in his knotted hands. "Now, now, man," I rebuked him. "You ought to be able to stand the sight of a little blood."

He looked at me, his weather-beaten face greenish under its stubble. "It ain't that." His pupils were dilated, his tone a half-whisper of almost religious awe. "It's not the blood." He swallowed with perceptible effort. "It—Doc! Do you—Could a man come to life after being drowned six months? Changed, maybe?"

"Nonsense," I snorted. "What on earth gave you such an idea as that?"

His head turned, slowly, reluctantly, to the figure on the couch. "When I came into the light I saw his face and—" A sigh as if of relief cut his sentence short. "No," he resumed. "I guess I was wrong. He's just a tramp. I guess I was just kind of kerflumoxed with all the excitement."

"I guess you were," I said dryly. "Look. The third bottle on the bottom shelf over there is whisky. Pour yourself a jolt. That's the best medicine for what ails you." I had no time for the vagaries of superstitious rustics.

"May I have some too?" a clear bell-like voice asked wistfully. "I rather imagine I could use it."

"Of course." I really saw the other girl then for the first time. Disheveled and disarrayed as she was, she was something worth seeing.

SHE WAS tall, but she carried that tallness with a singularly graceful poise, and there was singing rhythm to every line of her body. Ordinarily the harsh glare of my floodlight is cruel to feminine charm, but it merely emphasized the pearly sheen of her skin, the delicate modeling of her features. I found myself pensively wishing that I was not short and rotund, that there were no gray hairs in my Vandyke.

"You were in that accident, too. Are you hurt?"

"Just shaken up a little." She smiled briefly. "And bruised. Nothing to take you away from poor Hugh."

"Don't be too sure, Ann Doring." I knew her at once. "I'll look you over later. Meantime, if you'd like to clean up you'll find everything you need at the head of the stairs."

"Thank you. I'll take advantage of your kindness. But first, my drink."

"It's all poured out, miss," Parker said from across the room. "I've hidden mine an' I'll be running along. Marthy will be worrying about what become of me."

Miss Doring downed her drink and followed him out of the room. I turned to look at the tramp.

"I've cut his shirt and coat away," Edith Horne said as I came around. "So you won't have to bother with that." Competent as all get out, that young lady. I don't know a better nurse. I had hated to send her up to the lake, but she'd earned a vacation through a busy winter, and besides she was just right for the job. Strictly business and no feminine nonsense. "His clothes are so old they're moldy and rotted."

"Third and fourth ventral ribs caved in," I diagnosed aloud as I stepped toward the couch. "Look like they're driven into the lungs." But they couldn't be—I frowned. The fellow would be dead or writhing in agony if they were. He wouldn't be watching me with a curious detachment out of eyes as expressionless and blackly glinting as camera lenses.

His torso was of that distinctive gray whiteness one associates with long defunct corpses, and entirely aside from the costal depression on which I based my superficial diagnosis there was something grotesque about it. The word is rather melodramatic, but it fits the gross, lumpy malformation of that body.

Perhaps I may more clearly convey his appearance by saying he looked as if some child had thumbed out of putty an inept, three-dimensional caricature of a human form.

His flesh was clammy under my probing hands, and pecu-

liarly soggy, evoking from the mists of the long years a recollection of student days and my first formaldehyde-pickled
cadaver; I had been right! The bones beneath were free-floating,
torn from their anchorage. The man's stoicism was remarkable.
He should have shrieked under the pressure I applied, but he
did not make a sound. I glanced at his face, wondering if he
had fainted.

I knew that face. Or rather, I knew the one it had been ineptly
molded to resemble.

The card file in my mind presented the appropriate memo:

> NAME: Elijah Fenton. DIAGNOSIS: Fibrous tumor,
> right side of neck. TREATMENT: Excision of growth. RE-
> SULT: Successful. POST-OPERATIVE CARE: Weekly
> dressings, discontinued because patient drowned, 12/11/33.

I laughed shortly. Was I as credulous as Jethro Parker, letting
a chance resemblance suggest impossible things? This could
not be Fenton. Fenton had been drowned last winter in the
tragedy at which all Albany shuddered.

A feathery chill brushed my spine. There, from clavicle to
point of the right mandible, *was the healed scar of the incision my
own scalpel had made!*

I V

Dr. Courtney Stone's account, continued:

I CONFESS THAT for a brief moment I was jolted out of
the scientific attitude and almost believed that lying before me
was a *revenant*, somehow returned to life after being nine
months dead. Then I saw that what I had taken for a scar was
merely a groove across the tramp's neck. To continue the simile
I have used before, if the fellow had been sculptured from putty
the awkward artist might have used Elijah Fenton as a model
and attempted to reproduce the result of his operation along
with the rest.

It was coincidence pure and simple, of course. If the investigators of so-called psychic phenomena would remember the frequency of such accidental duplications they would not make such fools of themselves.

Nevertheless I was grateful for the interruption of Miss Horne's steady, "Mr. Lambert's wound is still seeping and I'm ready for you. Would you want to take care of him first?"

"Perhaps I'd better. He can't stand the loss of much more blood." She was waiting for me with operating gown and sterile gloves as I turned. "Think you can take an X-ray of this fellow's chest without help?" Artery clamps, sterile sponges, cat-gut-threaded needles were laid out on a towel-covered instrument stand next to the examining table. "I'll have to see what's inside him before I can do any thing."

"Of course." There was no hesitation in her reply. "I'll wheel in the portable machine and have the picture ready for you by the time you're through with Mr. Lambert."

The artery wall was cleanly cut, the tissue firm, holding the suture without tearing. The care with which Hugh Lambert always kept himself in condition paid him dividends now. Sewing him up, I heard the rumble of the portable X-ray machine behind me, the *click-click* of the exposure and, as I finished, Nurse Horne was beside me, handing me the bandage and tape I required.

"The plate's in the developing bath, doctor," she said. "Are you going to give Mr. Lambert a shot of tetanus antitoxin?"

I felt Hugh's pulse again. It was dangerously feeble. "No. I don't think he could take it without the shock putting him out. He seems pretty weak. Get me a blood-count on him. On the tramp, too, while you're about it. I'll get to the darkroom meanwhile and take a squint at the Roentgenograph."

I lifted the film out of the hypo, washed it, adjusted it against the ground glass of the viewing frame and switched on the light behind.

The outline of the torso was clearly visible. I made out the bony structures, the fractured costal cage and the vertebral column, traces of musculature and circulatory system. But that was all. Where the shadowy outlines of the soft organs—the heart and lungs and the membranous sacs enveloping them—should be there was only a dark, amorphous blur!

If that plate was to be believed, my patient was nothing but a bag of skin and flesh stiffened by an amateurishly articulated skeleton and stuffed with something like a thick jelly. But the picture lied, of course. We'd have to take another.

THE GLARE of the surgery blinded me as I stepped out into it. Then I saw Edith Horne emerging from the laboratory. Her lips were colorless. "Doctor Stone! Hugh's—Mr. Lambert's count is under two million."

"Phew!" I whistled. "That's bad. I'll look up the list of professional donors while you type his blood."

"I've already done that. And—and it doesn't fit into any of the four groups. Its serum agglutinates the corpuscles of Type Four, and none of the standard sera agglutinates it."

"You must have made a mistake. If you were right about that, Lambert's would be the only case of that kind ever found."

"Not the only case," she said. I was disturbed by the husky quaver that had crept into her tones. The atmosphere of the camp seemed to have badly impaired her professional impersonality. "The other sample, that from the tramp, reacts the same way. I've cross-typed the two bloods too, and they match."

"There's your answer," I pointed out. "You must have made the same mistake with both. I'll soon find out."

But what I found out when I repeated the simple technique in the laboratory was that she had made no mistake. Only a scientist will understand the elation I felt as I racked the four test tubes that confirmed her report. In my mind I was already drafting the paper I would write for *The Journal of the Medical Association…*

Then I realized that the result of the tests I had just made was a virtual sentence of death on my friend. Being the sole

*We were hurtling toward that jagged cliff at
a speed that would smash up to pulp!*

possessor on earth, as far as science knew, of this unheard of
blood type doomed him assuredly as a noose around his neck.
If he did not receive transfusion within a half hour at the outside

there was no chance to save him, and there was no possibility of finding a donor for him.

There *was* one. There was, by a weird, impossible coincidence—a sheer, lunatic fluke, the tramp. How badly injured he was, I did not know, but there was no doubt in my mind that any drain on his vitality would lessen his chances of recovery to the vanishing point.

No. That was out. Every principle of medical ethics forbade my taking the chance of tapping his veins. Every principle of the law, too. If he died under the operation I would be guilty of murder.

Back in the surgery, Edith Horne lifted from Hugh's recumbent form. "Low," she whispered. Her face was drawn, the sprinkling of freckles across the bridge of her pert nose vivid against a white pallor. The eyes she raised questioningly to mine were no longer a golden brown but dark with distress. She was far different, in that moment, from a nurse to whom the conflict against disease and death is a matter of emotionless routine.

"You were correct," I told her. "It will be impossible to find anyone whose blood will match Hugh Lambert's."

Her hands closed, slowly, on the edge of the table. She said tonelessly, "The tramp."

I shook my head. "No. I have no right to choose between them."

"Right!" The corners of her mouth twitched in a smile more bitter than tears. "Have you a right to do otherwise? Look at them." My gaze went from Lambert, clean-limbed, strong-jawed, to the miserable derelict on the couch. "Think what they mean to the world. And then tell me have you no right to make a choice." The one is a sodden hulk, I thought, useless to humanity and to himself. The other has already brought back from civilization's frontiers outstanding contributions to science, will accomplish far more—*if he lives.*

My eyes came back to her and read a fierce challenge to be for once a man and not a scientific machine.

"The Medical Board," I temporized, weakly. "The law. If the tramp dies…"

"If he dies, only the two of us will know why."

I made my decision. Not in words, but in an almost involuntary gesture of assent. Only afterward did it occur to me to wonder why the tramp had said not a word through all this, and by that time I had something far more amazing to wonder about.

EDITH HORNE gave me no time for a change of heart. In almost less time than it takes to write it, she had the Unger transfusion apparatus set up between the table and the couch, had laid out antiseptic and hemostats and ligatures, had handed me a scalpel and was waiting for me to begin.

I did, God help me!

I shall not go into details. Medical men know the procedure, others will not be interested. Suffice it to say that I connected the tramp's artery to Hugh Lathbert's vein and permitted the blood of one to flow into the other.

I saw the ruddiness of health again tincture Hugh's cheeks. Edith watched him with an intentness that excluded all else. I turned, then, to check on the tramp's condition.

My jaw dropped. My hands shook on the stopcocks I was so carefully manipulating. Ice molded my body, tightening it.

The tramp was shrinking! Visibly and with increasing rapidity he was growing smaller! Every part of him was diminishing, at once and in proportion, as if he were a motion picture image from which the camera was being withdrawn at express speed. As if he were a pricked balloon out of which the gas was rapidly emptying.

He was the size of a child, then of a doll, and in no time at all of one of those bangles that women wear on their wrists… He was gone! The tube that had ended in his arm dangled loosely in mid-air.

The table on which he had lain was empty. Absolutely, impossibly empty!

I swear by Hippocrates, of whom I am a humble follower, that I saw that man shrink and vanish, there before me, and leave no trace whatever, that he had ever existed.

> Affidavit of Edith Horne, R.N.
> State of New York,
> County of Albany,
> City of Albany

Edith Horne, being duly sworn, deposes and says:

I have read the account of Dr. Courtney Stone as to the events occurring at his home at about midnight on the morning of August 16, 1934, and aver that as to such matters that I could have seen or heard, the said statement is true.

I did not actually see the disappearance of the man we called the tramp. My attention was wholly concentrated on watching the condition of the patient, Hugh Lambert, to whom the said tramp's blood was being transfused, but I affirm that said tramp was on the operating table in the surgery when the transfusion started, and that when I looked up at a sort of strangled cry from Dr. Stone, he was no longer either there or anywhere else in the room. I further depose that I was in such a position that even if the tramp had been in condition to move he could not have gone out through the door into the entrance hall without pushing me aside, and that the only other exit from the room is through Dr. Stone's office, which was locked.

There is no question in my mind that the said tramp actually vanished in the manner described by Dr. Stone.

In witness whereof I set hereunto my hand and seal this 5th day of December, 1934.

(Signed) Edith Horne, R.N.*

Dr. Courtney Stone's account, resumed:

I MUST automatically have shut off the stopcocks of the

---

* Editor's Note: To save space, the *jurat,* or notary's statement of the administration of this oath, has been omitted from this and succeeding affidavits. The originals, however, are on file at my office and may be examined there by any one presenting credentials from a recognized scientific society.—A.L.Z.

transfusion apparatus, for that is how they were when I was recalled to myself by Nurse Horne's startled demand, "Where is the tramp? What's become of him?"

I didn't reply. What could I have said if I had tried to? I sought sanity in ligating Hugh's vein, in suturing the wound I had made. Edith helped me.

By the time the task was completed I had got more nearly back to normal. "He must have managed somehow to get off the table while I was watching the gauges," I said. "He must be somewhere around. We'll look for him."

We did, in the laboratory, in the X-ray dark room. Even in my office, though the door to that was locked. It was impossible for the tramp to have gotten in there, but not as impossible as the other thing I thought I had seen. We didn't find him.

Edith turned to me finally, her face inscrutable, and said, "Well, that solves our problem, doesn't it?"

"How about Jethro Parker and Miss Doring? They will be asking for the tramp."

"That's easy. He wasn't as badly hurt as he seemed, refused treatment and went away. He refused even to give his name and there is no way to trace him. And that's what we'll tell Hugh Lambert, too. We won't even tell him about the transfusion. Glass cut his arm as well as his leg, and in the excitement he didn't notice it." There was everything in favor of the course she proposed, nothing against it. We returned to the surgery and I examined Hugh.

"He's coming back strong. We'll fix up a bed for him in my study and he'll be good as new in ten days or so, with proper nursing."

"You can be sure I'll give him that. I—"

"No, Edith. Your job is back at the camp. There are half a hundred kids there to be watched over and I wanted you there because I wouldn't trust them to any of the other available nurses. I'll have the Registry send someone over for Hugh."

"That won't be necessary, doctor." The opening door admitted Miss Doring. "I was pacing the hall," she explained, "and couldn't help overhearing you. I'm coming to stay here and take care of Hugh."

"Very commendable, my dear," I met her proposal. "I'm sure you're anxious to do something for him. There really will not be anything to do requiring training, but helping at the dressing of wounds such as his requires courage from one who is not used to the sight of blood. I can't have you fainting just when I need you."

"You wouldn't be afraid of that, doctor," it was Edith who replied, "if you had seen Miss Doring grasping Hugh's leg to stop that artery. She saved him, when she couldn't have been sure that she was not herself badly hurt or so badly cut that her career was ended."

"I wasn't doing him much good. It was the bandage you put on that really saved him. I—"

"Wait a minute, you two," I growled. "Stop throwing bouquets at each other, and let's get this matter settled. I'll take you as Hugh's practical nurse on Miss Horne's say-so, but aren't you being somewhat impulsive? It seems, to me I read somewhere that you were flying back to Hollywood to start a new picture at once."

"Hang the picture!" Despite her earnestness there was a twinkle of elfin mischief in Ann Doring's eyes. "Let Ratskoff do a little worrying about me for once."

And that ended the discussion. I forebore to ask Mrs. Small what she thought on her return to find that she was being called upon to chaperon a glamorous motion picture actress, but I confess I found myself hurrying through my day's work to get home a half-hour earlier. Somehow my bachelor domicile had taken on a new allure.

But it was not to last long. Hugh gained strength rapidly, and the third day after these events insisted on being taken back to camp to finish his convalescence there. Ann Doring went with him.

V

Sundry telegrams from the files of the New York Office of World Pictures Corporation:

HOLLYWOOD CAL 8/17/34

JENNINGS
WORLPIC NEW YORK
READY SHOOT HEARTS DESIRE BUT NO DOR-
ING STOP SHIP HER FIRST PLANE WEST STOP
NEVER PULLED TRICK LIKE THIS BEFORE STOP
IS SHE GOING TEMPERAMENTAL ON US
RATSKOFF

NEW YORK N Y 8/17/34

RATSKOFF
WORLPIC HOLLYWOOD CAL
DORING LEFT WALDORF IN HER ROADSTER
MORNING FIFTEENTH STOP NO WORD SINCE
STOP HAD RESERVATION TWA NIGHT DE-
PARTURE SIXTEENTH STOP DISAPPEARANCE
SHOULD BE SWELL PUBLICITY STOP SHALL I
GET TO WORK ON POLICE AND PRESS
JENNINGS

HOLLYWOOD CAL 8/17/34

JENNINGS
WORLPIC NEW YORK N Y
PUBLICITY DANGEROUS STOP REMEMBER
DISAPPEARANCE ORETTA SWAN STOP REPORT-
ERS FOUND HER FOR COSMO AND HOW STOP
DO YOU WANT SOME OF SAME
RATSKOFF

NEW YORK N Y 8/17/34

RATSKOFF
WORLPIC HOLLYWOOD
NOT DORING

JENNINGS

HOLLYWOOD CAL 8/17/34

JENNINGS
WORLPIC NEW YORK N Y
SO NEW YORK STILL HAS ILLUSIONS STOP I
WOULDNT TRUST SHIRLEY TEMPLE STOP DOR-
ING ANNOUNCED FOR HEARTS DESIRE STOP
MUST HAVE HER STOP GET BUSY STOP HIRE
PRIVATE AGENCY STOP HIRE TWO PRIVATE
AGENCIES STOP FIND HER STOP IN FACT FIND
HER OR LOSE YOUR JOB
RATSKOFF

CHAPTER I

Narrative of Hugh Lambert, B.S., M.Sc., F.A.G.S., F.R.G.S., etc.

COURT STONE IS the salt of the earth and a wizard with the scalpel, but he's a damnable fussbudget about his patients. I had a devil of a time getting it into his head that I had a job to attend to and couldn't be bothered nursing a couple of scratches.

Perhaps I'm being unfair to him. Whom has he treated, after all, but a pack of soft and flabby city dwellers emasculated by the countless comforts of civilization? Could he understand how little the loss of a quart or so of blood meant to a man who'd fought a hundred and fifty miles of Chaco Arica jungle with his arm and side shredded to rags by a jaguar's claws; who, deafened and blinded and maddened by fever, had driven by curses across ten days of burning desert a caravan of Touaregs while they meditated his murder as an act of devotion to their deity?

I was sorely tempted, I'll confess, to let the argument slide. I've had a pretty tough time of it, working my way through Dartmouth and batting around the world's waste spaces ever since. Lying around, relaxed and catered to and pampered, made that study of Doc's a little bit of Heaven.

It had its angel too. Ann Doring.

All my life I'd been searching for something. Not the ruins and fossils and artifacts of peoples who were already civilized when my own ancestors still gnawed raw meat from the bones of mastodons, but something more personal, the fulfillment of some lack in me, some indefinable, but poignant hunger.

I had never known what it was, however, till I saw Dick Doring, grinning all over himself, dragging his sister up to my table in the mess hall. Then I knew that I'd found it. Ann Doring did something to me, in the few seconds Dick blurted out an introduction I didn't hear, that no woman had ever done before.

It was nothing I could put words to, but it had tingled in my palm when Ann's palm met it, and it throbbed between us, there in that room.

I had her all day to look at and dream about. I had Court Stone in the evening to engage me in man talk, his clipped Vandyke bristling, his eyes growing bright as he told me of the daily battles against death, battles as bitterly waged, and often with as much peril, as any of my own fights against ravening savages. But I was restless and uneasy, and the walls of the house seemed like the walls of a prison.

I had on my mind, of course, that we were in the last two weeks of the season, when the staff goes quietly mad with the need for keeping routine going, while preparations for breaking up become more and more febrile. If anything went wrong now it might wreck my hopes of wangling Tony Wagner into financing the diggings at Peth Ankor in Mesopotamia where the fate of certain theories of mine as to prehistory lies buried under some hundred yards of detritus. But I was also vaguely aware of an urgent necessity for me to go back to Wanooka, a demand for my presence there that inexplicably seemed to have nothing to do with my responsibilities.

Peculiarly enough this feeling was not nearly as powerful while I was fully awake as it became when, as a result of my weakness I suppose, I would drift into a dreamy half-doze. It bothered me a lot, because I couldn't understand it.

I have always slept dreamlessly, but now I would come awake at night, and lie wide-eyed, desperately endeavoring to recall some nightmare that had slipped into oblivion at the instant of consciousness' return.

I stood two days of that. On Saturday morning I announced to Court that he and all Albany's police force together couldn't make me stay put any longer.

He spread his pudgy arms, at whose end those slim surgeon's fingers of his seemed so incongruous, and yielded with the physician's invariable formula. "All right, Hugh. I can't keep you here against your will but I won't be responsible for the results." None of my protests would avail to keep Ann from accompanying me. At that they were perhaps none too vigorous.

Doc evidently had phoned ahead, for Nurse Horne met our car at the gate and packed me right off to the infirmary shack. Lord! I'd rather try to get my own way from ten Cairo dragomen, indubitably the most mulish males in this large world, than one red-headed gal with a conscience and me the subject matter of that conscience.

Show Edith a patient and the devil himself won't stop her from taking care of him. She'd laid down the law to us before she'd been in camp two hours, and made us like it. Made us like her too, man to man, because she did her job without fuss and feathers, and because she asked for nothing in the way of special privilege on account of her being a woman.

Yes, that gal was a good soldier. The kind you could take along on a trek into the wilds and never have to worry about her going soft or, which is more important when there's business to attend to, flirtatious. All of which is to explain why, after all the mischief I'd raised to get here, I meekly let her bundle me up in bed and as meekly swallowed the sedative she handed me.

That potion was a mistake. It put me to sleep, all right, but it didn't keep me from dreaming. I don't recall much of what I dreamed, but for the first time bits of it stayed with me.

The sense of something drawing me was in it somewhere, not satisfied with my being at Wanooka but still dragging at me, wanting me to do something I could not understand. There was a crystal wall, metal bars and levers screwed to it in an orderly sort of jumble, much like one of those switchboard panels of gray slate one sees in electric power houses. Hands, white and slender and definitely feminine moved along those levers, but they seemed puzzled, uncertain.

Remembering those hands afterward, I realized that I had accepted as natural, like one does in a dream, something quite unnatural about them. Between each finger there had been a translucent membrane, expanding and contracting as the web of a frog's feet do.

I recall one thing else out of that dream. A face that made it a nightmare!

It was a little blurred as though it were looking at me from the other side of a window of slightly impure glass. I had the impression that the glass was more of a barrier to its vision than to mine, so that it could not quite make one out, and that the rage that darkened its eyes was due to this fact.

It was a narrow face, sharp-featured as a falcon's and as soul-lessly cruel. The eyes were fierce black lights within slitted, lashless lids. The mouth was a tight gash in its swarthy, leather-textured skin, yet something about their shape made me feel that behind those compressed lips were not teeth but sharp fangs. There was rage in that face, as I've said, but there was also ineffable threat. Confronted by it, I knew the meaning of terror, I who can say without boasting that never before had I really known what fear is.

I awoke from that dream trembling and bathed in cold sweat.

I stared at the darkness till it grayed with the dawn, and when Edith came in to see how I was, I demanded my clothing, telling her I was through with being a pampered invalid once and for all. I must have spoken to her pretty sharply, for she flung them at me and went out of the room without a word of objection.

I was at once sorry for that. I had been angry at myself for a blithering sap and I had taken it out on the first person I saw. Which, again, was utterly unlike my usual self.

I OVERTOOK her on the way down to breakfast, apologized to her, and felt better. The clean, sharp tang of the pines was pulling into my lungs, the needle-carpeted earth was springy underfoot and the chill morning wind was grateful on my cheeks. This was what I needed to make me whole again; I'd been cooped up in a house too long.

Edith put her hand on my sweater sleeve. "It's all right, Hugh. We'll forget it. But take care of yourself. Please."

I laughed. "I've been doing that for a long time," I said, "and I think I can manage it without help for a little while longer. Quit worrying about my few lacerations, will you?"

"It isn't that." She wasn't laughing with me, as she ordinarily did.

"What is it, then? What's got you looking so washed out? I'll be blessed if there aren't dark circles under your eyes. Look here!" A thought struck me. "There hasn't been a measles or whooping cough case out in the junior bunks while I've been laid up? Or something like that?"

"No." She pulled away from me. "No, you fool." And then she was running away from me, down the path to the mess house.

I might have gone after her, tried to find out what was jangling her, if Ed Hard hadn't barged out of the councillor's bunk just then, roaring a welcome at me in his gentle way. After that, mess call blew and I forgot all about the incident.

I got a thrill out of the way the kids cheered when they saw me at the head table. It was the real thing, no mistake, and it meant a lot. I'd been a strict disciplinarian, and once or twice I'd wondered whether those brats out of rich homes didn't hate me for it. The way they yelled told me.

Ann got it, too. I knew that by the way she looked at me, starry-eyed. "You can't fool boys," she whispered to me as I sat down after getting a little thank you speech past the lump in my throat. "I've got a brother and I know."

I got into harness right after that meal was over. It was Sunday and outside of their swim the campers were free to entertain their relatives, who started flocking in about ten, but I had plenty of work cut out for me. Besides an accumulation of mail only I could attend to that had piled up on my desk, there was the schedule of activities for the final fortnight to work out with Ed, arrangements for baggage packing and transportation to the city to get underway, the last Saturday entertainment and the break-up banquet to be planned, and the Lord alone knows what else.

I drove my assistants and my office staff hard, but I drove myself harder. There were a hundred interruptions, of course. Fond papas came in with checks (the more money a man has the longer he likes to hold on to it) and had to be chatted with. Fonder mamas came in with complaints (the better satisfied a kid is the more his mother finds to kick about) and had to be mollified. Giggling sisters and cousins came in for no good reason at all and had to be combed out of my hair. Just before lunch Dick Doring showed up and got me aside in a corner.

"Listen, Uncle Hugh," he whispered. "Sis don't want to be bothered with autograph signing and such, so she's keeping out of sight till this mob of visitors beats it. She don't even want them to know she's here, so will you please ask the staff not to say anything? I've already tipped off the fellows, and they've clammed up."

"Oke," I grinned, knuckling his cheek. "Mum's the word." He's a well set-up lad, the tallest of our youngsters, clean-limbed and frank-eyed. "Now run along and have fun." I passed the word around, decided to have my lunch in the office so that I should have at least one hour's work in peace.

WE GOT back to normal at camp Monday morning, and I had the office work going well enough so that I decided I could be spared for a swim with Ann during the boys afternoon rest hour. I warned her to keep inside the line of buoys that marks off a space sufficiently large for even the strongest swimmer.

"The sun warms the water enough," I told her, "in this end of the lake where it's fairly shallow, but the rest is icy. It can be negotiated, but it's no fun, and it's dangerous, so we just don't swim beyond the markers, and even keep our canoes within reach of them."

Her dive cut into the lake without the hint of a splash. I contrived to match it. We raced for the big raft. She was a marvel of graceful speed and I beat her only by five feet. I was a little miffed at that. My face must have shown it, because her clear, merry laugh rang out as she clutched the raft ropes.

"If I had my health," I grinned, "It would be different."

The echo of Ann's laugh came back from the mountain, coarsened so that it did not seem her laugh at all. Someone indistinguishable called from a canoe farther out. I shoved the soles of my feet against the side of the raft, straightened, rolled over, filled my lungs and dove to swim back under water.

It seemed colder than usual as my arms pumped. The imprisoned air tore at my chest. I have always made the distance easily, and an idea glimmered in my mind that perhaps I had been foolhardy to go in so early in my convalescence. I plunged up to the surface, *whooshed* the air from my lungs, glanced up to see how near I was to the float.

I wasn't anywhere near it! I had veered, somehow, under water and had been swimming up the lake, parallel with the shore, and was already well beyond the buoys. No wonder the water was so cold! I'd have to get back, and quickly, too.

I started swimming again. But I did not turn. I wanted to. I sent the message to my muscles, or thought I did, but I kept right on pumping toward the far end of Wanooka. The icy water seethed along my sides, and the cold seeped deep into me. I was numbed, lost all sense of feeling. I thought: stop it, turn around, make for the shore; and swam straight on, not even slowing, though I should have with my muscles freezing.

The cold got to my brain and I did not think any longer. I was conscious of nothing but the urge, the terrible urge to get to the north end of the lake. Yes. Somewhere deep inside of me there was still a kernel of awareness that I was swimming to my death. It seemed some other person who knew that.

My arms beat, my legs threshed, my body cut through the water. Faster. Faster… My hand hit something hard! My head bumped it.

A voice screamed at me. For a moment it was just shrill sound, then it made words: "Hugh! What are you trying to do?" It was Edith Horne's voice. "You fool. You unutterable fool. Are you trying to kill yourself?"

My head cleared a bit. I became aware that it was a canoe into which I had bumped. Edith was in it and she was yelling at me. She had been out on the lake and she had cut across my suicidal course.

"I—I don't know…" I gasped. "Cold."

"I should say you must be cold. Get in here, quick."

I was so numbed that it was almost an impossible job, but I managed it somehow with Edith helping me. Her paddle slashed down, driving the canoe to shore.

Her face was sultry, her eyes blazing. "You've got yourself a case of pneumonia now," she stormed, "you unmitigated ass. What made you do it?"

"I didn't mean to. A current had hold of me and I couldn't fight it," I lied. There had been no current. There had been nothing palpable about the thing that had drawn me to inevitable disaster.

I suspect that Edith knew I lied, but the canoe's bow crunched on ground and saved me from further lies.

"Jump out and run up to the infirmary as fast as you can go," she commanded. "We've got to get your blood circulating."

I jumped, and ran. Her voice was like a whip, lashing me.

"Faster! Run faster!" I couldn't go very quickly, I was so frozen, and she kept right behind me. "Faster!" It irritated me, but I obeyed. It would have been senseless to do otherwise.

I glimpsed Ann standing on the raft, watching us, her hand to her mouth as if she had just realized the implication of what she had thought a bit of bravado. I waved her in signal that I was all right, but Edith wouldn't let me stop. Anger flared in my skull.

In the infirmary she flung an armful of towels at me.

"Get into that room, strip and rub yourself down. Hard. Tear the skin off. Then get into bed."

I did as I was told. Then Edith piled heated blankets over me, raged at me till I downed a tumbler of hot whiskey, and went out, slamming the door. The heated liquor knocked me out, so that I was in a dreamless sleep almost at once.

WHEN I awoke I knew it was very late. The infirmary is set a little away from the camp. From my window I could see only the woods, and through their trunks the north end of Lake Wanooka, but from the position of the stars I could tell it was well on toward dawn.

The moonglow glimmered on the water, silvery except where that queer circular path of light showed, about which I had often wondered. Was I mistaken, or had it moved nearer the bank? Much nearer?

I had always meant to investigate the thing, but the routine of the camp had kept me too busy. Now I was sorry I had not, for, from nowhere, I got the idea that it was the source of the strange attraction that had bothered me ever since my return from Court Stone's and that was stronger than ever tonight.

A strange thing, that vague, intangible drag at me. Hard to describe. It was something like the Whisper in Kipling's *Explorer*. Remember?

> *Something hidden. Go and find it. Go and look behind the Ranges—*
> *Something lost behind the Ranges. Lost and waiting for you. Go!*

Yes, it was like that, except that it was I that was lost, and the hidden *Something* was calling me back to it.

And that instead of a promise there was an element of dread in that call.

Suddenly I stopped pondering it and shoved up on my elbow. The high, rank weeds down near the lake edge were rustling in a straight line, as though something were threading through them. Then they were quiet. But there was movement under the trees through which the moonlight was sifting. The movement of shadows.

There were shadows, but there was nothing to cast them. Not even a rabbit. A little muscle twitched in my cheek.

There was something eerie about those drifting shadows, something nape-prickling... Lord, I was getting jittery! They could be nothing but the shadows of branches stirred by some vagrant breeze in the treetops. I made myself lie down, and closed my eyes.

And I was dreaming once more. Of a city of strange, squat buildings on which a weird light lay though there was no sun in a sky I could not see. Of a topless crystal shaft within which, although it was solid, rainbow-hued clouds swirled and billowed, so that it seemed informed with an awesome other life divested of all mortality. Of the terrifying dark face again, more vulpine than before, shrewder, somehow, with a reptilian shrewdness.

I saw another face, too, this one small and winsome, tight black curls capping it, fathomless gray eyes wide-pupiled and puzzled and afraid. The face of a maid over whom some brooding fear hovered.

I knew, in my dream, that her name was Leeahlee.

Clipping from the Albany Gazette, August 23, 1934:

The authorities at the Postgraduate Hospital are puzzled by two cases of a hitherto unknown malady that have been brought to them for treatment during the past week. The first, Adath Jenks, 48, of Four Corners, was admitted August 13th; the second, Job Grant, 57, a farmer living some five miles northeast of Lake Wanooka, on Tuesday, August the 21st.

These cases resemble *encephalitis lethargica,* sleeping sickness, in that both men have been continually unconscious since they first became ill, but the germs of that disease have not been found in their cerebral fluid. Their strength is being steadily sapped, however, and Jenks is at the point of death.

Dr. Courtney Stone, of the hospital staff, said when interviewed that progress is being made in diagnosing these two cases, and that there is no cause for alarm as no indication has been found that the illness from which they are suffering is contagious. He suggests, however, that the inhabitants of the Helderberg Mountain region boil all their drinking water as a precaution.

Hugh Lambert's Narrative, resumed:

Rather grudgingly I shall have to admit that Edith Horne's treatment was efficacious, for I suffered no ill effects from my adventure. I was hard at work again at once and the countless demands upon me gave no time for sickly maundering. No time even for Ann, except in the evenings. We spent those in the rec hall. Edith must have talked to our visitor, for Ann insisted on our remaining indoors, despite my persistent suggestions that we stroll along the lake in the moonlight. That redhead was making a pest of herself, taking my temperature morning and night, giving me the devil when I forgot my sweater on a cloudy day, and behaving altogether like a hen with one chick. I found myself wishing that a couple of mild cases of grippe or something would show up among the boys, to take her mind off me, but they remained disgustingly healthy.

Ann was a trump. She kept out from underfoot during the day, and took one big load off my shoulders and that of the dramatic councillor.

To make Wanooka different from other, cheaper camps, I had organized it along the lines of a nation of primitive men instead of an Indian tribe. Our different age groups were called clans, the office was the *Kave of the King;* and so on. Pretty childish stuff, but the brats ate it up. For the last Saturday night I had devised a Tribal Council Dance, drawing both on memory and imagination for its details. I had the arts and crafts councillor building a big hide-headed drum, the nature councillor cutting out fur costumes from some hairy hides I'd purchased, and everybody busy with something or other.

Ann took over rehearsing the kids in the dance that was to be the grand finale and did they hop to it for her! The free period wasn't enough for them; they begged me to let them go at it again between supper and taps, and I consented.

That meant I had only about an hour alone with her, and it wasn't enough. Something had come between us. I don't know whether it was my own irascibility or what. We'd fuss around wordlessly in the dim, vast reaches of the big social hall, and often as not I would jump up, stride to the window and stand staring out at the lake.

She'd put a record on the phonograph when I did that. The first time it was some crashing jazz tune, and I whirled around, snarling at her to take it off. Which was queer too, because that was the only kind of music I liked.

"What do you want then?" she came back at me. "Wagner?"

"Go ahead," I answered, ashamed of the way I was behaving but perversely continuing. "It couldn't be worse than that blare. There are some Wagner records in the corner."

I could just see the luminous disk at the end of the lake. It was very close to the shore now. Curse these women anyway, I thought. If it wasn't for them I could go down there right now and figure out what made the light come up through the water like that.

Then I heard the *Ride of the Valkyries* begin behind me. The first sonorous notes took hold of me and lifted me up, and I soared away on the tumbling, fierce rush of its wild stream. For the first time I appreciated the breadth and the depth and the swift impetuosity of that master music. When it was finished I demanded more.

After that there was no more jazz in the rec hall after taps, but Wagner. All of it was soothing magic to me, but it was the *Song of the Rhine Maidens* I demanded most, the sirens chanting from beneath the waters of the treasure they guarded, of the mysteries beneath the blue depths. Listening to it, the pounding in my wrists would subside, and the ache behind my brow fade away.

The record would come to an end. Ann would say, "That's enough for tonight, Hugh. It's ten o'clock, and Edith says you must get your rest."

REST. THERE was no more rest for me. I wasn't sleeping. I didn't tell Edith that or she would have thrown a conniption fit, but that was the crux of what ailed me. I'd climb the hill to my room behind the office, so exhausted that I stumbled as I walked; get undressed and get into bed; and then lie there wide awake, wondering if I was going crazy.

I had cause enough for thinking that. I was seeing things! At first they were no more than the shadows of Monday night. As the week wore on, however, they became more distinct until every now and then, peering from behind a tree, dodging behind a rock, I would glimpse a little man. A man not more than a foot tall!

I saw them only at night, and only fleetingly, so I knew nothing about them except that they were so incredibly small. But I shouldn't have known that much about them. I shouldn't have seen them at all. They could not be real. They could exist only in my mind.

I dared to speak to no one about them. I dared not test out whether they were visible to me alone. I knew what the answer would be, and I knew what it would mean.

There was the call of the lake, too, clamorous now in the long dark hours. Tugging at me, tearing at me to come to it. It was part of my madness, of course. Part of this thing that had happened to me.

I tell you, I was glad when morning would come and the numberless petty details calling for my attention would help me to forget the night; I welcomed every paper thrust at me, every question the councillors had to ask, every one of the thousand and one problems that would come up for me to solve. It was hard work; and ordinarily I should have hated it with every atom of my being, but it kept me from thinking. I resented the smoothness with which matters were going. I should have liked it better if the railroad had wired that cars wouldn't be available to take us to the city, or the expressman that baggage trucks could not be obtained. That would have given me an excuse to get away from camp.

That was what I wanted most of all. I had a notion, reasonable enough, that as soon as I got away from camp I should be back to normal. As soon as I got away from the lake.

But nothing like that happened. There was one incident, though, that was disquieting enough. Saturday morning Ed Hard came to tell me that Jim Symes, on night patrol, had seen a rather rough-looking man prowling about in the woods back of camp. Jim had called to him and he'd run away.

There isn't much about Wanooka worth anyone's stealing, except what's locked in the safe in my room, but one doesn't overlook a report like that when one is responsible for the welfare of a bunch of youthful heirs to fortunes aggregating billions. I told Ed to see that the councillors kept all the kids in sight at all times, and to have them take shifts patrolling the camp borders by day as well as by night.

We had the canoe and swimming regatta that afternoon. I had to go down to judge it and distribute prizes, though I had shunned the cribs since Monday. I was rather glad I did so. Cribs and floats were gay with bunting, the sun was bright as midsummer and there was certainly nothing ominous about the lake. Edith, crisp in a new white uniform, forgot to pester me and Ann grew hoarse with cheering, especially when Dick won both his Senior Life Saving Badge and the canoe tourney.

Dick was proud as Punch, and Ann was pleased and gay.

Right after that there was a fifteen minute intermission, and I took the opportunity to walk up to the end of the lake with Bob Falk, who was to relieve Hen Corbin on the patrol we were maintaining even through the gala. Hen looked a little per-turbed as we approached. Close to the shore when he saw us coming, he bent and picked something up.

"Look here, Mr. Lambert!" he exclaimed as we reached him. "Look at this!"

He shoved his hand at me. There was something on his palm, a brown-furred little animal, not two inches long. It was alive, as I could see by its heaving flanks, but its legs were tied to-gether by bits of string.

"What's that?" I asked, wondering at Hen's none-too-well repressed excitement. "A field mouse?"

"No, sir. It's a muskrat."

"A muskrat? Maybe you're nature councillor, but you're way off this time. No muskrats are this small, even new-born, and whatever this is, it's adult."

"It's a muskrat," he insisted. "What's more, I think I saw it get as small as that, though I still can't believe it. I was in the bushes here, heard it splashing out in the water and watched it. It was full size then and it was swimming toward shore. Just as I saw it, it got into that—that kind of slick place there, and it got small, all of a sudden. I caught it as it scrambled out on the land and tied it up."

"Nonsense," I grunted. "The muskrat you saw dived, and this pigmy one came up just at the same time." But I was looking it the "slick place" he had mentioned and my throat was dry. Tangent to the bank, it was circular in outline, and I knew that by night it would glow with a peculiar violet light. "Come on back to the cribs and forget about it."

Maybe he would forget about it, but I would not.

IT WAS dusk by the time the regatta was over. I plodded up the hill between Ann and Edith, trying my best to comprehend their chatter. Abruptly two blasts of a councillor's whistle shrilled from the north end of the camp grounds. In our code that meant trouble. I muttered some excuse to the girls, started away. Ed Hard angled to meet me. We held ourselves to a fast walk until shrubbery screened us from the youngsters and then broke into a run.

Bob Falk had hold of the arms of a lean, blue-jeaned man. "Found this fellow sneaking through the woods, Mr. Lambert," the councillor gasped, "and copped him."

"Good work," I panted. And then I demanded from his prisoner, "What are you up to here? Can't you read those signs? Can't you see these grounds are posted?"

"Yeah," he grunted. He wasn't struggling. He was standing quite still, with his arms pinioned behind him and his eyes on the ground. "I know it's posted, but you ain't never kept us farmers around here from berrying and fishing on it."

"You have no pail and no rod, so you were neither berrying nor fishing, and I have my doubts about your being a farmer."

"I farmed on Waley Road when you wasn't dry yet behind the ears. You can ask anybody about who Jeremiah Fenton is."

I had hard work understanding him. His voice was a thick-tongued mumble oddly taut with—was it pain? Desperation? But what was once Waley Road is now the numbered highway into which the camp road descends and only an old resident would know its former name. I moderated the harshness of my tone.

"All right," I said. "You're a farmer then. What were you doing here?" His shoulders hunched, as a balky mule's will, but he remained silent.

"Come on," I growled. "Spit it out."

Fenton's head came up. Tiny muscles crawled under the wind-seamed leather of his countenance and hysteria jittered in his eyes. His grimly defiant face seemed vaguely familiar.

"Rats!" Ed Hard grunted, behind me. "There's only one thing to do with the guy. Turn him over to the cops."

"That's right, Mr. Lambert," Bob acquiesced. "They'll make him talk."

"No!" the farmer yelled and wrenched out of Falk's grip. His lanky length fairly hurtled away from us, up the hill. Bob whirled to go after him; Ed plunged past me. And then both halted. Fenton had snatched up a fist-sized stone from the ground, was crouched, an animal at bay, his lips snarling back from discolored teeth, his nostrils flaring.

"Let him go, boys," I called. "No use getting your skulls cracked." But I was wondering why he had stopped. There was no one between him and the road and that unexpected leap of his had taken him far enough away to make it improbable that we could overtake him. "Go on, Fenton. Get off the camp grounds and stay off."

The farmer gave no sign of having heard me. He wasn't looking at me. He wasn't looking at Ed or Bob. He looked past us, at the lake.

And startlingly he hurled himself through the narrow space between the two councillors, pelted down the hill, straight for those frigid waters! Realization blazed through me that he was going to throw himself into Wanooka's bottomless depths. My muscles exploded. I ran. I caught his shoulder barely in time.

"You fool!" His arm swung back, the rock clenched in his

gnarled fingers. My own free hand spatted open-palmed, against his cheek.

The stone dropped to the ground. I felt a long shudder run through the farmer, saw sense come back into his eyes. His mouth twisted.

"It almost got me. The hankering. It almost pulled me into the lake. I couldn't stand it no more."

My palms went moist, suddenly, and a pulse pounded in my temples.

Ed came up. "He tried to conk you."

Ed's fist closed on Fenton's one arm, Bob's on the other. "It's the police for him, all right."

"No," I said, very quietly. "Let go of him, Bob. Let go, Ed. Please get my car from the garage and run it up into the woods so that we can get to it without the whole camp seeing us. I'm taking Mr. Fenton home."

Hard looked at me queerly, but his hand dropped away.

"All right," he said, "I'll tell Jim to take charge of camp till I get back."

"That won't be necessary," I told him. "I'm going alone."

He started to protest.

"I said *I'm going alone.*"

MAYBE I was sick. Maybe I was crazy. But I still could get out that top sergeant's roar that makes them jump. Ed went off without another word.

"You'll say nothing about what happened here," I told Bob Falk, and then I was moving away from him, climbing up through the woods toward the road. Fenton went with me, quiet again, docile, all the hysteria, all the ferocity, gone from him.

Here was someone else to whom the lake called, I was thinking. He had fought its mysterious spell till he could fight no longer. I had to talk to him. I had to question him, alone.

But, driving him home, I could get nothing much out of Jeremiah Fenton, except that the "hankering" had come on him only recently, about the day Ad Jenks was took sick, and that it had been getting "worse and worse" ever since. I hinted about the Little Men without result, but my efforts in that direction brought from the farmer a strange tale.

I may have given the incident of which he told me, and his own interpretation of it, too much importance. If so, that is because of a rather heretical theory to which I incline that the advance of civilization and science has obscured almost as much from the knowledge of mankind as it has revealed. Is it not possible that those who live close to the soil, who work with Nature and commune with her, may be aware of eternal truths we have lost the capacity to even comprehend? Once, in the Haitian hills…

But I digress. The story Jeremiah Fenton told me then, haltingly, gropingly, was this:

He was a bachelor and lived alone in the ramshackle, sprawling farmhouse where I left him eventually, since his twin brother Elijah, also unmarried, had been drowned in Lake Wanooka the preceding winter. Jeremiah told me the two had been engaged in their nightly game of chess when the sleighs that were carrying a gay party to undreamed of tragedy drew up at their gate and called them out.

"I had the Black," Fenton recalled, "and all I had left was my King, on his Queen's Bishop's two. Elijah's King were on his Queen's fourth, his Queen on King's eighth, his Bishop on King Bishop's five, and it were White's move. I seen I was licked. 'You'll get me in six, ten more moves,' I said. 'I resign.'

" 'Six moves nothing,' Elijah says, 'I'll mate you in two moves.'

"Well, I thought he was talking through his hat, and dared him to do it. He ponders a minute, lays his pipe on the table and stretches out his hand to his Queen. Just then Jethro Parker bust in, hollering for us to hurry up.

"Elijah didn't make his move. 'We'll finish when we get back,' he said. Jethro was making so much noise Elijah even left his pipe lyin' there. Well, he never come back to finish pipe or game. The lake ice broke and—"

"Yes," I broke in. "I know what happened."

"I left the board lie just the way it was, pieces and pipe and all. Taking them away would of been kind of like—like pulling down the shade on my recollection of him. Like—"

"I understand," I murmured, wondering what all this was leading up to.

"It was just like that a week ago tonight. I finished my supper and went out in the front yard to pump a pail of water for washing the dishes. I was gone maybe five, ten minutes. When I got back there was a smell of tobacco in the kitchen. I don't ever smoke till after the dishes is done. I looked over to the little table where the chessboard sets, half expecting to see Elijah waiting for me to come and start our game.

"He wasn't there of course. But I saw right away that one of the pieces had been moved. It was the White Queen and it was resting on White Queen's Knight's fifth now."

I know a little about chess, enough to understand what that meant.

"Black King has to go to his Queen's square, and White Queen mates in the next move. Clever!"

"Clever's right. But who had moved that Queen? There wasn't no one in the kitchen."

"You had done it yourself, without thinking. You had been milling the problem over and did it mechanically."

"Maybe," Fenton said slowly. "Maybe. But I saw by marks in dust that Elijah's pipe had been moved too, and when I touched it, it was hot. I didn't light it and not even no tramp would of touched that black old corncob. Nor they ain't nobody around here good enough at chess to figure out that move. No. I get a notion that Elijah, not being buried in consecrated ground, can't rest; and that his hankering for me brought him back to where I was, just like my hankering for him is drawing me to Lake Wanooka. We was like as two peas, and that close…"

I didn't hear the rest. I didn't listen to it. Fenton's mention of a tramp had given me the clue to the resemblance that bothered me. It was the tramp I had run down of whom he reminded me.

Was there any connection between my injuries that night and what had been happening to me ever since? Doc Stone had been evasive about just what they were. *Edith would know.* I dropped Fenton yards from his gate, wheeled the car around and went back to camp as fast as I dared drive.

A shout to one of the boys brought the information that Edith was in the infirmary. I pounded in there, stiff-legged, saw her checking a shelf of supplies, grabbed her arm and twisted her around to me.

"What did that accident do to me beside cutting my leg and arm?" I demanded. "What are you and Court keeping from me? Was I hit on the head?"

Her eyes went wide, and her face gray.

"You're hurting me, Hugh."

"All right, I'm hurting you," I growled, but relaxed my hold slightly. "Now tell me about it. Hurry up. Tell me what happened. I've got to know. Do you understand? I've got to."

She told me—about the transfusion and about the tramp's disappearance. It didn't make sense. But then nothing since had made sense. I was as much in the dark as ever.

THE REST of that afternoon, supper that evening, went by with me in a daze. But I pulled myself together afterwards, because the Tribal Council was beginning and I wasn't going to have the boys' big night ruined. The contests, the games, went off slickly. Then came the moment when I climbed the platform that had been erected a little back from the shore and draped to simulate a high boulder. This was the Medicine Rock, and I was the medicine man who was to drum for the dance.

The boys, faces grotesquely painted, furred skins thrown over their shoulders, took their places below me. In the wavering, red light of a huge bonfire they seemed indeed a gathering of cave men.

I picked up the padded drum stick, started to beat on the tom-tom. The shuffling, shambling dance Ann had rehearsed began. The mountains took the hollow *boom, boom* of the drum and multiplied it, so that the whole bowl within which Lake Wanooka lies was filled with measured thunder.

It beat back at me, beat into my blood. My blood was beating in tune with it, in a runic rhythm that went faster and faster, in a thumping, cadenced frenzy that was the ancient pulse of the world, the systole and diastole of the world's hot core. This measure I beat was not the one I had rehearsed. This dance, this prancing, savage interlacing of skin-clad primordial brutes below me, was not the dance they had been taught. Something spoke to us, something older than antiquity, of the death of summer. It spoke to us of the cold death from which *this time, this time, this time* the trees in which we hid, and the grasses upon which we fed, might never come alive again.

It wasn't I who beat upon that drum. It was something within me, some ancient memory within me, that beat the booming rhythm these mountains had not heard for uncounted centuries. It was fear that *pound, pound, pound* fought; fear of the gigantic beasts that roved the forest; fear of the flying things that darkened the sky and pounced upon us to devour us. But above all fear of the Little Men who brought to us a terror the more awful because we could not understand wherein it lay.

There they are, the Little Men, coming up out of the lake, coming on to the land on either side, just beyond the fire's red glare. They do not see them, my dancing tribesmen, but I see them; I, the Medicine Man; I, the one to whom the dread night has whispered its secrets. But they will all see them soon, they all will know the terror the Little Men bring, unless I drive them back, drive them back by the furious *boom* the magic *boom, boom, boom* of my drum.

They are retreating, step by step, inch by inch. They are fading into the trees, into the lake, unable to withstand my power, the power of my furiously beaten drum. There is only one left, their leader, hawk-faced, vulture-eyed. He stands there just without the circle of light and defies me. Him too I am driving back, by the power of my arm and my primitive drum.

No! It is not I who drive him back. He has sensed that one among us has wandered off into the night beyond the fire and the protecting sound of my drum. He has darted after her…

A scream comes to me, almost drowned by the thunder of that drum! *Ann's scream!*

"Take it, Ed!" I shouted, remembering even then, even in that instant of my recovery from the strange spell that had seized me, that the boys must not be alarmed.

Then I leaped from the back of the platform and was racing up the hill.

Afterward I realized that I alone had heard it because I was higher than the rest and so the hill had not blanketed it from me. But now it did not occur to me to wonder why no one went with me as I raced to Ann's rescue. I was aware only that she had screamed to me and that I was going to her.

I saw figures in front of the deserted rec hall; two men, one with his hand on Ann's arm, the other's head hunched forward, fists knuckling at his sides. I shouted, and left the ground in a flying leap that ended with the smack of my knuckles on a hard jaw, and the pound of a sodden body on the ground. I whirled to the second man.

"Hugh!" Ann shrilled. "Hugh! It's all right. I'm all right. Stop, Hugh. Don't hit him."

"No, it ain't all right, lady," the fellow on the ground groaned. "He's broke my jaw."

Ann clung to me, holding my arms, half-laughing, half-crying.

"What is this?" I panted. "What's going on here?"

"They're from the company," she jabbered. "From World Pictures. The man you hit is a private detective who traced me here, and this is Frank Jennings, vice president in charge of the Eastern office."

"But you screamed—"

"Yes, I did. Irving Ball, who's on patrol tonight, came down and told me they were waiting for me at the gate. They had wandered into camp, and popped out at me unexpectedly from behind this house, and I did scream. But it was just because I was overwrought by your drumming and was startled."

"Listen, Miss Doring," Jennings intervened. "We haven't got any time for all this talk. If we start out right away we'll just about have time to make the first plane out of Newark in the morning."

"But I'm not going," Ann replied. "I'm staying right here."

"Do you realize it's costing the company ten grand a day to keep that stage waiting for you?"

"World Pictures can afford it. I've made enough for them."

"All right. But how about the fifty or a hundred extras you'll do out of a couple of weeks work if the picture's cancelled? How about the other leads, and the technical people?"

Ann's expression changed at that from obduracy to indecision.

She looked at me.

"What shall I do, Hugh?"

I didn't want her to go. Lord, how I wanted her to stay! She had been my only hold on sanity, with her alone I had found a little peace. If she went now—

"It's your job, Ann," I said quietly. "You have to go."

She winced at that, and the light died out of her eyes.

"All right. I'll go." Then her hands flung out. "But you'll come to me, Hugh. You'll come as soon as you can."

"As soon as I can," I promised. But I knew that it would not be soon. I also had a job to do. It would take me half around the world and keep me there for two years at least, two years I knew would be a hell of longing.

CHAPTER II

Hugh Lambert's narrative continued:

TIME BLURRED AFTER that. All I did was a blur, though I must have done properly what I had to do, for there were no complaints. All I can remember of those days are flashes of the bustling camp and always, somewhere around, Edith Horne, watching me, always watching me, trouble growing in her anxious eyes.

But I can recall the nights, too distinctly. I can recall the leader of the Little Men stalking me, following me along the night-shrouded paths of the woods, peering through my window at my sleepless tossing. He hid no longer. He was no longer furtive. I had full opportunity now to study the vulpine features of his visage, that seemed to be carved out of a fist size knot of dark mahogany. I knew what that miniature, foot-tall body of his looked like, how it was clothed in some skin-tight, shimmering fabric that seemed to be woven out of metal lustrous and flexible as silk.

I knew now that he was visible only to me. He had stood right in front of Ed Hard and me, one night, and Ed had not seen him. I almost pointed him out, checked myself just in time, remembering the Little Man was a figment of my imagination.

I must get away from him. I must get away from camp. When distance lay between me and Lake Wanooka I should be healed. But I had to stay. I had to finish my job.

Wednesday came at last. The boys' trunks were a high pile on the campus, waiting for the trucks. The Break-up Banquet, a long nightmare of speeches and songs and cheers, was over. I almost ran to my room behind the office to pack. This was the last night, the knowledge pounded in my brain, the last night. Tomorrow morning I would be driving down to Albany, and Lake Wanooka would be a thing of the past.

My hands shook as I dragged my flat stateroom trunk from against the wall, as I opened the door of my closet and started to take the neat piles from it and lay them in the trunk. With release at hand I could think of just how I would talk to Tony Wagner after we were through with the final affairs of the camp, how I would sell the Mesopotamian expedition to him.

I'd say—what was this? I was at the closet but I wasn't taking anything from it. I was putting something into it. I was piling my khaki trousers on the shelf where they belonged. But these trousers were the first thing I had put into the trunk! The trunk—I turned—was empty!

I had had it half packed, and now I had emptied it! I wasn't going tomorrow. The lake would not let me go!

That lake was an obsession with me. And I knew how to cure it. Suddenly I knew how to cure it. I had been shunning it, shunning the thought of it. That had been my mistake. If I went down to it, if I stood on its bank and looked straight at the weird light that came up through it, fought the infernal pull of it and defeated it, I should once and for all be free of it.

I flung around and went out of the office door, went down through the woods toward the north end of Lake Wanooka. Someone spoke to me. Bob Falk, once more on patrol. I answered him, almost gaily, that I was going down to say goodbye to the lake. Then I was past him, and on the shore, and I was staring at the glowing circle of luminance that was now right against the bank.

"Here I am," I said to it. "Now do your worst."

It leaped out at me. Right out of the water it leaped and enveloped me in a blinding, violet blaze!

Affidavit of Robert Falk, graduate student, Columbia School of Engineering:

State of New York
County of New York
City of New York

Robert Falk, being duly sworn, deposes and says:

I was, on August 29th, 1934, a senior councillor at Camp Wanooka for Boys, and was on night patrol. At approximately twelve-fifteen I saw and spoke to Mr. Hugh Lambert, director of said camp. He was walking down the hill toward the lake, and said something rather queer about saying goodbye to it.

My beat was along the northern border of the camp grounds. Since there had been some reports of prowlers about the camp I was vigilant. The trees there are set quite far apart, it was bright moonlight, and I am certain that I should not have missed seeing Mr. Lambert had he returned.

At approximately eleven-twenty I went down to the shore to speak to him. He was not there.

I found his clothing in the rank, tall grass that comes almost to the bank there. The garments had not been taken off in the ordinary manner. They could not possibly have been. For they were one inside the other, as they are worn, and every button, every buckle, was still fastened.

In witness whereof I set hereunto my hand and seal this 10th day of December, 1936.

(signed) Robert Falk.

Hugh Lambert's Narrative, resumed:

The violet glare was gone almost at once, and I was in pitch darkness, struggling with a swathing of coarse cloth that had been thrown over me. As I fought it my head found an opening. I pulled out through it, came to my feet.

Fist size rocks bruised them. I was nowhere I had ever been before. I was in a forest. A jungle rather, but such a jungle as no man has ever set eyes upon. Stalks curved gracefully up from the oddly coarse-grained earth to heights varying from barely greater than my own to fifty feet. They were not tree trunks, but great veined sheaths of plant fiber that curled in on themselves. The shorter ones flattened out near their dipping upper ends and narrowed gradually to pointed tips. From within the taller, stems issued three-quarters of the way up.

Some of these branched, others thickened into club-like rods long as a tall man. There were no leaves, but each bore such fruit as may grow on some distant planet but never on earth.

One type was teardrop-shaped, furred with short hairs, a barbed spike protruding from the sharper end. Another was an elongated cup of leafstuff studded with leprous blisters and stiff hairs. Still another...

But there is no profit in describing them all. Enough that this nightmare display was flooded by a nightmare, violet luminance. Enough that I shivered as much with the impact of the delirium setting into which I had emerged as with the cold that lay like ice against my skin.

My skin! *I was stark nude!* Not a single garment, not even the bandages on my arm and leg, remained to cover me!

I perceived all this; the incredible jungle, my nakedness; not *seriatim* as I am forced to set them forth but in a single sledgehammer blow upon my brain. Then movement glimpsed out of the corner of my eye whirled me around to the left.

I crouched, my jaw hardening, my hand snatching up a stone with the instinctive clutch for a weapon which the wilds breed into a man's very bone.

Five paces away, a serpent was outstretched, inches thick and long as a man is tall. Its blunt, eyeless head was lifted a bit, as though it had located me by smell alone and was making up its slow mind whether to dismiss me as not worth its attention, or go after me.

Experience has taught me that few savage things, mammal or reptile, will attack a motionless creature unless they are hunting food. I tautened my muscles to immobility, cramped as they were, and waited with pent-up breath for the monster's decision.

If the toss went against me, I would throw the stone and leap aside. Yes. But that would be a thousand-to-one chance at best. I have good reason to know a great snake's appalling invulnerability to anything but a blast from an elephant gun; and the lightning-like speed with which it can move.

I waited—The nape of my neck bristled with warning of a malign gaze upon me, of a threat to which that of the serpent was insignificant.

Some sixth sense made me look upward. Hovering over me, apparently unsupported in mid-air, was a creature into whose gargantuan body all terror a man can know was crammed.

That body, two feet in diameter, was globular, purple-furred. It had eight double-jointed legs, longer than the repulsive torso from which they angled. But the acme of the beast's horror was in its head, its sharp fangs protruding from diamond-shaped, cruel jaws; its tremendous eyes from which glared the black fires of Hades.

IN THE instant I glimpsed it, it crouched and hurled itself down upon me. My leg muscles exploded, hurled me out from

under it at the last possible instant of escape, hurled out of the forest and into a clearing floored with tumbled, jagged boulders. A wave rolled up on them, splashed me with its spray.

The monster had not followed me, and I'd lost sight of the serpent. I stared wildly around.

Only the brush of a Doré could limn that scene. I was a lonely midge in the heart of an inconceivable immensity steeped, saturated in a violet radiance that was not light bathing it from some outside source but luminance exuding from the very texture of all it made visible. Before me stretched a shoreless infinitude of billowing waves.

Behind me was the outré jungle and behind it, sweeping away from me on either side and curving so I sensed that somewhere, worlds away, it closed upon itself, a darkly purple barrier rose.

It piled aloft, mile upon mile, league upon immeasurable

league, till my mind reeled with very inability to comprehend its vastness. High, high it loomed, so that the sky was not above it but pinned to its bastion; the vaulted sky that alone was black save where bright violet dots were patterned into—a familiar constellation of a familiar world.

I saw Cygnus, the Swan, and just beneath its lowermost star the Great Barrier shaped itself into a peak I knew, a peak that I had gazed at, many times, from the campus of Camp Wanooka. Somehow, incredibly, this weird, other-worldly landscape was situated on the very spot, the very location, of the camp!

"Hughlambert!" I whirled to a deep voice that had spoken my name, making one word of it. I saw a man, straddle-legged on the shore, watching me. A man whose misproportioned frame was clad in a skin-tight garment of some metallic cloth that had the lustre and sheen of silk. A man whose dark face was lean, hawk-nosed and vulture-eyed. That face was the face of my dreams. And it was the face of the Little Man who had stalked me, night after night, about the camp.

But he was as tall as I!

"Who—who are you?" I gasped inanely, while the fingers of fear closed on my throat.

"Vanark," the deep voice replied. Then his left arm swung out, horizontally before him, his fingers spread so that I could see the webs joining them, and he said something I was to hear many times. *"Gor Surah."*

Strangely without will, I threw my own arm out, and answered, *"Gor Surah."* That was mechanical. My brain was not on my act or my words. It was reeling, dazed, with a sudden discovery.

The Little Man was not as tall as I. I was as small as he. Somehow, through some unbelievable chiromancy, I had shrunk to the height of twelve inches. Everything clicked into place. The vast barrier was the mountain rampart encircling Lake Wanooka. The giant jungle was the patch of rank weeds along the shore. The serpent was an earthworm, the monster I had barely escaped a spider. This limitless, billowing sea was the lake itself.

"Come, Hughlambert," Vanark said as his arm dropped to his side. "Don this and come." I took a dark bundle from him, mechanically as I had given the strange salute, mechanically obedient to his command, to some inner command that was like, but stronger than, the pull of the lake against which I had fought so long and so unavailingly. I had in that moment no will of my own. I had only some strange outside will in response to which I moved.

Its folds fell apart as I took the bundle, and I saw that it was another such garment as his. I squatted and struggled into it, feet first through the neck opening, knowing with queer surety that was the way to put it on. The stuff tingled, as if it were alive and consciously shaping itself to my body.

It was on, and I stood up, and in imitation of Vanark I pulled over my head a hood that was fastened at the back of my neck. It enveloped my head completely and melted into the neck hem of the garment to make a seamless joining.

And then, obedient still to that strange power that had supplanted my own will, I followed Vanark into the sea.

I could see through the fabric, and breathe through it. I could breathe through it even when a wave rolled over my head, swamping me. The curious textile seemed to possess the ability of a fish's gills to strain oxygen out of water!

A second wave took me off my feet. I started to swim—halted the motion in mid-stroke as I saw Vanark lay motionless on the surface, motionless as far as his limbs were concerned. He was gliding, with no effort at all, through the water.

I kept close behind him, realized that I was being towed by some force I could not sense otherwise than by its effect. Faster and faster it pulled me.

I was beneath the surface! I was going down, straight down into Lake Wanooka's unfathomable depths! Not sinking. Being

drawn down at ever increasing speed, while ahead of me, *below*
me, was the blurred, foreshortened form of Vanark.

I have dived, pearling in the South Seas, to a depth of twenty
fathoms, which is the deepest an unprotected man can go and
live. This was not diving, it was a plummet-like descent, a hurtling fall into an immeasurable water abyss endless and awful.

THAT STUPENDOUS descent continued endlessly. I was
aware that I dropped, at a rate too rapid to be called sinking,
straight down into a water-drowned valley whose floor was
miles beneath. By the eerie violet light that permeated those
infernal depths to which the brightest sunlight never had penetrated, I could see Vanark's blurred form below me, always
below me. I was even conscious that, instant by instant, the
distance between me and all that was familiar tremendously
increased.

Yet, incredible as it may seem, I felt neither amazement nor
fear. Not, understand, because of any courage or any super-
human stoicism of mine. The fact is that, for an unmeasured
period, my mind was literally numbed by the enormity of the
experience, my brain unable to apprehend it.

That suspension of thought, that stasis of emotion, must have
blocked off the mental chaos in which I had been lost since the
auto accident, for when I recovered the power to think, I knew,
definitely and beyond question, that I was and always had been
wholly sane. I knew that nothing, the tramp's vanishment of
which Edith had told me, the tug of the lake, the Little Men
visible only to me, had been other than actuality. I was not, I
never had been, mad. I wanted to shout it: "I'm sane! I'm *sane!*"

Strange reaction of one who minutes before had dwindled
to a sixth his normal size; of one who even then was gripped
by some occult force that dragged him at appalling speed down
into an awesome void of liquid light!

I had lost all sense of elapsed time. Of distance. There was
only myself, and the limitless lavender light all about me, and
the darker shape of the Little Man beneath me.

Outré as the week's occurrences had been. I now began to realize there was a weird inner consistency among them, a macabre pattern fitting them each to each.

The nexus of that design seemed to be the tramp. I had been wholly normal till his blood had been mingled with mine, then Lake Wanooka's strange attraction had begun to manifest itself. Jeremiah Fenton had felt it, too—and was there not his vague yet definite resemblance to the tramp to tie Fenton into the pattern?

Edith had described the tramp as shrinking to nothingness. I also had shrunk, except that the process had been halted when I was a foot high. The violet light…

My speculations were halted, abruptly, by a subtle, but ominous change in my surroundings.

It was at first merely an intangible adumbration of bounds to a space that hitherto had been boundless; insubstantial as that which might bring to a blind man awareness that he was within, say, Madison Square Garden; but almost at once I descried walls sloping in under me to make a roughly elliptical funnel still so vast I could not discern its lower limits.

I now had something by which to gauge the speed of my descent, and it was breathtaking. Those slanting sides of rock fairly leaped up at me!

Vanark was suddenly *beside* me, instead of below. Our course had changed. We were moving horizontally now. We were shooting toward one precipitous facade, the fanged rock now so immense its concavity was no longer perceptible. We were hurtling toward that jagged cliff at a speed that would smash us to a pulp!

I flailed the water with frantic arms and legs, in a frenzy to brake that suicidal swoop, to swerve it. The effort was as futile as an aviator's catapulting parachuteless from his plane and attempting to halt his fall. In a final terrible moment every detail of that cruel wall etched itself on my retina, the last thing I was to see in life…

We darted through an opening where no opening had been. There was a flash of solid rock slitting, gulping Vanark and me, and then there was only the water again and the sickening feel of the fluid compressing me, cushioning me, robbing me of motion!

My feet found some solid footing, but I still swayed with the eddying of the currents set up by our sudden halt and Vanark was a blurred shadow swaying beside me. I made out rock ahead of me, on either side of me, a yard or two above me. I turned to gape at the sudden aperture through which we had been swept.

There was no opening. It had closed again, swiftly and silently as it had appeared. Intelligence had chiseled the smooth rocky walls out of the submarine mountain. Intelligence had constructed the gateway in the cliffside, had opened it to receive us and had shut it behind us.

Vanark moved. I saw his arm reach out to touch the wall nearest him. It must have been a switch that he touched, for at once the flooring on which I stood and the liquid mass that engulfed me were pulsing with the slow, ponderous *throb-throb* of some gigantic machine.

The water tugged at me, pressed against me. I braced myself against its force, realizing that it was seething to some drain I could not perceive, was rushing out through it. Rapidly, for there was distance at once between the water's surface and the inwardly luminous roof of the carved-out cave, distance that grew from the moment I was aware of it.

The surface of the water came down to my head, to my chest, swirled down along my sides. The machine was emptying the enclosure. I realized that it was a water-lock permitting communication between the lake and—and *what?*

There must be another, greater hollow within the mountains. A cavern? A labyrinth? Some open space, at any rate that needs must be protected from the incursion of the lake, some space inhabited by living beings.

This much I reasoned out while the water seethed away. I was right, as events proved. But my wildest imaginings could not have predicted what lay within the bowels of the Helderbergs!

A SUCKING noise proclaimed the rock floor almost dry. "Hughlambert!" Vanark's voice said sharply. I turned, saw his gnomelike head, too large for his body, uncovered and projecting from his skintight garment. It leered at me its thin lips twisted in a mocking smile. "Doff your hood!"

"What is this?" I demanded. "Where is this?"

"Obey!" His tone an inflection such as is used only to members of a subject race, ridged my jaw with sudden anger. I had used it myself to coolies in Suiyuan, to bearers on the slopes of the Mountains of the Moon. "At once!" It was the impersonal contempt, the gloating triumph, in his beady eyes that seared me.

I snarled back at him, an iron band constricting my forehead, my thigh muscles cording.

He made some slight movement. Perhaps I thought he was about to attack me. Perhaps my latent wrath at what had been done to me, at myself for the meekness with which I had responded to Vanark's earlier commands, needed only the tiniest of sparks to bring it to full flame. I launched forward, clutched his shoulder and slammed him against the wall.

"Answer me!"

Vanark's countenance darkened with malign fury.

"You dare touch a Surahnit,"* he said whitely angry. "*Taphet!*"

I didn't know what the epithet was he spat at me, but I knew its intent. He had called me, "Pariah!" It put the final touch to

---

* Note: Some time after this incident I realized that from the moment I had been reduced in size I had understood and spoken a language utterly new to me, comprehending it as though it were my mother tongue except for terms such as these, that have no counterpart in our lexicon. Sometimes, in what follows, I shall substitute for the names of objects, functionaries, their nearest English equivalent translating for the reader of these lines (if they ever have a reader).

my blind wrath. My arm jerked back, my fist knotted to smash that hateful face…

And stayed that way! I couldn't deliver the blow. I could not move at all for one nightmare moment of paralysis!

In the next instant I did move, and what I did was infinitely more terrifying than doing nothing. The fingers I had on Vanark's shoulder loosened and dropped away. I stepped back, my shoulders bowed. My left arm, the one that jerked back to hurl hard knuckles at the swarthy man, threw itself horizontally before me fingers spread.

"Gor Surah!" The syllables came from my lips, but I swear they were not formed in my mind. Nor those with which my voice followed Vanark's brief acknowledgment of the strange salute. "Your pardon, master." *Master!*

I lifted my hands to my head and stripped back the hood that had covered it. I detested myself for the humble gesture, the spineless apology, the gesture of obedience to the glowering Vanark's command. I, the real Hugh Lambert, had nothing to do with them. Some substanceless compulsion had hold of me; a will not my own had begun to replace my will up there on the borders of Lake Wanooka. My rage had momentarily released me from it, but now it had regained possession of me. I came now to the full realization of its strength, because now for the first time I had come into direct conflict with it.

Conflict? There was no more conflict than there is between marionette and the puppeteer who pulls its strings. Save only this: Whoever, whatever, it was that dominated me had stolen my body from me; my muscles, even my tongue; but it had not vanquished my brain.

Nor my soul. Appalled, I might be, filled with dread of this strange thing that had come to me. But not conquered. Not conquered yet, not till reason itself should be blotted out. I swore that to myself, standing there powerless to defy another's will.

MY FINGERS were still stripping off the metallic fabric that had acted as gills through that terrific dive, when the scrape of rock on rock jerked my head around to the cave wall opposite to that through which we had been swept. A vertical gash appeared, rapidly widening until the lock chamber was open on the side away from the lake.

"*Gor Surah!*" A figure, poised where the vanished wall had been, flung out a horizontal arm in salute, its webbed fingers close together.

"*Gor Surah!*" We responded, imitating his gesture in unison. Vanark added a name, "Talim!"

This second of the Surahnit with whom I came in contact was young, a mere lad. Except for the strange misproportion of his head and limbs, he might have been one of my own senior campers. He had about him the same air of lithe eagerness, the same joy in a life just taking on meaning. There was a quick dart of his dark eyes to me; curiosity and some obscure excitement glinted in them. Then they were cast down, and Talim was backing away from before us as we wordlessly advanced.

But there was a more fundamental difference between Talim and my lads than mere appearance. Not even the youngest of them would ever have manifested quite the subservience that subtly cloaked Talim as he backed into a niche in the wall of a long tunnel while we continued past him.

I forgot Talim, I forgot even my resentment at the stolid submission with which I followed Vanark, as the tunnel ended and we came out on a narrow, shell-like ledge that clung to the side of a colossal cliff.

High as the towering rampart of the Helderbergs had appeared, it shrank to insignificance in contrast with the vertiginous fall of this mighty escarpment. How far above me the precipice towered I did not immediately observe for I gazed down over the brink before me and my senses reeled with awed wonder.

A landscape stretched below, mile upon distance-dwarfed mile, to another tremendous wall hazily remote. I saw hills and valleys and ruler-straight roads. I saw isolated dwellings, structures clumped into small clusters that might be villages, and two larger groupings one of which might well be the city of my dream.

I was too far above all this to discern the detail of even the largest building. But I did have an impression of *difference* from the world above.

That difference was not alone a matter of shapes and contours. For an eye-blink of time I sensed only a dream-like, eerie quality suffusing the scene, a weird wrongness that was infinitely ominous. Then I saw what the difference was.

There were no shadows. Nowhere, not where a sharp-sided mesa jutted from the ground nor where, to my left, a tremendous tumulus of splintered, rectangular boulders was piled against the distant wall of this hollow within the earth was there a single shadow.

I glanced down. There was no shadow on the stony shelf where I stood. I myself cast no shadow. Vanark cast none…

"Come!" Vanark said, and was striding away along the ledge. I followed him, impelled by the alien will to which I was subject. My gaze returned to that vast stretch of terrain below. Everywhere upon it tiny specks crawled. Though I could make out nothing of their form, they moved too purposefully to be anything but animate, intelligent creatures.

This was no cave, no mere subterranean cavern. Here was a nation, a world within a world, inhabited by thousands, perhaps by millions of the Little Folk whose messenger was Vanark.

And I was their captive.

IT IS difficult to select out of the welter of thoughts and speculations and fears that seethed in my brain at this time the ones which are most significant. Perhaps, since its nature was then becoming a little clearer to me, I should discuss the spell that dragged me so helplessly in Vanark's wake.

I obeyed it, willy nilly, as one obeys some post-hypnotic suggestion, unconscious of its source. Yet it did not continuously control me. The jerk of my head toward the sound of the lock's opening inner portal had been my impulse, as had been my pause just now at the edge of the ledge. My command over the movements of my body was not obliterated, but superseded.

I resolved to remember that. Some time I might have a chance to use it.

There was more. The fact that Vanark had *spoken* his order to me, just now, seemed to indicate it was not he to whom I was enslaved. But when I had been halted in the very act of striking him there had been no one else in the chamber, and we had been enclosed by solid rock. Even now I could locate no one near enough to make me out as anything but an almost microscopic animalcule crawling along the looming cliff. Were there invisible eyes upon me, watching me every step? How could that be?

I decided upon an experiment. I would whirl, run off in the other direction. Vanark was ahead of me, could not see me. I would take good care he did not hear me.

Now I would do it. *Now!*

I kept right on going, a half dozen paces behind my leader. There had not been even a twitch of my smallest muscle in response to the fierce effort I had made, or tried to make.

Quod erat demonstrandum! I was master of myself only when what I wanted to do did not contradict the Other's commands.

I was not, you see, beaten yet. I was testing the forces arrayed against me. I was preparing myself for rebellion against my captors. I had no plan. To make one I must know what it was I schemed against. I must know my own weaknesses, my enemies' strength.

I must also gather every iota of information I could about my surroundings. The weird world below was a map without detail from this height. I turned my attention to the face of the looming cliff.

There were other openings in it, intermittently along the

ledge. Some of them were roughly framed, the exits of natural caves. Others were manifestly hewn, as the lock had been, out of the perdurable rock. I tried to glance into one of these as I passed it. I saw nothing. My sight was blocked by a screen of *living light!*

It was a curtain of radiance, an impenetrable sheet of coruscant purple fire, so shimmering that it seemed endowed with some other-worldly sort of sentience. It was made up of sparks, of tiny-explosions, of darting violet infinitesimal stars, and all of them streamed incessantly, endlessly, out of the very substance of the cliff.

The rock itself, the towering precipice was aglow with light. And not only the rock. Vanark himself, hurrying ahead of me, was visible by the same intrinsic radiance that glowed from within his very flesh.

My own hand, too, was softly lambent. To its qualities of form and color another had been added, as inherent as these. Light!

That was why there were no shadows in this amazing terrestrial hollow! There was no sun, no mode, no external source for its pervading illumination. Everything here, living and inorganic matter alike, shone with its own brilliance. Light casts no shadow.

There was infinite beauty in that omnipresent luminance, and—infinite threat.

THAT THREAT was vague, a product simply of strangeness. But there was nothing vague about the terror that struck at me seconds after my attempt to peer within the opening had failed.

We had gone by a half dozen of such light-screened portals when the ledge curved around a jutting fold in the cliff face. The protuberance hid Vanark. I went around it.

There was no one on the ledge. It ended abruptly, a scant three yards in front of me, and beyond was nothing but a sheer dizzy drop, without hand- or foot-hold, to the base of that incredible precipice.

Utterly impossible for a man to take more than three strides more and live. I gasped—*and paced on, utterly unable to halt!*

One step I took. Two. All of me, every shuddering nerve and cell, recoiled from the fearful plunge. The third-stride brought me to the very brink. A scream formed in my throat as my foot lifted for the step that must be my last...

I turned, *was turned,* toward the cliff!

My foot came down on solidity! I was within the arch of an opening the sparkling motes of whose curtain parted to let me through. I was in a tunnel once more, and Vanark was a dozen feet ahead of me, and the sound of our footfalls reverberated hollowly in my ears.

The passage pitched downward for a space, twisted sharply to the right. I reached the turn, went around it, came out on a gallery running along one smooth concave wall of a huge cavern.

Still moving swiftly, I contrived to look down to the floor of this great cave, fifty feet below me. It swarmed with the tiny creatures of this outré world.

The *tiny* creatures. Though they were no smaller than myself, my perspective was restored! For, lying there below me, row upon ghastly row, were the corpses of humans, human-size; the cadavers of men and women and of little children, gigantic by contrast to the ghouls bustling about them—busily, purposefully.

They were human beyond question, and by unmistakable, gruesome signs I knew them to be long dead. Then they were screened from me by hulking machines that whirred and clashed violet-gleaming rods, that spun cogged wheels and hid the grisly morgue. But far at the other end of the vaulted space there was a raised platform, and this I could see over the tops of the machines as I was hurried along, unable to stop, unable to cry out, unable to do anything but gape at what was happening on that dais.

A half-dozen Little Men were clustered about a naked human corpse lying there. There was something grotesque about the recumbent shape, something clumsy in its formation. It was too far away for me to be sure of what there was about it that troubled me, but it was not too far away for me to see that a foot-high creature lay beside it, and that there was some connection between the opposed arms of each, something that dimly resembled a transfusion apparatus I once had seen Courtney Stone use.

The group of Little Men swirled with some obscure excitement. And then—and then...

The dead human quivered! His free arm rose, moved across his chest and fumbled at the other, as though his first sensation were discomfort of which he must be rid.

The dead human quivered... his free arm rose.

A wall cut off my view, the wall of another tunnel, into which my swift course had taken me. I tried to convince myself I had been mistaken. The human had not been dead. He had not come to life again as I watched him, life pumped into his veins from the veins of a Little Man.

Why should I have thought, just then, of a tale I had heard, was it days or eons ago? A tale of a drowned farmer returning to his home and moving a piece on a dusty chess board? Why should the fingers of a gelid dread have tightened on my heart?

Was it only because I had seen, screwed to a dead lad's moldering, green-scummed* shoe, a rusted ice skate? Or did there already glimmer in my mind some inkling of the fearful truth, some suspicion of the ghastly scheme that was maturing in that balconied cavern?

I think it was then that, for the first time since my plunge into the lake, I thought of the world above and wondered how my disappearance had been taken there. How had Ann Doring reacted to it?

---

* Editor's Note: Observe that from this point on Mr. Lambert begins again to mention colors other than violet in his descriptions. This is not because there was any change in the character of the illumination in the strange underground universe but because his brain had learned again to interpret in terms of the normal spectrum the retinal impressions it was receiving.

CHAPTER III

Letter from Richard Doring, Senior Bunk, Camp Wanooka, Cadet Major U.S. Grant Military Academy, to Ann Doring, c/o World Pictures, Hollywood, Cal.

Camp Wanooka, Thursday,
Aug. 30, 1934

Dear Sis:

I guess you're surprised to see that I'm still at camp. Well, you're no more surprised than I am.

I woke up in the dark, last night, which was queer in the first place, because it's usually hard enough to wake me in the morning. I thought it was just because of all the skylarking on account of the Break-Up, and I lay there thinking about all I was going to do in New York the three weeks before I had to leave for school.

Pretty soon I began to see, through the open window over my cot, lights flashing in the treetops. There was a lot of whispering too, and it was all very mysterious.

The night seemed full of a hushed sort of excitement. I looked at my luminous watch. It was almost one o'clock, which is awfully late for here. I knew, then, that something was up.

Well, it couldn't be like me to have anything going on and not stick my nose in it. I slid out of bed, slipped into my bathrobe and sneakers and tiptoed out.

Catfooting out of the door, which was open, I stumbled on something and had to grab the jamb to keep from falling. Funny thing was, when I looked to see what had tripped me there wasn't anything there. Nothing at all.

I was real scared for a second. Creepy scared. Then I decided I must have tangled my leg in the skirt of my robe. It hadn't felt like that, though it had felt as if my shin had been bumped by something solid—and alive.

The flashlights were flicking around up at the north end of camp. I went toward them, keeping in the dark as much as I could, got past the office shack and stopped dead in the edge of the woods just beyond it. Ed Hard and Bob Falk were prowling through the brush, their flashlight shining on the ground.

"It's funny," Bob was saying, "that we can't find his tracks anywhere."

Then Ed said that somebody'd been acting upset lately and maybe he'd jumped in the lake. I saw Bob's torch shake a little. They were talking about Mr. Lambert, and Bob said that he'd never do a thing like that, and look at the way his clothes are piled on the ground. Then I heard Nurse Horne yelling at me, and Ed and Bob came running, and before I could answer they started to bawl me out.

But Miss Horne told them to let me alone. She said as long as I was there they'd have to tell me what'd happened and depend on me to keep my mouth shut. Her face was tight, kind of, and awful pale.

I know I can trust you not to repeat a word of what follows. So here goes.

Mr. Lambert had disappeared. He'd gone down to the lake about an hour before and then had vanished clean off the face of the earth!

We looked for him awhile longer, but it was no use. Bob Falk had been on patrol at that side of camp, Ed Hard on the side along the road, and Miss Horne had been awake, packing all the medicines and stuff in the infirmary. Mr. Lambert couldn't have got out of camp without one of them seeing him, but he wasn't in it. We gave up at last, and they started to talk about what they should do.

The councillors wanted to notify the police, but Miss Horne wouldn't let them. She said they mustn't get the boys excited. They'd go home and tell their folks and that would ruin the camp next year. There really was nothing to worry about. Mr. Lambert must have his own reasons for going away like he had, and if he'd been able to take care of himself in the wilderness he certainly could be in America.

That's the way she talked but I had a funny hunch she had more on her mind than she was saying and that she was frightened to death.

Well, I went back to the bunk and I was so tired I fell right asleep. When the get-up bugle blew I dressed in a jiffy and rushed out but Mr. Lambert wasn't anywheres around.

The bus that came, right after breakfast, wasn't big enough to take all the bunch, so it was decided that the four seniors in my bunk were to be run down to Albany in the camp sedan. That's why it wasn't till the bus left that anyone noticed Charley Dorsey hadn't showed up.

Ed Hard went to get him. Charley was still asleep, and Ed couldn't wake him up!

Dr. Stone, whom they phoned for right away, said that Charley has a queer disease, something like sleeping sickness only it isn't. There's two cases like it in the Albany Hospital, both from around here so it may be contagious and Doc has quarantined our bunk.

Charley is in the infirmary here and the rest of us; me, Roger Norton and Percy White; have to stick around. Besides us fellows there's just Miss Horne. Ed, Bob, and Morphy the cook, left in camp.

Morphy's a queer duck. He's an old Irishman, with a face like the ones we saw cut out of toast in that store on Lexington Avenue. We all ate lunch in the kitchen, except Charley of course. By that time Rog and Perce had started asking questions about Mr. Lambert and Ed decided it was best to tell them what had happened, swearing them to secrecy.

"It's the leprechauns has got him," Morphy said. "We won't see him no more."

"Leprechauns!" Rog asked. "What's that?"

"Them's the little people that's older than the hills themselves," Morphy said. "The little people that owned the Earth when it was young and we wasn't yet thought of." He had a frying pan in his hand. There was a queer, faraway look in his eyes just then that made me shiver a little. "They never die, and some day they're going to take the Earth back for themselves."

Rog laughed. It seemed to make Morphy angry.

"You can laugh, young fellow," he said. "But I seen them myself, coming out of Lough Neagh. They was a queer purple light on the water and—"

"That will be enough of that," Ed interrupted. "We've got enough on our minds without your Irish fairy tales."

"Fairy tales, is it? Irish, is it? What about the trolls the Germans tell about? What about the black pigmies of Africa no explorer has ever seen? What about the gnomes that carried Rip Van Winkle

away right in these here very mountains, the ones the Dutchmen used to say made the thunder? And what about the fairies and the elves themselves? There's good and evil among the little people, just like there is among us."

"I said that we'll have no more of that sort of talk," Ed, growled, and that shut Morphy up. Perce said something to me but I didn't hear him. I was watching Nurse Horne. She just sat there, staring at the cook, and her face was like it had been the night before, pale and tight and awful scared.

This is a long letter but I didn't have anything to do except write it. Camp is awful empty with almost everybody gone, and those who aren't worried sick and trying not to show it. I'll have to close now, though, because Doc Stone's going to town and he's going to air mail this for me. He's coming back later. He's going to spend his nights here. He says that's on account of Charley but I'm pretty sure it's on account of Mr. Lambert.

I've asked Doc to bring back some games, like Mr. Ree and Pick Up Sticks. Will you be a good sis and wire him the money to pay for them? My balance in the camp bank is all used up.

> *Your affectionate brother,*
> *Dick.*

Hugh Lambert's Narrative, resumed:

THE TUNNEL THAT led from the great cavern where I had seen, or thought I had seen, a human corpse weirdly revived, ended abruptly in a circular, dome-ceilinged room some ten feet in diameter. I came to a halt beside Vanark.

This cubicle was entirely bare, and there was no exit from it. *There was no entrance! Following* the rounded walls with my eyes, I was aware that they had made a complete circuit and had encountered no break in the gleaming rock. Startled, sure that this must be illusion, I put out my hand to feel for the opening through which I had just come.

A sharp cry of warning from Vanark was drowned by a whistle that leaped high in the scale to a tremendous, humming

roar. The wall rasped the skin from my fingertips, flung my hand up and away from it, so violently that I was thrown off balance!

I did not fall. I was poised on one foot, my body canted at an impossible angle, but I did not fall!

I stared, bewildered, at the wall. It was not speckled with light-points as the face of the cliff or the tunnel sides had been. It was striated by multitudinous vertical lines of brilliance that wavered and were never still.

No! The walls were motionless. It was we who were flashing downward, so fast that we were weightless; so fast that I gasped with sudden fear lest the floor drop away from beneath me and I crash against the ceiling. I cowered beneath that threat, looked upward.

There was no ceiling! There was only a tight-lined cone, coming to a point immensely far above me.

I was in no enclosed car. I was on a platform and the cone up into which I stared was the shaft down which it shot.

Somewhere in that shaft there had to be a vent for the air beneath the close-fitting stone disc that carried us downward, and that was the source of the unbearable roar that beat in my ears.

The shaft, the platform, vibrated with the fearful sound. It took hold of me and shook me, so that every separate atom of my body was in its grip. In the next instant, or the next, they must disintegrate. The pain of it was excruciating. I was all pain, all agony. I could hear, see, nothing.

I threw out my arms, wildly, actuated only by some instinct of self-preservation, some brainless impulse to combat the terrific vibration that was tearing me to pieces. My hand struck something soft, warm. Flesh, Vanark's flesh. Vanark's throat.

My fingers closed on that throat. Somehow the fingers of the other hand joined them.

I was stripped of sight, feeling. I was stripped of reason. I was suffering torture. But I knew, my hands were on the throat of my enemy. For this one moment he was at my mercy.

Mercy! A savage laugh ripped from me and my fingers closed on the neck they clutched. I felt flesh squash beneath them. I felt windpipe gristle crumple.

Hands seized my arms, my waist, dragged me from my victim. Silence throbbed in my skull, silence that was like thunder after the roar that had accompanied that awful descent. The fall was ended. There was a door again in the wall of the great shaft, and men were crowding in through it. Men had taken hold of me, had dragged me erect, their froglike fingers digging into my flesh. One knelt to Vanark, whose face was blue with strangulation, the bruises my fingers had made livid on his throat.

I wrenched an arm free from the clutch on it… and then I was rigid. I stood meekly, abandoning the struggle. Not because of resignation. Because once more the Other had seized control of me.

"ANOTHER TAPHET bustin' out," a low voice muttered, behind me. "They're sure looking for trouble these times."

"Yeah," another responded. "If I was the Council I'd quit

tryin' to bring 'em to their senses in the labor squadrons. I'd line
'em up and *coret* the whole crowd." He touched a short-barreled
device at his belt, fashioned from some dull red metal, beyond
doubt a weapon of some sort.

"Well, this one won't get to no labor squadron if I know
Vanark. Not after what he done to him." *

There must have been a dozen of these men crowding around
me, youths like Talim. They were all dressed alike, in queerly
cut costumes of what appeared to be a dark green, pliable leather,
evidently a uniform. The one massaging Vanark's throat was
probably their officer. He was older, his uniform better fitting.
Some insignia decorated its sleeve and his belt supported,
instead of a *coret,* a short-handled, flint-headed ax. An ax of
the Stone Age!

"Silence!" he commanded, not turning his head. "There's too
much chatter."

Vanark spluttered. He thrust a hand against the floor, shoved
himself up to a sitting posture. The officer helped him to his
feet; stepped back and saluted him with horizontal arm, spread
fingers, and the inevitable: *"Gor Surah."*

Vanark responded perfunctorily, turned to me. His countenance was a frozen, expressionless mask, but his eyes were red
balls; worms of rage crawled within their lurid depths.

"Coret this man," he blurted out, thick-tongued.

The officer straightened. I think he clicked his heels. "There
has been no court," he protested. "The decree—"

"May at all times be superseded by a member of the Council,"
Vanark interrupted. "You know that, Subaltern Hafna. I will
cover you. Obey my command."

"Very well." Hafna wheeled crisply to face me, jerking the
ax from his belt.

"Attention, men!" he snapped. Feet shuffled. The green-

---

* Editor's Note: Mr. Lambert here evidently attempts to convey by elisions and
ungrammatical construction some difference in the speech of these men from that of
the more cultured Surahnit.—A.L.Z.

uniformed men were ramrod-stiff. "The execution detail will be Fator, Latta, Kut. March the prisoner out."

"No," Vanark countermanded. "I want him slain at once!" His urgency seemed not to be wholly due to his desire for immediate vengeance. I caught a flicker of his glance to the entrance. "Here!"

"The concussion may injure the shaft mechanism, Councilman Vanark," Hafna objected. I rather resented his temporizing. I had no chance of escape, no chance even to die fighting. The quicker it was over and done with the better.

"Have him taken to your guardroom," Vanark yielded. "But no further."

The subaltern gave the command. I was marched off the platform through the doorway. This side of the guardroom was the lambent rock of the cliff, the others were of a whiter, softer appearing stone. The room was sparsely furnished with appointments queerly shaped out of the same alloy as the guards weapons and the handle of Hafna's ax. A rack of *corets* hung on one wall. A tool of that strange, red metal hung in an embrasure of the one opposite the shaft entrance.

I was paraded to the third wall, and stood against it. The detail Hafna had named lined up, facing me. The officer strode stiff-kneed to the end of the line. "*Corets!*" he barked. Three hands snapped to three belts. "Draw!" Three hands jerked in unison. Three dull red barrels snouted at me.

"Wait, Subaltern Hafna!" I exclaimed. "Nal Surah has need of me and even Vanark cannot save you from his wrath if you destroy me."

THE WORDS came from my lips, but I swear I did not say them. How could I? I had not then yet heard the name, Nal Surah, was unaware of its transcendant power. It was the Other who had spoken with my tongue. The Other invisible, intangible, but aware of what was happening here.

Hafna hesitated, his head turning to Vanark, his eyes ques-

The dead human quivered... his free arm rose!

tioning. I could not read the latter's expression, but what he said was clear. Too clear. "He lies."

"But," the subaltern began, "would it not be wise to make certain. I think…"

"Your duty is to obey, not to think. Am I not of the Ratanit? Do I not know Nal Surah's mind? Give the command!"

Hafna shrugged. His fleshless lips parted. Now, I thought. This is it. This is the end...

"Who is it that knows Nal Surah's mind?" It was a woman's voice, indolent, low, almost intonationless. "What passes here?" But there was something in its timbre that spoke of an assured power.

Hafna spun to it, his arm flinging out parallel with the floor. *"Gor Surah!"* Vanark's gesture was this time no mechanical acknowledgment of an inferior's salute. It was a greeting to an equal. Or a superior? I could not be quite sure. "Nalinah!" one of the guards muttered.

She leaned against the jamb of the outer doorway, open now, flicking a lithe thigh with a thin silvery rod that was tipped by a filigree representation of the same insignia that was on Hafna's sleeve. There was a pantherine grace to her small body. A short-skirted, rainbow-hued frock was kirtled at her waist but tight about her bosom so that it did not conceal the soft curves it covered. Her head, crowned by an aureole of flaxen hair, was canted slightly to one side, like a curious bird's. The curl of her lips, the color of old rose, hinted at a smile but there was no smile in her blue eyes.

"What goes on here?" she repeated. "Answer me, Subaltern Hafna."

Against the sun-brightness of her hair her complexion was oddly dusky. Her features had the racial sharpness of these Folk, yet in some evasive way they brought to mind not the vulture Vanark's resembled but the parakeet. There was the same pastel beauty there, the same fragile loveliness.

"We execute this Taphet, Ra Nalinah," the officer spoke up. "He attacked Rata Vanark and would have slain him had the elevator been but an instant slower in its descent."

Nalinah's face hardened. "Why is he not delivered over to a

court, as the Council has decreed, that the execution may be a public warning to others of his ilk?"

"Rata Vanark commanded to the contrary."

"Ah, Vanark. That was why you claimed to know Nal Surah's mind. But I recall that in Council you cast the deciding vote for the public punishment of rebel Taphetnit, when I opposed it. Strange you should forget the decree."

"I did not forget it," Vanark responded. "Nor did I forget that at my suggestion authority was reserved to us of the Council to order instant execution at our will. I am exercising that authority now."

I listened to all this with a curious detachment. There seemed no question but that one way or another I was to be executed. It made little difference to me whether I died at once, or a little later.

Nalinah smacked the rod against her skirt. "You have the right! Get it over with. I have been informed of a new experiment, the most successful thus far, and am in haste to inspect it."

"Thank you, Nalinah," Vanark said, and I thought there was a mocking undertone to his voice. He turned away from her. "Subaltern Hafna!" he said. "*Coret* this Taphet!"

The officer saluted, wheeled smartly. Well, I thought, that's that. I should have preferred to have seen the sun once more before I died.

Facing those strange weapons of the green-clad guards, watching them lift to blast me with whatever lethal charge they held, an old speculation drifted across my mind. Could they kill me, these macabre little Folk? Or was I not so different in structure from them, so definitely from another plane of existence that the effort would merely result in returning me to the world from whence I had come, the world of green, growing things of limpid, rippling waters?

In that moment of final threat, my only emotion was a nostalgia for all that was my own, my birthright!

Account of Courtney Stone, M.D. resumed:

THERE COULD be no doubt that the boy, Charles Dorsey, was affected by the inexplicable malady that had struck down the two natives in the hospital, Adath Jenks and Job Grant. Driving down from Camp Wanooka, I tried to force myself to concentrate on that problem, tried to review once more the little we had learned about the wasting disease of which there was now a third victim. I found it impossible, however, to keep my mind from straying to other problems, that were hardly therapeutic but no less pressing.

There was, for one, the question of the quarantine I had imposed on the few left at the camp. There would be no trouble about the Dorsey lad. He was an orphan and the ward of a trust company. A wire to the proper officer would forestall inquiries. I carried letters from the other three youngsters to their relatives which I hoped would delay an incursion of these for at least a week.

What bothered me in this respect was whether I had been right in permitting the other campers to scatter to their homes, when a phone call could have caught them at the station. Were they carrying some epidemic broadcast?

The three cases of that coma during which the vitality of its victims seeped slowly away were definitely endemic to Lake Wanooka. That spoke of a focus of infection in that locale. We had isolated no germs, no filterable virus by which we could transmit the affection to any of our test animals. This, I concluded, justified me, in my course of action.

Perhaps it was a bit of sophistry. I wondered what I should have done had I not been aware that an investment of several hundred thousand dollars depended on my decision. Big Money is scary, and irascible. Not five per cent of Wanooka's clientele would return next year if I insisted on a general quarantine.

I persuaded myself that this aspect of the situation had not influenced me but I could not deny that I had agreed to keeping Hugh Lambert's disappearance secret for any but personal motives.

The reputation of the camp had entered also into this equation. The fear of kidnapers is a peculiar affliction of the wealthy, and certainly Wanooka's patrons would be justified in arguing that if its director could vanish mysteriously from its precincts, their sons would not be safe there. This was not, however, the clinching argument for silence.

Edith Home had put it like this: "Whatever's happened to Hugh is tied up with what we did the night of the accident. It's useless to bring the police in on this unless we tell them about that. And we dare not."

"You mean—that tramp?"

"I mean that they won't believe us if we tell them what happened to the tramp. Nobody would. They'll think that he died as a result of the transfusion and that we—we—"

"Disposed of his body somehow. To hide—"

"Murder."

I knew a moment of terror as she said that word, quietly, without perceptible emotion. Then I rallied. "But Edith," I protested. "We can't let that stop us. We've got to do everything we can to find Hugh. If it means trouble for us we'll have to stand the gaff. I'll try to cover you up somehow, but he's my friend and—"

"Your friend!" she broke in. "What do you think he is to me?"

Her hands were at her breast. Her eyes held mine. I looked into their agonized depths, and read her secret there.

"Do you think there's anything, in the world or beyond it," she asked, "I would not do to help him? But we can't help."

I didn't understand. I said so.

"Doesn't the way his clothes were found mean anything to you?"

I perceived her drift. "You think that—"

"The same thing happened to him as happened to the tramp, or something very like it. What else can I think?"

"Then he's gone," I groaned. "Hugh Lambert's gone. We'll never see him again!"

Thinking it over as I drove down the road, I realized what utter nonsense it all was, but with Edith's eyes upon me, I had believed it. Strange how a man trained in science could have been swung so far off his base by a superstitious woman!

"No," Edith had responded to that hopeless exclamation of mine. "I have a strange feeling that he is alive, somewhere. And a strange faith that he will win through and come back to us. But we can only wait; and hope that sometime, somehow, we shall find a way to help him. If we're to be ready for that, we must be free to act. That is why we must act like criminals, with a secret that would put us in the chair if it were found out."

A criminal with a secret that would put me in the chair. That was what I felt like as I reached New Scotland Road at last and saw my home ahead of me, at the end of a long block. Waiting for a red light to turn, I actually cringed inwardly at the sight of the blue-uniformed traffic cop who manipulated it, gasped with relief when he released my car.

A man stood looking at a pile of debris on the edge of the sidewalk in front of my gate. I recalled that Mrs. Small had started one of her periodic convulsions of housecleaning that morning, remembered that the phone from camp had caused me to forget to call the rubbish cart.

It was Jethro Parker who looked at the heap of papers, broken curtain poles, pots that had outlived their usefulness. I braked the car.

"What brings you here?" I asked. "You look pretty healthy."

"I am," he answered. "I come to Albany to see Marthy, my wife, off on the train. She's goin' to Providence to visit her brother for a fortnight. I was kind of at loose ends and I thought I'd drop by and ask you how that tramp made out, that had the accident up near my corn lot."

"The tramp?" I hoped nothing in my face showed the sudden panic that leaped within me. "Oh, yes, I remember now." To hide my confusion I fumbled with the car door, stepped out on the sidewalk. "He—wasn't hurt badly at all. He was suffering from shock. Surly chap. He refused to let me do anything for him. Got up and went out without even telling me his name. I've a notion he was afraid to. Maybe the police were after him."

"Got right up an' went out," Parker drawled in his nasal twang. "Just like he was?"

"Yes."

"That's funny."

"What's funny about it?"

"Well, I could swear that them rags—" he pointed at the heap of my housekeeper's off-scouring—"is the very clothes he wore when I picked him off the road."

They were! When Ann Doring had come into the surgery I had stuffed the filthy moldering garments behind an instrument cabinet, and forgotten them. I stared at them now, wadded on the very top of that mound of debris, tattered, mud-slimed, and accusing!

Hugh Lambert's narrative, resumed:

TIME HAS a way of slowing up at moments of stress. I saw the little muscles at the corners of Subaltern Hafna's mouth gather themselves to open for the command that would blot me out. I saw the trio of green-uniformed guards waiting for that command. I saw the girl in the doorway, her look bent on Vanark, studying him. I had time, even, to recall that not once, while they had discussed my fate, had she glanced at me.

"Ra Nalinah," I was surprised to find myself saying. "I am no Taphet. I am the one who has so long been sought in the Upper World. I am the one whom Nal Surah awaits."

The words were gibberish to me, but they brought a sharp,

"Hold it, Hafna!" from her. She sprang erect, stepped into the room to stare at me. Her eyes widened. Her lips parted, showing a white gleam.

"He is fair-skinned," she murmured, thinking aloud. "But he has not the look of a Taphet. It may be. It may well be."

"It not only may be, but is." Weird sensation, that, to hear my own voice saying things I not only did not think; but did no comprehend. "Ra Vanark is no subaltern of the labor squadron guard. Ask him how he came to be alone on the platform with me, if I am a Taphet. Ask him why I am clad in this suit of *sibral,* as he is. Ask him."

Nalinah did not take her gaze from my face. "What say you to that," she purred, "Rata Vanark?"

Realization flashed upon me that the unseen wielder of that ineluctable control over my acts and my speech was fighting for my life, had been fighting for it from the moment the guards had seized me. With the omniscience of which he had proven himself possessed, he had known Nalinah to be on her way here; had spoken, through me, exactly at the proper instant that would delay my execution sufficiently long for her arrival to interfere with it.

"What concern is it of yours?" the man responded to Ra Nalinah's demand. "For what I do I am answerable to the Nal alone."

"And to the Folk!" She turned to him, her brooding eyes upon him. "The Creed seems to have faded from your mind. The Folk is all," she chanted. " 'I am nothing. The Folk will is my will, the Folk weal my weal. I die, the Folk exists forever.'" There was a religious, almost fanatic fervor in her tones. "The Folk is the master, Vanark, the Ratanit but its voice. Even the Nal. Even Nal Surah."

Vanark's swart lip trembled, as if it would lift in a sneer, but dared not. There was a long minute of silence, electric with tension, with bristling antagonism.

I sensed, from the amazed look on Hafna's face, from the

startled glances among his men, that this strife was new in the relations of these two, or if not new then newly manifest. Was it to bring this about that the Other had delayed speaking through me again till Vanark had committed himself to a lie?

Had even my attack on him been directed and not, as I had thought, a voluntary act of my own, freed from control by the swiftness of that descent?

IT WAS Vanark who broke the silence. "This is he for whom I searched in the Upper World," he admitted. "But I have found him imperfectly controlled, more likely to defeat our purpose than serve it." He was desperately trying to convey the impression that he was explaining his act, not apologizing for it. "I decided it were best to destroy him and return to our first design."

"You decided!"

He spread his arms wide. "Perhaps I was too hasty. Perhaps it were better to place the matter before the full council. I shall conduct him…"

"I shall conduct him to my own quarters," Nalinah cut in, "and hold him till the Ratanit convene. You consent, Vanark? Or shall we refer the matter to the Nal, repeating to him all that has passed here?"

Vanark didn't like that. I could see he didn't like it at all. He hesitated.

Nalinah lifted her silvery rod. A low hum came from it. The device at its tip seemed to glow more brightly. With some surprise I perceived that its pierced pattern showed a central orb and nine others, smaller and of various sizes, circling about it. It looked amazingly like a representation of the Solar System. But how could that…

"There is no need to disturb the Nal!" I was almost sure Vanark's exclamation was edged with a quiver of fear. "No need for him to know there has been any dispute between us. It is a matter of small moment. You may do as you wish."

The humming stopped. "Thank you, Rata Vanark." Nalinah

said it gravely, but as she turned to me, I surprised a dancing light in her eyes, of impish amusement. With somewhat of a shock I realized that she was little more than a girl. She had been so dignified, so almost regal, until then.

"What are you called?" she asked me.

"Hugh Lambert."

"Hughlambert." She ran the syllables together, as Vanark had done. Evidently there were only single names here, terms such as Nal, Ra, Rata, being titles. "It is too difficult to say and to remember. I shall call you Hula. Come then, Hula."

She turned and went out through the doorway.

I strode across the floor. As I followed Nalinah out into the open I felt Vanark's eyes on my back. They seemed to bore into me. I knew that whatever the attitude of the others here might be to me, I had one implacable, malignant enemy...

If I seem to have related these events in too great detail, I have this excuse. From every word that had been spoken, almost from every shadow flitting across the countenances of the swart speakers, I had gleaned some bit of information to add to my pitiful store. I was commencing to apprehend the weird web in which I was entangled, the nature of the strange internecine strifes.

Most of this was still tantalizingly vague, but one fact stood out clearly. There was nothing accidental about my being brought here for some definite purpose. Though that purpose was as yet hidden from me, I knew somehow that it affected not me alone but the world from which I had been snatched. Somehow dread crept sluggishly through my veins, seeped blackly into my brain.

How terribly justified that dread was, what the amazing intent of the Surahnit was, and how—desperately, hopelessly— I strove to defeat it, will appear as my narrative proceeds to its astounding climax, the issue of which I do not yet know.

Will appear, I write. I smile, wanly, bitterly, as I set those two words down. No human, no man or woman of the Upper World, will read this narrative if the die I have cast rolls against me and *them.*

I STRODE out of that guardroom where I had so nearly met my end. Somewhere over me there was a roof upon which great mountains rested but I was aware of it only as a murky, clouded sky. I was more immediately conscious of the loom of rock towering just behind me, yet even this was so incredibly altitudinous and ran to such sightless distances on either side that I could no longer conceive of it as a precipice. It was, rather, a limit to space, a boundary to reality itself. To all intents and purposes I was in the open.

The ground across which I was being impelled was not earth but stone. It was imbued with the eerie glow that permeated all things here, but here the luminance was dark and secretive, and the uneven surface within which that glow seemed imperceptibly to pulsate was the surface of a frozen flow.

This was rock that once had been molten, rock that was rigid now in whatever queer twisting of shape the fading of its heat had left it. It was igneous rock. It was the naked primal matter of our whirling planet.

I knew now how very deep this land must be, how close to Earth's heart I had penetrated, and how remote I was from the world I had known.

It rolled away from me, this plain of congealed stone, and it lifted as it rolled so that its cresting ridges circumscribed my vision within a radius of perhaps a hundred yards. Motionless now, some twenty feet ahead, Nalinah awaited me, her dusky lips curved in a half smile, and beside her was something new to my experience.

I guessed this thing to be a vehicle of sorts, because, and only because, it was poised in the center of a wide swathe of rock evidently artificially smoothened to make a road running off, straightaway to some unguessable destination.

At its highest the contrivance rose barely above the golden glory of Nalinah's hair. From there it curved forward to a bulbous nose and pitched backward to a pointed tail. Its sides and its bottom duplicated the curve of its roof so that, albeit with an amazing appearance of rigidity, it was balanced on a single point of its under structure.

Puzzling me almost as much as how this could possibly be accomplished, there was no aperture visible anywhere in the dull red walls of the device; no door, no window.

"Have you then, Hula, no *lusan* in that Upper World of yours," Nalinah purred as I came up to her, "that you appear so bemused?"

"Is that what you call it?" I asked, inanely. "How do you get into it?"

"See." She twisted to it. Her heel caught in some inequality of her footing and she stumbled against me. I threw an arm around her, to save her from falling.

A pulse pounded in my wrists. She was crushed against me, soft, and yielding, and ineffably feminine. The fragrance of her was in my nostrils. Her hair brushed my cheek and her warmth enfolded me, an aura of exquisite allure. My arm tightened...

I heard—I distinctly heard, I tell you—a strain of music, *within me!* The blast of a warning horn. Full-throated arpeggios, like the blast of a soaring wind. The rush of wings, of the wings of the Valkyries. The twittering calls of the harpies, beautiful as heaven—and evil as hell itself.

Abruptly I was back in Wanooka's rec hall, poignantly conscious of Ann Doring's nearness... I set Nalinah firmly on her feet, releasing her.

"See," she said again, and it seemed to me there was a quiver in her voice. She touched the *lusan's* side with her wand. A circular hole appeared in the metal wall, widened from the point of its first appearance as a camera shutter's iris diaphragm opens to uncover its lens. At once there was an aperture large enough to admit a man. Within I glimpsed a cushioned seat, a brightly gleaming lever.

Queerly I still heard the rush of wings, the twittering, faint now, and trifling sweetly. But it was no longer music and it was no longer within my skull. I looked up to whence the sounds seemed now to come.

The sheer, unearthly beauty of what I saw caught me by the throat. High above, a covey of white birds paralleled the cliff in graceful flight. Their bodies were chastely white, but their outspread great wings were a shimmer of iridescent color, frail webs woven from light that had splintered into all the infinite hues of the spectrum. They filled the air with multihued facets of jeweled motes. Each was a glittering glory in itself, the whole was a sparkling rainbow, a congeries of a million rainbows, sweeping across the sky.

Over them arched the drab vault of a gloomy sky. Backgrounding them was the ominous gray of that gigantic wall.

A single bird veered, abruptly, out of the flock and darted for that wall. The twitterings rose to a chorus of alarm. A pencil-thin, scarlet beam streaked up from the ground.

The bird's shriek was a scream of human agony! One of its marvelous wings had vanished! Its companions shot away, too evidently abandoning it to its fate. It sideslipped, plummeted downward.

The remaining wing caught it, held it suspended for one heart-breaking instant.

"That's no bird!" I gasped. "It's a woman!"

The slender, delicately formed body, contorted now in agony, was a white-clad human shape. Long hair, lustrously black, cascaded about a staring, tortured face.

The slender, delicately-formed body was contorted now in agony...

The wing's momentary hold was gone. She went down, was hidden by a jutting vertical fold of the precipice. I heard a sickening thud.

A moment later, a green-uniformed man left the guardroom entrance, his *coret* in his hand. He strolled leisurely along the base of the cliff, toward the spur that hid his victim from me.

"Kut's aim was poor," Nalinah said behind me. "I must have Hafna instructed to send him back to the ranges."

I whirled to her. "That was a girl!"

She seemed mildly surprised at my perturbation. "A Taphet, Hula," she shrugged. "Their women are the worst." Then, as if that was explanation enough for the murder, she said, "Come. Nal Surah awaits us."

Her hand gestured to the *lusan*. I had to enter it.

Account of Courtney Stone, M.D., resumed:

I WAS uncertain whether Jethro Parker's questions had been as casual as they seemed, or whether he had deliberately trapped me. Whichever it was, I knew that I could not now deceive him by any hastily contrived tale of having given the tramp one of my old suits before he left. Parker would have known instantly that I lied, if only because, in that case, I should have at once gotten rid of the disease-breeding rags he discarded and not kept them around for two weeks.

They may be uncouth, these farmer folk of the Helderbergs, and ungrammatical in their speech, but they have a native shrewdness most scientists might well envy.

They have also insatiable curiosity and a straight-lined honesty with which it is impossible to tamper.

Parker, I was certain, would not stop now until he had unearthed exactly what had happened to the tramp, and he could not be kept from reporting the occurrence to the police.

"Yes," I said. "There isn't any doubt those are the tramp's clothes. Come inside and I'll tell you about him."

I took the farmer into my office and shut the door. "Sit down," I said. "I always take a snifter about this time in the afternoon. Will you join me?"

Parker rubbed his great, bony hands on his knees. He was perched on the edge of the chair I had indicated and he was looking about him uncomfortably. Laymen are always ill at ease in the purlieus of a physician's office.

"That was grand liquor you give me the other day," he said. "Sure, I'll have a drink."

I went into the surgery and brought back two medicine glasses filled with the dark amber liquid. I gave him one. He downed it at a gulp.

I thumped my own emptied glass on the desk, and said, "All right, now, Parker, I'm ready to confess."

"Confess!"

He was so startled his glass fell from his fingers.

"Yes!" I leaned over him, my palms on the desk. "Remember, you thought there was something strange about the tramp, that night, and I laughed at you? You were right and I was wrong. He was a strange bird."

The man's eyes widened. "Strange," he said huskily. His eyes widened; but the irises did not. My gaze shifted to his forehead, where the throbbing of the sinistral temporal artery, was quite visible. "As how?"

"I don't know how," I whispered. "I don't know. But wouldn't you call it strange if a man vanished right in front of your eyes, if he got smaller and smaller while you watched him, till he wasn't there at all?"

"The tramp did that?" He mumbled the words, thick-tongued. "Got smaller…" The pulse in his temple slowed perceptibly, his pupils were shrinking to pinpoints.

"And vanished. You believe me don't you?" I whispered. "You believe what I am telling you?"

"No." I had expected that reaction. "No."

He shoved himself up out of his chair.

"You—you're foolin' me. You're lyin' to me. You did somethin' to him and now you're tryin' to lie out of it."

I threw my arms wide. "All right, Parker," I murmured. "You can't blame me for trying."

"I'm—I'm goin' to—the cops and tell 'em." He started for the door. "Let them figure out what to do."

"Wait," I called quietly. "I'm going with you. I thought I would try the story out on you. If you believed it maybe every-body would believe it. But I see it's no use. I might as well go with you and give myself up."

I had my hat and coat on and I was going out through the hall with Parker. He stumbled a little and I caught hold of his arm just as I saw my housekeeper's face peering over the upper railing of the stairs.

"Mr. Parker is ill," I called to her. "I'm taking him home. Please phone the hospital I will not make rounds today, and mail the letters I've left on my desk." To the farmer I said, low-toned, "No use telling her yet. She will know soon enough."

I had to support him as he went down the path, had to almost lift him into the car. I got around to the left, got in behind the wheel, and he slumped against me.

"Straighten up," I snapped at him, savagely, as I let in the gears. His obedience to that command was almost purely reflex, but he sat erect enough to attract no attention from neighbor-ing cars, from the traffic officer at that light on the corner. When he finally slumped down in the seat and went frankly asleep it did not matter any longer. We were on the open road and I was driving, as fast as I dared, toward Camp Wanooka.

The dose of chloral I had measured into his glass had been exactly right. I had distracted his attention from its distinctive taste by startling him. With exact timing, guided by my ocular taking of his pulse, I had contrived to have him walk out to my sedan under his own power before the sedative took full effect.

I would satisfy the men at the camp, when I drove him up to the infirmary, by saying I had stopped at his home on the way down and finding him in coma had decided to bring him there so that I could give him more of my personal attention than he would receive at the hospital. After that, Edith and I could keep him asleep until—

Until when? That was as far as my plan had formed. The rest was in the lap of the gods.

I had done all this, I, Courtney Stone, M.D. In the parlance of the underworld I had doped a man and shanghaied him. It wasn't pretty. But, given all that had gone before, what else was there for me to do?

Edith Horne had convinced me, you see, that for Hugh Lambert's sake we must both be at liberty, free to help him when he should call for our help. If I had not silenced Jethro Parker we should both have been in prison by night.

It needed no imagination now to make me out a criminal. I was one in very truth. Curiously enough, I rather liked the idea. My life till now had been so much a matter of stodgy, deadening routine.

CHAPTER IV

Narrative of Hugh Lambert, resumed:

NALINAH CAME INTO the *lusan* and took her place beside me. The opening shut itself. I have said the strange shell had no window. That is true. Yet enclosed within it, I still saw the smoothed road ahead.

No, the metal was not transparent. A screen was suspended vertically before us, and on this the road was pictured, vividly and in its natural colors, as though on the eyepiece of a periscope; except that this image was right side up and not reversed.

I wondered why the builders of the vehicle had gone to the trouble of contriving what must be an intricate optical device when a pane of glass would have been so much simpler. Nalinah touched the lever, and then I knew.

The ridge at which I was gazing flashed down and out of the screen. The long, straight road seethed toward us out of a vast, dreary plain. On either side of us there was only a rushing,

featureless gray blur. No glass thin enough to be transparent could have withstood that incredible speed.

There was just room enough for the two of us between the *lusan's* curving walls. I was clothed only in that single, tight garment of *sibral* and it was evident that under the girl's rainbow-hued frock there was not much more.

Recalling Nalinah's shrug, her unfeeling comment on the death of that gorgeous creature of the air, a steel plate might as well have intervened for all the effect her closeness had upon me.

"Why did she have to be killed?"

"It is forbidden for a Taphet to approach the wall," Nalinah replied, "except under orders and closely guarded."

"Was her crime so great that she had to be killed?"

"There is only one crime in Mernia, disobedience of the Law. There is only one punishment, death." The harsh statement seemed utterly incongruous coming from those tender, girlish lips. "The Folk cannot tolerate unsocial conduct, no matter how slight."

I asked, "Is life then so cheap in your Mernia?"

"Only the life of the Folk matters, only its weal. The guard who flashed her with his *coret* did not slay that Taphet. She slew herself. From the moment she violated an edict of the Law, she was dead. Kut merely disposed of a body that had forfeited its right to existence."

I shook my head in bewilderment. "I don't understand."

Nalinah's brow wrinkled. "Look you, Hula," she said, speaking slowly and distinctly, as if explaining something to a child. "Do not some cells in the body of one of your kind, having been injured or altered by some disease, sometimes cease to perform the function for which they are designed?"

"Yes. Of course."

"And do they not then become a danger to the body of which they are a part, at first latent and then actively as their nature changes and they become maleficent? Diseased?"

"Yes."

"Do you permit these cells to corrupt other cells, till the whole body rots and is destroyed?"

"Naturally not. We get rid of them, cut them out or burn them out, or destroy them with some—some antiseptic."

"Is not the Folk, the state, a living organism composed of a multitude of smaller living organisms, just as your body is composed of cells?"

"Yes."

The small oval of Nalinah's face lit up with triumph. "They why is it not right, that when some of these smaller organisms, these individuals, fail to function properly for the welfare of the whole body, the whole Folk—why is it not right that they too should be destroyed, mercilessly, lest remaining they corrupt other individuals till the whole state is rotten and is destroyed?"

IT WAS a ruthless philosophy, I thought, gazing into the screen. My eye followed the streaking ribbon of road till, infinitely distant, it narrowed to a point. The landscape there was too far off to be veiled by our speed, and I was able to make out some of its details. There were nowhere any trees, any greensward. There was only the dead rock; barren, infertile, desolate.

"Your argument is specious," I said slowly. "But the analogy on which it is founded is a false one. The important thing in the conglomerate of cells that compose a human body is the body itself and the soul it houses. The important thing in a nation is the individuals that compose it. Cells exist to serve the body. The state, the social organization, exists to provide for the well-being of its citizens."

A gray mass appeared on the horizon. It grew rapidly as we neared it, became a high-piled, frowning wall. We topped a rise higher than most and for an instant I saw over that wall. There were buildings within it, streets swarming with traffic.

"Calinore," Nalinah said, answering the question in my eyes. "Home of the Taphetnit." She returned to our discourse. "You have no laws, then?"

"Yes. Of course we have laws, but they are made and administered for the greatest good of the greatest number. I heard you repeat what you called your Creed, a little while ago. We too have our fundamental Law, and it states its object thus: To establish justice, insure domestic tranquility... promote the general welfare, and secure the blessings of liberty to ourselves and our posterity..."

There was a wistful quality to Nalinah's smile.

" 'Insure domestic tranquility, promote the general welfare, secure the blessings of liberty…' How beautiful it sounds. Does your Law do all these things, Hula?"

"It was so intended."

"I asked if it *did* them."

I thought of two lines of men I had seen on the docks of San Francisco, grimly facing one another; those composing one gaunt-faced, pinch-bellied, and bitter eyed; the others blue-jowled, stalwart shouldered, their gnarled fists grasping tear-gas bombs, waiting for the word to throw them. I thought of hollow-eyed, dull-faced little children bent over the treadles of a spinning mill, the sun not risen yet; and I thought of a court that had said the law of which I boasted forbade the stopping of this crime.

I thought of all this, and far more, and I said: "The Law would do all these things if we lived according to the spirit of the Law. It does not wholly succeed because, of the men we choose to interpret and administer it, some are selfish, some venial, some merely fools."

"Selfish. Venial. Fools. Are there none among you who are unselfish, unbribable and wise?"

"A great many."

"But why permit the others to carry out this wonderful Law of yours?"

How naive that question was! And yet…

I kept silent, the changing images in the screen my excuse. We had flashed past Calinore, and now there was a change in the plain. It seemed softer, warmer somehow in hue. There were crops of some kind growing upon it.

What those crops were or how they were induced to grow out of the rock, I could not make even a guess, for when they were near enough for me to have examined them closely they were swallowed up in the streaking gray blur of our speed. Nevertheless their being there at all was yet a scientific miracle.

"I am convinced." I realized the Nalinah was no longer speaking to me, but thinking aloud. "Nal Surah is right. We have

The fingers of a gelid dread tightened on my heart,
as I looked upon him who had been dead.

tarried here too long, in this barren and desolate land. Our place
is in the sun."

"You will be welcome," I said. It was for this, then, that I had
been brought to Mernia. I was to be an ambassador from the
Little Folk to the Upper World. My forebodings had been

unwarranted. "I am sure I can arrange permission for you to come among us." My mind was already busy with plans. Although the fertile regions of Earth's surface were overcrowded, a people who made livable a land of bare rock would find in our deserts, our tundras, a veritable Paradise.

"Permission?" Nalinah seemed surprised. "We shall *take* what we wish."

I didn't get it, at first. "Take!" I chuckled. "Maybe we'll have something to say about *that*."

"Your people will have as little to say about it as you, have had about coming here, my Hula, and what you have done since you came here." There was nothing grim, nothing threatening about the way she said it. Her tone was quite matter-of-fact. "When we are ready to bring the blessings of Mernian civilization and science to your barbarian race, your benighted race who do not know even how to govern themselves, we shall do it, and you shall be helpless against us."

She is talking nonsense, I thought. What can they do against us, these tiny people against the giants that we were to them, these few against our hordes?

And then I recalled what I knew already of their powers. I recalled how the tramp had vanished. I recalled how utterly unable I had been to struggle against the grip they had upon me. I remembered the corpse I had seen brought back to life…

"We need only to learn a little more about those whom we shall conquer," Nalinah was saying. "It is you, Hula, who shall tell us what we need to know."

"I'll be damned if I will!"

She laughed at me. The *lusan* was filled with the trill of her girlish, merry laughter.

There was something horribly sinister about that laugh.

RA NALINAH'S laugh was sinister with its implication of my utter helplessness against the forces of which she and her people were masters. Yet curiously enough, it warmed me to her, calming in the moment it was born, the rage her astounding statement had aroused in me!

There was in that silvery trill and in the glorious countenance she turned to me, a soft caress, almost as if she brushed my lips with the dusky velvet of her own.

More than any other of the strange folk who people this adventure of mine, which is too fantastically unreal to be a dream, I shall carry the thought of Nalinah with me into the oblivion that is death. Since first she had appeared in the doorway of what so narrowly had missed being my execution chamber. I had seen her imperious and regal as an affronted empress; wide-eyed and fluttered as a sub-deb at the sight of a new male; artfully seductive as a courtesan of the *Petit Trianon;* callously cruel as a Borgia. She had been, only a moment ago, a keen-minded analyst of politico-economic systems; as the representative of a super-race she had announced their intention of a world-conquest that would brook no opposition and conceived no possibility of defeat.

Now Nalinah, wise with the ageless, instinctive wisdom of her sex, covered with a laugh her heartache over the man child who strutted brash defiance of a doom she knew must overwhelm him.

Yes, there was mocking gaiety in her laugh; but there was also pity!

Because of that, the interior of the rushing *lusan* was chilly with a fear that struck into my very bones. But I said quite calmly, quite steadily:

"If you and your people, Ra Nalinah will come among mine as friends, I shall be happy to do everything in my power to help you. If you come as enemies, Satan himself could not compel me to stir so much as my little finger to aid—"

A screaming hell of sound battered at me. Nalinah jerked the *lusan's* control lever toward her, her pupils abruptly widened to dark pits, her face lined and suddenly pallid! I catapulted out of my seat, crashed agonizingly against the visual screen!

My legs, arms, skull burst with the surge of blood forced to them by the sudden checking of our tremendous speed. Half stunned, I heard Nalinah's scream, managed to twist.

The girl's clutch tore loose from the lever. In the flashing split second before she would strike it, I thrust myself sidewise along the wall to which I was pinned, took the impact of her soft form on my own, cushioning the blow that certainly would have maimed her.

What little breath I had left was smashed out of me. I pounded with Nalinah down into the narrow space between screen and seat-base. Then we were falling again.

Jackknifing in mid-air, I contrived to get between the girl and the metal just as we struck. I folded her in my arms. I saw the lever spearing down to impale us. I jammed a foot into a corner, crooked a knee over that threatening handle, and clung like that while the crazy, bounding, roll continued.

It slackened, stopped…

The floor of the vehicle pitched steeply forward. Nalinah was a limp, unconscious bundle in my arms. I shifted her, and twisted to get my knee free of the lever. The screen came across my vision and, oddly canted in its depths, I saw a field through whose stand of some vividly orange crop ploughed the wide furrow of the *lusan's* mad plunge. Across this field a score of white-faced Taphetnit, their outspread wings a rainbow shimmer about them, streamed toward us with high, awkward bounds.

Dazedly lifting Nalinah to the seat, I wondered why our rescuers were not flying.

The image of their leader expanded to fill the screen like a movie close-up. I saw that those glorious wings of his were cruelly cropped, and knew why they did not fly.

He went past. Behind them I glimpsed a green-uniformed soldier on the ground, contorted and very still. I saw another guard; his belly ripped open. I caught sight of the road from which the *lusan* had been flung.

Grating metal whirled me to the side wall. It was pierced by a circle of light that opened out from its own center. The Taphet was right outside, waiting for the aperture to grow wide enough to admit him.

I crouched. The murdered guards, my flashing glimpse of a pit in the road that had been skillfully masked to trap the *lusan*, had warned me that the wreck was no accident, but a trap.

The Taphet leaned in reaching for Nalinah's recumbent form. I leaped, smashed a fist into his face. Bones crushed under my knuckles. My momentum hurled me out of the *lusan*. The Taphet went down, but I snatched at the edge of the entrance, managed to hold to my feet.

Another of the winged men sprang at me, flailing something that looked like a hoe at my head. I ducked under it, buried a one-two in his midriff.

Hands grabbed my ankles, living weight pounced on my back. I stumbled flailing out, and was swamped under a heaving, tossing mass of the Taphetnit. I was on the ground, my face being pressed into rock, my arms, my legs pinioned and useless.

Blows battered me, stinging but ineffectual because the attackers were in each other's way. That gave me a moment to realize that I was overwhelmed, that they would finish me off first, then…

Their twitterings, shrill, excited, told me they were getting organized. One by one they extricated themselves from the pile.

WHEN I judged only one or two Taphetnit remained on my back I heaved upward, came up easily. Too easily! I whirled to face the marauders.

One sprawled headlong where he had been flung by my leap. Another staggered, fighting to catch his footing.

There were only two of them! Where were the others?

The standing Taphet was suddenly rigid. Then—I pulled a hand across my eyes—he was *blurring!*

The surfaces of the winged figure at which I stared were

wavering and losing definition. Details merged into one another as though he were a waxen statue exposed to the blasting heat of a furnace. Just like that he was melting, was running together!

There was agony in the Taphet's face, such agony as I hope never to look upon again, and then there was no face at all. There was no Taphet, only an irregularly shaped pillar whose outlines changed constantly as it shrank. Runnels of viscid liquid dripped from it. It toppled, splashed in a great pool that glistened yellow on, the ground, dissolved.

The beat of frantic wings tore my gaze from that horror. The last Taphet was fighting to get to his feet. A flash of light flicked to him, and he was immobile, his frozen pinions shining with splendor. At once he too began to melt.

The flash seemed to have come from the direction of the *lusan*. I looked there. Nalinah was tensed just outside its entrance. She held her curious wand high before her and the tiny sun at the center of the device blazed hot and dazzling as if it were veritably a miniature sun.

The glare was fading, its lethal task accomplished. Of the score of Taphetnit who had attacked us, nothing but that glistening pool was left. The grisly fluid lapped around a half dozen metallic implements whose use I could not make out; then settled to a gruesome stillness.

At the very edge of the pond a single iridescent feather floated.

"They *planned* to kill me, Hula." Nalinah brought me back to realization that we were both alive who, were it not for the awful power of her wand, would be corpses now. "See there," she pointed, "behind that tumbled stack of harvested *fortlik*, the opening of the tunnel they bored to undermine the road. When they saw my *lusan* approaching they killed their guards and sought to slay me."

There was in her tones only a kind of uncomprehending wonderment. Just so had a small boy I once overheard in

Gramercy Park sounded as he said to the nurse from whose side he had strayed to become embroiled with an urchin of the slums, "He hit me, Nana. I only said hello and he hit me."

I went gingerly around the yellow pool to the girl's side. I forced my lips to grin, wryly. "It was a good thing you came to so quickly."

I tried not to think of why it was a good thing. I tried not to think of that slip of a maid deliberately, coldly, efficiently, extinguishing twenty living beings.

"Yes," she agreed, and turned to gaze at the *lusan*. "It is staunch," she pondered. "It is injured not at all. If it could be gotten back to the road it would function as well as before."

I was bruised, battered, aching with pain and exhaustion. Twice in the cataclysmic moments just past I had saved her from injury, from death, and she knew it. If she had thanked me I should have disclaimed her gratitude. But this calm acceptance of what I had done, this matter-of-fact ignoring of it, angered me.

"Look here," I burst out, hotly. "Do you realize—*Look out!* There are more of them coming!" I grabbed her arm. "Get into the *lusan!* We'll be able to defend ourselves better from inside."

She twitched out of my grasp, swung around.

"Where?" she gasped.

I flung a pointing finger to the dots I had glimpsed speeding toward us across the flaming terrain. "There. Don't you see them?"

She was laughing once more, laughing at me! "Those are not Taphetnit, my Hula. They are an emergency troop of the labor squadron guard. It has taken them long enough to appear."

I saw then that though only one small group was in motion, other figures speckled the horizon, completely circumscribing us. Silent silhouettes against the drab sky, they watched us from afar, and it came to me that, wing-cropped as the Taphetnit had been, they could not possibly have hoped to escape that ominous ring.

I said something to that effect. "Yes," Nalinah agreed. "They knew that in attacking me they condemned themselves to certain death... Just think what such devotion would be worth to the Folk, were the Taphetnit willing to serve Mernia as they serve their own fantastic philosophy."

I recalled that futile sacrifice later, when I learned what philosophy it was she called fantastic; but now I had no time to respond. The foremost of the oncoming guard had reached us.

HE CLICKED heels, saluted. *"Gor Surah,* Ra Nalinah," he greeted her crisply.

"Gor Surah, Colonel Skoolteh." She went through one of her amazing metamorphoses, and was once more a figure of imperious hauteur. "How is it that this outrage could occur in your district?"

"Outrage?"

She told him what had happened. "You reported this region completely under control," she ended angrily.

"I did," Skoolteh was taller than Vanark or Hafna, older, the tight black cap of his hair graying at the temples. Every line of his erect form spoke of the habit of military dignity long ingrained. "The Taphetnit laboring here had been altogether amenable. We were short-handed and I had every reason to believe it would be safe to leave only a skeleton guard here, transferring the men thus released to the fields nearer Calinore where there have been so many outbreaks of late."

"It is evident that was part of their scheme," Nalinah retorted. "They had observed that I always followed this route on my visit to Gateway Wall during the past few *steena* [periods of approximately a week]. Apparently the conspiracy is widespread. They contrived that the Taphetnit working here should be as scantily guarded as possible, so that they might carry out their attack on me with little risk of discovery or interference."

"Not *their* plan, Ra Nalinah," Skoolteh glanced around. His men were drawn up in rank, well beyond earshot. "No Taphet has the capacity to scheme so well. They carried out the plot but it could only have been formed in the brain of a Surahnit."

Nalinah's nostrils twitched once. "You but seek to minimize your shame, that you should have been so deceived by the flutter-minded Taphetnit," she said coldly. "You know as well as I that no Surahnit could be so recreant to the Folk weal."

"No?" The officer's smile was as frosty as the girl's voice. "Has the Ra forgotten the Surahnit Battalion that formed the spear-point of the Taphetnit attack upon our city of Tashma seventeen *sloonit* [years] ago?"

"What Mernian tot has not been taught that tale? It is you, Colonel Skoolteh, who seem to have forgotten how the wrath of Nal Surah went out against the traitors, and how they were extirpated root and branch."

Nalinah gestured to the pool at our feet, drying already and green-scummed. The small motion made plain how the rene-gades had been punished.

"The wings of the rebel Taphetnit were cropped, and from them the labor squadrons were formed, so that through the rest of their life they might expiate their crime," she went on. "But of the Surahnit who led them not a drop of blood was left in all Mernia. From Wall to Wall they and their families were hunted down, and they were herded in the Central Plaza.

"I was there, Colonel Skoolteh. It is my earliest memory, how my mother held me high, a tot of two *sloonit,* so that I could see over the heads of the throng and watch them perish— old men and young, mothers, wives and sisters, sons and daugh-ters—in the glorious purge."

Something of a long ago horror, never obliterated, crawled in the cerulean depths of her eyes, belying the adjective with which she had described that holocaust. "None escaped. None at all."

"*One* did escape." Skoolteh was a graven image, staring straight ahead of him, only his lips moving. "A baby boy. A subaltern then, I had become separated from the squad of troops

I commanded. I saw him borne off between the wings of a fleeing Taphet. I could have brought both down with my *coret*, but I did not.

"That boy, if he still lives, would be eighteen now. Ra Nalinah! Some *roha* [hours] ago it was reported that our search rays have spied out a Surahnit in Calinore, where by the Law no Surahnit may dwell. A lad of about eighteen. The Nal has already made demand for his delivery. There has been no reply as yet. If that reply should be negative, it will be my duty to lead a force against Calinore and take the boy from the Taphetnit who shelter him."

The girl appeared not to have heard the latter part of Skoolteh's statement. "You permitted the offspring of a traitor to escape the purge?"

"His mother was the wife of my dearest friend."

"He ceased to be your friend when he turned renegade."

"I had ceased to be *his* friend long since. The boy—was my son."

"Your son!" Nalinah paled with fury. She took a step toward the colonel, her wand rising. "You violated the strictest law of Mernia, committed a second and more loathsome crime because of your offense. You, most trusted of the Nal's officers!"

Skoolteh's hand darted to his belt, flashed away again, a *coret* clenched in his webbed fingers. Before either of us could move, a scarlet ray streaked from the weapon's splayed muzzle.

The smell of burned flesh stung my nostrils. The body that crumpled to the ground in front of me had no head. I saw the charred place where it had set so proudly. I saw the edge of a green uniform-collar smolder briefly and black out.

Colonel Skoolteh had resigned his command.

Clipping from "Sound-Stage Secrets," Gossip Column of the Hollywood Herald, Thursday, August 30, 1934:

There's a grin around town so wide one jitters lest it slice off the head of the fellow wearing it. *** The grin's the property of Carton Ford, World Pic's ace megaphonist. *** He's doing *Heart's Desire* for Tycoon Ratekoff and it's the work of Ann Doring in that epic that's got him dancing on the Boulevard. *** "She reaches right into your chest and plays the *Lost Chord* on your heartstrings," Carton burbled to your correspondent. *** "She was good in *Love's Repentance* but she's great in this. *Great!*" *** Well, we always said our Ann would show the other gals something when she came down off that ice-cake she's been using as a perch. *** What? *** She's been scarcer around the nite spots than ideas in a contract writer's skull since she came back from her trip East. *** Yeah, but there are whispers it took a strong arm squad to *bring* her back. *** One of the toughies is said to be nursing a jaw busted by a very masculine fist. *** Seems clear *someone* has been teaching La Doring things she never knew before. ***

Hugh Lambert's Narrative, resumed:

"HE'S KILLED himself," I exclaimed. "He—"

"Yes." Nalinah's somber look came away from Colonel Skoolteh's beheaded corpse. "He has cheated the Law."

She fingered that silvery wand of hers. Recalling the agony that had been on the Taphet's face in the moment before it was a face no longer, I knew very clearly why the man had chosen the *coret's* death.

"But the evil he spawned still lives. I must get to Tashna at once." She turned toward Skoolteh's squad, beckoned.

They had remained at attention, so rigid their discipline that they had not stirred even when they saw their commander drop. Now, at Nalinah's signal, one stalked stiffly toward us. He halted two paces from the Ra and saluted her. His toes almost touched the colonel's body, but for all the expression on his swarthy countenance the ground might have been bare.

Nalinah's arm dropped from her answering salute. "Sergeant," she snapped, "have my *lusan* replaced on the road, on the Tashna side of where it was undermined."

"Very well!" the non-com responded. He saluted, spun on his heels. His left arm shot above his head, jerked in swift, crisp movements to either side of the vertical.

From the point on the horizon he faced, some of the watching forms vanished. I understood that he had semaphored an order, was being obeyed.

"Let us move aside," Nalinah said to me. "We shall be in their way here."

I was glad she made the suggestion. The stench from the puddle over which we stood was unpleasant to say the least. We walked a little way off; the girl very silent and thoughtful at my side.

The tall orange grass she had called *fortlik* rustled against our knees. The luminous stalks were about the diameter of my forefinger. They rose almost straight from the ground. The broad, pointed leaves sheathed the stems with their bases, and then curved gracefully outward. Here and there along the plant's height, oval clumps, the thickness and length of my thumb, were tipped by tiny tassels of a silken, lighter colored fiber.

I plucked one of these, stripped off its covering. I was holding a wee ear of corn, its kernels just about the size of grains of wheat.

But if this were corn already ripe, I thought, the stalks should be well above our heads. Then for the first time since I had passed through the grisly morgue high within what the girl had called the Gateway Wall, I remembered the diminished scale I must apply to everything I saw in Mernia. By the measurements of my own world, this corn was four inches tall.

There was no soil. There was only lava-like, darkly glowing rock. It was deeply scored by lines too straight to be anything but the handiwork of man. Within those almost thread-narrow ruts, running water glistened, washing the *fortlik's* roots!

This great field, the whole vast expanse of growing things I had glimpsed on the *lusan's* rushing journey, was artificially irrigated! The Little Folk had with infinite labor scratched into hard rock a myriad of tiny channels to make its barrenness fertile!

"Where does the water come from?" I voiced the next question that came to me. "I've seen no streams anywhere."

Nalinah came out of her reverie. "It seeps out of the Western Wall."

"I can imagine that some porosity in the rock there might permit sufficient water to seep through from some subterranean stream to give you enough for your needs while not threatening to overwhelm you as long as its use keeps pace with its inflow. But plants need more than water to grow. Is that seepage also imbued with the food they require?"

"No. That which flows out of the Wall is water only. It is led to certain great basins there in the West, to which also are conveyed all the debris from our living and the bodies of our dead. Our scientists process these things and impregnate with the result the water out of which the *fortlik* grows."

"*The bodies of your dead!*" My voice was thin with shock. "You eat the grain that grows out of the bodies of your dead!"

MY FACE mast have portrayed the revulsion, the horror, that crawled within me, for Nalinah stared at it with a curious mixture of non-comprehension and surprise.

"Now, what is strange in that?" she asked. "We know something of the life of your people. You slay living beasts and feed upon their burned flesh. This we do not do."

"But those are animals of a different species," I protested. "They are not our own kind. Our human kind we bury in consecrated ground and make certain that they lie undisturbed forever. We tend their graves, make them beautiful with grass and flowers that clothe forever the good fertile soil. They sleep forever—" I stopped suddenly. A query had sprung unbidden to my mind. Whence came the elements that mixed with what in the beginning was nothing but rock pulverized by wind and weather—rock that could support no life—to make it good and fertile?

Aeons of time raced through my thoughts. Out of a warm, salt sea, bits of living protoplasm crawled upon a sandy and barren beach, died, and decayed. Green things, as tiny, grew out of the silt. Once more the sea gave up a froth of microscopic life. This fed upon the green, and it was a little longer before dissolution claimed it.

Epochs wheeled by, uncountable tens of centuries. Now shaggy, brute-faced men prowled a steaming jungle. They killed for food, it is true, the monstrous beasts that shared their haunts; but they stuffed also into their fanged maws the tender fronds of the ferns, and the now forgotten fruits of a primordial verdure. The apemen died, and their corpses lay moldering in the jungle, and from what the chemistry of decay made of these corpses new verdure grew, whose fronds, whose fruits the children of the apemen stuffed into their fanged maws...

I thought of grass and flowers upon carefully tended graves, their roots drinking from fertile loam the life elements washed out of cracked coffins, washed out of that which lies within these coffins. The grass and flowers die at last, are mowed down and carted off, perhaps to fertilize some field so that it may become golden with waving wheat. Perhaps some child, spooning his breakfast cereal, will nurture his chubby little body with an atom or two that once lived in the body of his great-grandfather.

Not horrible, this. Somehow beautiful. Somehow, it lent a new dignity to death, a new and glorious symbolism to every gardened graveyard. *"Dust thou art, to dust returnest, was not spoken of the soul,"* indeed. But neither does the dust of the soul's brief shelter remain mere dust. *"In Flanders fields the poppies grow..."*

"Forever!" Nalinah was exclaiming. "They lie forever undisturbed. How profligate that is! How rich your Upper World must be if it can afford such waste! Here in Mernia we dare

not waste anything, dare not lose anything. Look you, Hula.
Since Skoolteh's traitorous corpse is not worthy of the honor
of serving the Folk again, it will not go to the Basins. Because
of this, because the scientists will not change it and so the crop
of *fortlik* must be reduced by just so much, some Surahnit child
must be denied the right to birth."

"Denied?" I was still dazed by the revelation, the new understanding, that had flashed upon me in a split second of
insight. "Birth?" I repeated. And then I comprehended the full
implication of her statement. "Your state does that? It grants
or denies even the right to be born?"

"But yes, Hula. It is necessary." She spoke to me with the
same patience, the same effort to understand that what to her
was matter-of-fact must be explained to me, as that with which
I have justified to some Arab of the trackless desert our law
that one may move on a highway only when a green traffic light
signals us permission to move. "Within the four Walls of
Mernia there is sustenance for just so many. The balance between
the needs of the Folk and the things that satisfy those needs is
so delicate, the margin between race-life and race-death, so
minute, that only by utmost care can the Folk hope to survive."

I saw her point. "Yours is a meticulously planned economy,"
I exclaimed. "Not by choice, but forced upon you by the condi-
tions, the poverty of your environment." I understand now the
reason for their Creed, for the rigorous, ruthless discipline of
their Law. "Your totalitarian state—"

I was halted by the drum tattoo of many hoofs, rushing upon
us. I wheeled. Horses were stampeding across the *fortlik* field—a
band of horses herded by riders in the uniform of the labor
guard. The cavalcade poured headlong through the swishing
grain and my pulses thudded with the blood-tingling sight.

They were almost upon us. The riders shouted. The animals
forelegs braked them to a halt, a troop beautifully trained. High-
spirited, they curvetted in their places. The guards leaped to the
ground. Some were busy at once buckling the harness straps

together, hitching the beasts into a team. Others snatched coils of leather strapping from their saddles, and commenced rigging it about the *lusan*.

Something odd about the beasts clamored for my attention. I moved nearer for more careful scrutiny. Its head was chunky, its jaws heavier than those of any horse I'd ever come across. It batted its great, lustrous eyes at me, shied away, neighing and pawing the ground. The luxuriant fetlocks of its legs made shaggy stockings completely veiling the pasterns. The hoofs beneath them—

Those were not hoofs! Not horses' hoofs. They were cloven into three indurated toes. Three toes!

My fist smacked into my palm.

If I were of Upper World height these horses would appear to be the size of St. Bernard dogs. Their hoofs were three-toed. They were not horses. They were the remote ancestors of our horses. They were *Eohippi*, the horses of Evolution's infancy. They were dawn-horses, the like of which have not roamed Earth's surface for fifty thousand years!

CHAPTER V

Statement of Edith Horne, R.N., dictated to the author:

MEN ARE SUCH fools! Any woman would have known by Dr. Stone's face that he was lying when he drove up to the gate Thursday night, Jethro Parker lolling all over the seat beside him, and stammered out a story full of holes. But Ed Hard and Bob Falk swallowed it whole cloth, and of course the three boys did.

Morphy, the cook, did look a little puzzled, as nearly as one can make out any expression on his walnut shell of a face. I decided that was nothing to worry about. Even if Shean suspected something, he was an unreconstructed Sinn Feiner, aversion to constituted authority a fetish with him. He might do a lot of thinking, but he would do no talking.

The four men carried Parker into the infirmary. We shooed out the cook and the councillors. While I undressed the farmer and made him comfortable, I learned what really had happened.

"There wasn't anything else to do," Doctor Stone finished. "We ought to be safe enough for the two weeks till his wife, Martha, returns from her

visit, and if we've heard nothing from Hugh by then there will be no point in keeping up the deception."

"You intend to keep him under chloral for two weeks, doctor?" I let no surprise, no protest, sound in my voice. "Hadn't you better review exactly what I should do when he collapses?"

"Collapses!" He stared at me. "I—I hadn't thought of that." I knew that. One of the first things a nurse in training learns is how to remind a physician of his lapses without appearing to have noticed them. "It won't work. We can't take a chance on killing him."

"We can't tie him up, either, but we must not let him go."

"If we talk to him, if we explain everything," the doctor faltered, "perhaps we can persuade him to keep silent, at least for a while."

I have seen Courtney Stone in the operating room, confronted by more than one emergency that would have appalled another surgeon, and he was always completely unperturbed, brilliantly efficient. Now out of his element, he was a bewildered man, utterly at a loss.

"No," I answered him. "You know as well as I, we'd never succeed in that, if he is normal. But there must be some way we can make him do exactly as we want him. Some drug, maybe, not as dangerous as chloral or an opiate. Didn't you say once, lecturing to the probationers, that a man thoroughly acquainted with the *materia medica* can play on the human body and mind as a master musician plays on his violin?"

"Some drug—" He snapped his fingers. "Of course. Hyoscine hydrobromide! An injection of that paralyzes the centers of voluntary action in the cerebellum, renders the subject amenable to any suggestion. I was reading only yesterday about Dr. Calvin Goddard's use of it in criminal investigation. Given one-hundredth of a grain of it, the suspect cannot refuse to tell the truth when so directed. We can inject it while Parker's still under the influence of the chloral. When he comes to he'll obey us as though he were a will-less cretin."

"I *knew* you would think of something," I exclaimed, admiringly.

"Boil up a needle while I go out to my car and see if I have any hyoscine in my kit."

"Your kit's here. I brought it in, and I am almost sure you have a tube of the tablets in it."

I knew he had. I'd looked, while they were carrying Parker in.

Affidavit of Edward Hard, Instructor at West End School for physical culture:

State of New York
County of New York
City of New York

Edward Hard, being duly sworn, deposes and says:
I was, during the summer of 1934, head councillor of Camp Wanooka for Boys, situated near Albany, New York. The camp of-ficially closed on the morning of August 30, 1934, but because of a possible contagion that had been discovered after the greater part of its members had left, there were quarantined within it the follow-ing: myself and Councillor Robert Falk, Nurse Edith Horne, Cook Shean Morphy, Campers Roger Norton, Percy White, Richard Doring and Charles Dorsey, and a neighborhood farmer named Jethro Parker.
Charles Dorsey and Jethro Parker were ill and confined to the infirmary. The rest of us were free to come and go about the camp as long as we kept within its borders. Dr. Courtney Stone, Chief Surgeon of the Albany Post-Graduate Hospital, was medically in charge and was spending as much time with us as he could spare from his practice.
At about eight p.m. on the evening of the said August 30th, 1934, Robert Falk and I were with the three well boys in the recreation hall. I was refereeing a doubles table-tennis game the others were playing. Doctor Stone and Nurse Horne were in the infirmary with their patients.
The players were absorbed in a spirited rally when I heard a soft tap on a window behind me. I turned. Shean Morphy's face was pressed against the pane. He beckoned to me, furtively. I nodded and he slid away.
I made some excuse and went outside. After the glare within the rec hall, I was blinded for a moment. I heard a rustle in the under-

brush, started toward it, calling softly to Morphy. Fingers gripped my arm. They were trembling with palsy.

"Ed! I seen them. The leprechauns. They're all about."

His breath smelled to high heaven of alcohol, which was un-usual. Morphy had been honest about this failing of his when Mr. Lambert, the director, had employed him, but during the season he had confined his sprees to hike days, when the camp was empty and they would not interfere with his duties.

His free hand pointed in the direction of the rustle I had heard. By this time my pupils had accommodated themselves to the dim-ness, but I saw nothing except the tree trunks.

I say I saw nothing. Remembering that I am under oath I must admit that for a moment I thought there was something there. The nearest I can come to describing it is that the air itself seemed to have thickened, to outline a human form scarcely a foot high.

It was imagination, of course, and the blinking of my eyelids dispelled the illusion. "You're seeing things, Shean," I said quietly.

"Seeing things, am I? Maybe it's the same way I'm hearing someone walking through the woods, way down at the end of the lake. But hush and you'll hear him too."

I listened. The muffled click click of the ball behind the rec hall's closed door made no impression on the close stillness of the moun-tain night. For some reason even the all-pervading shrill of the nocturnal insects was silenced, so that the sounds Morphy meant were quite distinct, despite their distance—the scrape of fabric against tree bark, a stealthy footfall, the snap of a dried twig un-der a heavy heel.

There was no doubt of it, someone was prowling through the camp grounds, there to the north. That called for an investigation.

"I'm going to take a look," I whispered. "Be quiet, I don't want the others to hear."

I had two reasons for that. In the first place, the youngsters had been greatly overexcited by the disappearance of Hugh Lambert, the camp director, and I didn't want to set them off again.

I hate to confess that my second reason for not calling out Bob Falk was my sneaking suspicion that he might have had something to do with what had happened to Mr. Lambert. The only reason-able explanation I could evolve for the way the vanished director's clothing had been found was that Bob had arranged the garments.

The prowler might be connected with that, might be trying to get in touch with Falk.

There was nothing I could do about Morphy except let him come along, but he we surprisingly quiet for a man in his condition. The skulker hadn't heard us, even when we reached the edge of the bushes at the lake front, and, halting, saw him standing at the very edge of the shore, stark naked.

An odd violet glow from the water silhouetted him. I recognized the farmer, Jeremiah Fenton.

He bent, picked up some objects from the ground. I made out a chessboard, a handful of chessmen, and a battered pipe. Then he was wading out into the lake.

"He's going to drown himself!" I exclaimed, and started out to stop him. Morphy caught my arm. His callused palm flattened over my mouth.

"Wait," he breathed. "Let's see what queer thing it is he's up to."

So absorbed Fenton was that he was unaware of us. He halted, knee-deep in the violet shimmer, held the things he had with him out over the water.

"It's our birthday, Elijah!" His tone was as matter-of-fact as if the non-existent person to whom he spoke were right there in front of him. "And I know you want these presents more than anything I could buy."

He opened his hands and their contents dropped.

The violet light exploded to meet them, enveloped Fenton! Shean screamed, dragged me backwards into the bushes. We floundered there, the cook yelling, myself trying to bat him away and get to my feet.

When I succeeded, Fenton was gone, although his clothes were still on the shore. I looked down at Morphy, gibbering on his knees. "You scared him away, you damned drunk," I growled.

"The leprechauns took him. Did you not see him get small in the midst of the light and the little men pulling a shining cloak over him? Did you not see them drag him into the lake, and themselves vanish under the surface with him?"

"No, I didn't," I snarled. "I haven't got the d.t.'s."

Falk and the boys were rushing up just then. We sent the kids packing and Bob helped me manhandle Morphy to his bunk, where

we tied him down. We got Dr. Stone to come down to give him a
shot of apomorphine, and after a while the camp quieted down.

Both men agreed with me that Morphy was half-crazed by the
bootleg applejack he had assimilated. Doctor Stone told me that
Fenton's twin brother had been drowned in Wanooka the winter
before, which explained his actions nicely. Those Helderberg farm-
ers are pretty sentimental, but they don't like to be caught at it.

Nobody tried to explain the way the light had flashed out of the
water. Nobody thought it needed any explanation.

In witness whereof I set hereunto nay hand and seal this 12th
day of December, 1936.

(Signed) Edward Hard.

Hugh Lambert's Narrative resumed:

RA NALINAH and I were once more in the *lusan*, and it was
again traversing the road. She had not been altogether right
about the vehicle's being uninjured by the accident. It had
started, true enough, when she pulled the control lever toward
her, but it did not attain the blurring speed it had before.

The girl bit her lip, pettishly jerked the gleaming rod; but
she could not get the *lusan* to move faster than what I reckoned
to be somewhere around a hundred miles an hour. At this
comparatively slow rate I had a chance to examine the shifting
images in the visual screen.

At first, though, there was only the undulating expanse of
the *fortlik* fields on either side, a great sea of orange luminance,
and scattered buildings too far off for me to make out their
nature. I began to lose interest.

"Hula," Nalinah murmured; nestling close to me, "from what
you said, back there in the *fortlik*. I gather that in the world
from which you come there is no such balance between life and
death as here in Mernia."

It was a question, and I answered it. "Yes. Of course there is
a balance of existence in the Upper World, not so very different

from what you have here. Every living entity contributes to the welfare of every other, and depends on every other for its own well-being. Plants and animals, for instance, complement one another; what is poison to the one is the other's food. I have just thought of the reason why your scientists go to so much trouble to grow this orange grain"—I waved at it in the screen—"when apparently, they are advanced enough to synthesize what food you need. It furnishes a perfect, and at the same time simple, example of that interlocking of function of which I speak.

"Your people, your animals—and ours—breathe in oxygen and exhale carbon dioxide. Your *fortlik*—like our vegetation of every kind—inhales the carbon dioxide and breaks it down into carbon, which it uses to build its substance, and oxygen, which it breathes out as useless to it. Without this supply of oxygen people and animals would perish. So it is with every other life process, with us as well as with you. Do you understand that, Nalinah?"

"Hula." She was looking into my eyes, her own suddenly agleam with elfin laughter. "When you are absorbed, like this, your face is palely handsome as a Taphet's and at the same time darkly strong as one of our Surahnit. The combination thrills me."

I felt like spanking her for that but I ignored it. "We, too, walk upon a narrow, unrailed bridge over a bottomless abyss that is black with the oblivion of our race's death. Till lately the bridge was a way so broad we could not descry its borders. Even then our safety depended upon that balance between our needs and their satisfaction, but we did not think about it or trouble to maintain it. Nature did that for us, and we thought Nature would do it forever."

Nalinah's high brow grew pensive, and she became wholly attentive. I was all at once tinglingly conscious again of her otherworldly beauty.

"Nature," I went on, my jaw ridging with my effort of self-control, "having started us off with her lush abundance, still watched over us. Kindly cruel and very wise, when either plants or animals outstripped each other in numbers, upsetting the balance she had set up, Nature restored it by drought or floods, by catastrophe or pestilence, by the extinction, even, of one species or the creation of another."

"Why do you speak in the past?" the girl demanded.

I did not reply at once. As the *lusan* mounted one of the great, smooth waves into which the bed of the Mernian cavern was folded, I caught sight, in the distance, of a clearing in the spread of grain. It seemed to be walled in by a gray palisade of stone, except where on one side a long, low building paralleled the road, and within that fence there seemed to be some sort of bustling activity.

"Why, Hula," Nalinah asked again, "do you say these things *have been?*"

"Because, like half-grown children, we have come to think ourselves wiser than she who fostered us. Over the whole face of the globe we have interfered with Nature's plans. We have drawn upon the stores which she laid up for us against a time of scarcity, and have wasted them. We have taken far more from the other forms of life upon the surface of our planet than we have given to them. We have even altered the span of life Nature decreed for us; even altered the ratio, between our own births and deaths—not for the good of the race but for our pleasure. We have weighed down the scales against us almost too far for a chance of retrieval, and Nature has given up the task of holding the beam level."

WE WERE now close to the enclosure whose appearance had intrigued me. Animals within the fence milled to escape some Taphetnit who worked among them. I saw one of the little beasts caught and dragged off into the windowless building. We flicked past.

"What are they?" I exclaimed.

"*Tivra,*" Nalinah gave me their Mernian name. "From their

skins come the leather from which all our clothing is fashioned, and all our cordage."

She called them *tivra,* but I knew them by another name. Most laymen think of prehistoric creatures as the incredibly gigantic reptiles of the Mesozoic, *Dinosaurus, Triceratops,* and king of all, *Tyrannosaurus.* True, these did stalk old Terra fourteen million years ago, but the Glacial Ages, beginning five thousand centuries before the birth of Christ and ending some five hundred B.C., are quite as prehistoric. As we know by the fossil record of the rocks, the fauna of those times were diminutive rather than enormous. They were the tiny ancestors of the mammals we know today, like the *Eohippi,* like the *tivra.* Deer scarcely larger than our present-day fawns, their full-grown horns mere knobs behind their ears, our unimaginative paleontologists have named them *Dicroreri.*

The people of Mernia were diminutive humans, the wings of the Taphetnit notwithstanding. The two specimens of their animal life I had seen (I suspected then and know now the *only* two) were miniature mammals known to Earth's surface as recently as the end of the Pleistocene Era, but vanished since.

My slitted gaze strayed to Nalinah's wand, where she had thrust it into her belt. The device at its tip was, beyond dispute, a representation of the sun and its nine attendant planets. What could these dwellers in the subterranean world know of our solar system? True enough, they had made some excursions to the surface, yet it seemed utterly incongruous that the tenants of our skies should be important enough, to them to inspire what was evidently the symbol of their autarchy.

There was some clue, in all this, to their origin. The answer hovered tantalizingly at the threshold of my mind, slipped away from me as Nalinah brought me back to our discourse.

"Hula! You seem dismayed as you speak of the situation in your Upper World, yet to me it seems still a very Paradise, compared to Mernia."

"I don't wonder," I grunted, my mind still busy with the problem suggested by the *Dicroreri*. "No, I don't wonder."

"You started with a lavish abundance and much of that remains. Our universe is a closed one, limited by the four walls, the ceiling and the floor, of this great cavern. Nothing can come into it save the water that feeds the *fortlik*. Nothing can go out of it. Yet the Folk have survived here, for thousands of *sloonit*."

"That is about all you have done," I responded. "Survive. Because you know nothing better, you are content to be ruled in all your thoughts, and all your actions, for every minute of your waking and sleeping lives by laws so rigorous that the punishment for their violation is a horrible death. You are content to be not individuals but mere creatures of your commonwealth, mere cells in a social organism, not free to live or love or even hate as you desire. You cannot comprehend how abhorrent such a life seems to me, how abhorrent it must be to any who has known the Upper World."

"We are slaves, Hula, it is true. Yet we go on. You are free, and your race rushes to its own extinction."

"Not yet," I snapped. "We can still save ourselves."

"How, Hula? How?"

"By turning from our reckless course. By conserving wisely that which is left to us of Nature's bounty. By restoring, in our relation to our environment and our relations with one another, that balance of which I have spoken. By remembering, as a race and as individuals, that we must contribute to the common welfare as much as we take from it. By planning our existence, and living according to that plan."

"Your people, every one of them, are so wise then, so altruistic that you can do this, Hula, without rulers to promulgate it as a Law, without dire punishments to enforce the Law? Are they, Hula?"

"Well…" I hesitated, then honestly compelled the answer. "No."

The hint of a triumphant smile shadowed her lips, warning me of the trap into which she insidiously had led me.

What I had proposed was exactly the planned economy of Mernia that I so pitied the Folk for having to endure; what the negative I had just spoken made inevitable was exactly the despotism of a ruler caste, the absolute subjection of each individual to the state, that I stigmatized as revolting!

I recovered myself. "But we shall learn to be, so that we may work our destiny as free, masterless individuals, and not as slaves. The alternative is already too clear to us. Some territories upon Earth's surface, isolated by the artificial boundaries we call national borders, have already gone the way you imply we all must go. We have our horrible examples, our totalitarian states built upon one fanatic doctrine or another, and we see what sacrifice of happiness, what misery, they entail.

"Perhaps all humanity is mortgaged to that doom by the race's instinct to perpetuate itself, accepting any fate rather than extinction; but that mortgage is not yet foreclosed."

"No, my Hula?"

"No," I flung at her. "We are not yet in the situation of your Folk. Our resources are not yet drained. We still have a margin of safety. We still can save ourselves from the dire necessity that afflicts you, not by imposed Law but by our own enlightened choice. I still have faith, Ra Nalinah, that joining hands in a great unselfish, democratic band, we shall yet march on to greater heights of happiness and well being than we have ever known."

Her smile was gone. She seemed troubled.

"Ah!" she sighed, "but if this is more than just your dream, perhaps we Mernians have no right to—"

THE *lusan* lifted, abruptly. Nalinah cut herself off, fell into a dark absorption. I turned to the screen, saw that the ground, bare and dark once more, was dropping away from beneath us. The road was now a ramp stalking across the land on tremendous stilts, and climbing. The pitch of the incline slowed the limping *lusan* even more, so that it was crawling.

I peered downward at the airy network of the trestle members, a little dizzy with the height to which we were attaining, troubled a little by a sense of insecurity. The girders of that scaffolding seemed far too slender, far too fragile to support itself, let alone the weight of the *lusan*. They seemed to sway perilously in the dead air.

Quite suddenly the lacy structure was no longer a scaffolding springing from solid rock but a flying arch, a feathery bridge over an awesome chasm. I looked down into that terrible abyss, down till my eyes ached with the strain, and I could not probe its depths. Bottomless it seemed, its black mystery plumbing Earth even perhaps to the eternal fires bubbling at its core.

We were no longer over that fearsome gulf. The trestle ramp had curved suddenly, had become an ascending spiral, a mile across. Within the embrace of its arc encircled by that incredible chasm, I saw the Surahnit city of Tashna.

I saw Tashna, but not for the first time.

I had seen all this; the strange buildings that spread beneath me, the great Central Plaza out of which soared a topless crystal shaft within which rainbow-hued clouds swirled and billowed while the whole city pulsed with a weird, unwholesome light— in my dreams!

Statement of Edith Horne, R.N., resumed:

The drug administered to Jethro Parker did all that we hoped it would. Friday morning he woke up and asked me where he was, what had happened to him. I told him, bluntly, not to bother me with questions. I fed him his breakfast, ordered him back to sleep. He obeyed like a babe. When Ed Hard came in to inquire after my patients only a practiced eye could have made out any difference between poor Charley Dorsey and the farmer.

The healthy youngsters, Roger Norton, Dick Doring, Ann's brother, and Percy White, were much more of a problem. Restless, full of life, they were continually getting into mischief. I had suggested to the councillors that they work out a schedule of activities, as near the ordinary routine of the camp as possible, and they had done so. I thought the water was getting too cold for swimming and forbade it. There had been quite a little argument about this, but I managed to win my point.

After I was through with feeding Parker at noon, and with the task of giving young Charley such nourishment as possible, there was nothing for me to do. Dr. Stone had run back to Albany to attend to his practice; Ed and Bob were giving the boys lessons in boxing; Shean Morphy, recovered from his indisposition of the night before, was busy in his kitchen. The thought of Hugh broke through the barriers I had contrived to erect against it. It was the uncertainty as to his fate that was so dreadful. I could have borne it better if I knew him to be dead.

With a queer idea that it might make him seem nearer, I went into the room where Hugh had slept the night after he returned from Dr. Stone's and again the night after he almost drowned. I stood at the window and looked out into the woods. It was down there, I recalled, that we found Hugh's clothing, each garment in its proper place. But he was not dead. I should have known it if he were.

And then I heard a scream from within the house, a man's hoarse scream that could come only from Jethro Parker!

I WHIRLED, dashed through the door into his room. He was out of his bed. His eyes bulged with terror and his great hands were pawing at his chest.

"Jethro!" I cried, halting in the doorway.

He tore something away from him. Those hands of his were spread apart, as though they held something between them. Their fingers were curled, as though they clutched something. Hands, arms, were shaking as though something were alive, were fighting frenziedly to get loose. But I saw nothing. Nothing at all, except the farmer, the familiar furnishings of the little room.

Parker's arms swept over his head, slashed down, as if he were hurling from him the imagined thing he fought. Glass crashed. The window pane had broken, just as if he had thrown some object.

"Jethro!"

He turned and stared at me, glassy-eyed. "Sucking my chest," he gasped, his hands back at his hairy breast but fumbling there now uncertainly. "It was sucking my blood."

Delirium, I thought. Hyoscine sometimes acts like that.

"Get back into bed," I snapped.

I crossed to him, felt of his brow. It was damp with cold sweat, but not feverish.

It could not have been delirium unless I, too, was delirious. Parker had had nothing between his hands. He had flung nothing at the window, that was four feet from where he stood—but someone had!

When I looked at Jethro Parker I saw, where his hairy chest was exposed by the open V of his night-shirt, a reddened spot on the skin—as though his blood had been drawn close to the surface by a tiny, sucking mouth.

Clipping from "Sound Stage Secrets" column of Hollywood Herald, Friday, August 31, 1934:

SCOOP!!! SCOOP!!!*** This one just made the last edition deadline. *** That grin on Carton Ford's phiz is gone. *** World Pic's prexy Ratskoff is tearing the last three hairs out of his dome. *** Their star turned out to be a Comet. *** Ann Doring *** Got a letter on the set this morning. *** Read it. *** Walked out of the sound stage door. Out of the Lot gate. Hopped a taxi and before anyone tumbled to what she was up to was out of sight. Gate-keep Flannery had sense enough to get the hack's number. But La Doring must have tipped the cabbie plenty. He "don't know nothing." "I didn't make no pick-up in front uh the World lot this afternoon an' if I did I don't know where I took her." *** Well, that washes up *Heart's Desire*—and Ann Doring. Unless she shows back before Ratskoff strikes the sets and writes half a million off the books. *** Exhibs won't take anyone else in our Ann's place. *** I promised the guy I got it from I wouldn't tell anyone. *** But I know I can trust you to keep it always a "Sound-Stage Secret." ***

Hugh Lambert's Narrative, continued:

In that dream of mine I had seen the stone-built houses of Tashna from the ground level. That way, they had appeared odd enough—hexagonal, windowless, their doors rectangular plates of the dull red metal I have learned is an allotrope of copper, called by the Mernians *lural.* Now, from the vantage of the slowly mounting *lusan,* I saw their real difference from any terrestrial structure. They were roofless! I could look down into them, as they were imaged on the vehicle's visual screen, and could see every detail of their internal economy.

This was, come to think of it, quite to be expected. There is no rain in Mernia, no snow, no wind. The temperature is unvarying.

The Mernians did not build their homes for shelter, but for privacy.

For privacy? Numerous small, railed platforms were bracketed to the legs of the trestles supporting the ramp-spiral that encircled the city, and the roads coming radially in to merge with it. On each platform a man stood, leaning over, the rail, staring down. I pointed them out to Nalinah.

"They are the Watchers," she told me. "Their duty is to observe any infraction of the Law and report it to the Ratanit for punishment. They seldom have a report to give."

"I don't wonder," I remarked, thinking of those never-sleeping eyes watching the city. "Have you got some way of spying on the people's thoughts, too?"

My sarcasm failed. "Yes," was the girl's amazing reply. "See there." She pointed to a corner of the screen, to a building larger than most. "That is the Listeners' Post."

I leaned forward. The houses of Tashna are divided within into six-sided compartments or rooms, some of their partitions double-walled to allow for interconnecting passages. The entire city is laid out on this hexagonal plan, its resemblance to a vast honeycomb corresponding so well to the Surahnit's beelike sociology that I think I might have been surprised had it been otherwise.

There seemed to be less of a bustle of activity within the structure Nalinah had indicated than inside the others, but it was distinguished by a sparkling glitter, as though it contained much polished metal.

"You listen to their very thoughts," I repeated, wonderingly. "I said that because I deemed it impossible."

"Impossible? Thought is electrical in nature,* every brain continually sending out etheric waves. All that is needed to pick these up is the proper apparatus. Look."

Nalinah's hand touched the edge of the screen.

The interior of the Listeners' Post leaped at me. I seemed to be right on top of it as it revolved slowly, with our slow circling about the city.

The walls of the hexagonal rooms were of crystal. Fastened to them was an orderly jumble of metal bars and levers, of angling bus-wires. Seated along these walls were hundreds of Surahnit girls, wires coiling from the electrical apparatus on the walls to disc-like contrivances clamped to their ears. Every now and then one of the girls would stretch out a white-webbed

---

* Author's Note: A recent newspaper report *(New York Times;* Dec. 12, 1936) deals with the experiments of Drs. Lee Travis and Abraham Gottlober of the University of Iowa along this line. Their results while not complete yet only tend to confirmation of the electrical nature of thought but of course the Mernian scientists are far in advance of ours in this field as in almost everything else.—A.L.Z.

hand to make some adjustment; otherwise they were immovable, visibly tense with concentration.

"The Listeners," Nalinah murmured in my ear. "Vanark has them well trained, has he not? Even in his absence they attend strictly to their duty. They are forbidden only to scan the thoughts of us on the Ratanit, and of the higher officers of the labor guard."

This, too, I had dreamed about. I had seen one of these walls, a white hand moving...

NOT QUITE. The wall in my dream had been somewhat different from these. The connections had been different, the levers. I noticed, at the very center of the honeycomb, a small cell that was covered over. "That—why is it hidden? Is there something special there?"

"Special? Yes. An invention of Vanark's not yet perfected." Nalinah's voice halted abruptly. When she spoke again, almost at once, there was a curious mixture of, speculation and excitement in her tone. "Or so he claims. But—curious—He seemed to have no doubt that you—Can that be the real reason for his eagerness to destroy you? To hide his mistake?"

"What are you talking about?"

"His experiment for which he promised so much." I realized she was so caught up by her train of thought that she did not realize I had spoken to her or that she was answering me. "Far beyond mere eavesdropping on thought, though based on the same principle. Control of the will itself. Remote control! He reported that it had temporarily failed with the first emissary we sent into the Upper World. But are you not subject to it? I did not realize... Hula! You did not come here willingly, did you?"

"No. I could not help myself. Something made me follow Vanark, obey him, in spite of myself."

"In spite—Wait... " She broke off, thought for an instant, was speaking again. "Hula! You *are* a human, are you not, reduced only to our size, but otherwise wholly a human? Yet—were you ever dead?"

"Dead?" I laughed. "Why, no! I'm living, breathing. Once dead, a man stays dead."

"Not always, Hula. The emissary—the one Vanark reported as lost—was dead once. Then he was alive again—the blood of a Surahnit in his veins, the blood through which, only, Vanark's invention could act on a human. It was not perfected. It could not reach efficiently through the mountains above us, and the emissary was lost."

She was thinking aloud again, again oblivious of me. "I see it! I understand! Vanark searched for the emissary while the other parts of the Great Plan moved forward. He reported that he had found him again and was returning with him to Mernia. It was you with whom he returned. But you are not the lost emissary. You are not like those who lie in the cave in the Gateway Wall. You were never dead. Yet your will is not your own. You spoke, back there, of matters you could not know. How can that be when there is no Surahnit blood in your veins?"

My pulse pounded. I had been thinking too, fitting into the weird occurrences of the past few weeks the weird things she was saying. Seeing the pattern almost plain now.

"Perhaps there is, Nalinah. There is another's blood in my veins, not my own. Perhaps the other was the emissary of whom you speak." The blood of the tramp had been transfused into my veins—of the tramp who gruesomely resembled the man, Elijah Fenton, who had been drowned! "If that was Surahnit's blood, then within me there surely courses blood of the Surahnit."

"That's it!" No doubt of Nalinah's excitement now. Her eyes were gleaming with it; her face was flushed. "When Vanark lost control of the emissary he lived for a while, blundering aimlessly about like a machine with its controls jangled."

Into the path of my car he had blundered, I thought.

She went on, "He no longer had a mind, but his muscles

might have retained some memory of the time when they were alive on earth, might have reacted in response to motor impulses not yet faded from the ganglia that are independent of the central nervous system."

A hand now dead, I thought, having blundered into old familiar surroundings, might have completed a chess move it had started months before. As Elijah Fenton had done.

Sooner or later, Nalinah ran on, the life loaned his dead body would be exhausted and it would dwindle, vanish to nothingness, as had been provided for should it be captured.

THERE IT was! The incredible thing that had happened in Court Stone's surgery was explained. Why I had been so irresistibly drawn to Lake Wanooka was also clear. That attraction had grown as the Surahnit blood that had been added to my own had invested mine with its peculiar chemistry. With that gradual change I had progressively gained the ability to see the Little Men who, invisible to anyone else, had been searching for the vanished tramp. When the change was completed, Vanark had obtained complete control of me, had carried me off…

"You are not the emissary, as Vanark pretended. If he deceived by that much us others of the Ratanit," Nalinah mused aloud, "he may be hiding more in his secret room. He may not have yet returned to it. Before he does—the search ray!"

She reached once more to the screen, pushed one of a series of disc-like buttons flush in its frame, so exactly the color of the metal that I had not noticed them before. The image of the house she had called the Listeners' Post was again enlarged so that practically the whole field of our vision was occupied by the lid over Vanark's secret room!

Nalinah thumbed another button.

The roof was abruptly transparent! I could now see into the chamber beneath it.

I saw more crystal walls, more gleaming metal bus-bars screwed to them. I saw gauges and levers, and a screen much like the one before me. There was only one girl in the cell. She was seated before the screen, was watching it intently. I gasped.

That which she watched was my own countenance, staring out at her! Nalinah's was beside it, the interior of the *lusan* backgrounding us!

The girl down there turned, and I saw her face.

It was small, winsome. Black curls capped it. Its fathomless gray eyes were not puzzled now, but terrified!

It was Leeahlee!

I was not surprised. If I had found the city of my dream, what was there astonishing in the fact that the girl who I thought existed only in that fevered dream dwelt within it?

The screen was blank! I realized that it was blank because I had reached out and jabbed the uppermost button of the series on its frame. Nalinah snatched at my wrist, tried to drag my hand away. I fended her off with my shoulder.

"Hula," she cried. "What are you doing? I thought I saw another there, a stranger. I must—"

The *lusan* jolted to a stop. There was the grate of metal on metal and the vehicle's side was opening. Just before anyone outside could have seen what I was doing, I had released Nalinah, had settled back in my seat as if I had never left it.

I had intended to do none of all this. I did not know why I pressed the button, nor that my pressing would blank the screen. I did not know why I fought Nalinah to keep it blank. Once more the Other had taken control of me.

I knew that Other's name now. Leeahlee. I had seen her white fingers flash among the keys before her as I had acted as I did.

A labor guard subaltern appeared in the *lusan's* entrance. "Seal the covered cell in the Listeners' Post," Nalinah cried, whirling to him. "At once! Before anyone within it can escape."

"*Gor Surah*, Nalinah," the officer saluted; and then he clipped, "I cannot obey your commands. By order of Nal Surah you are suspended from your powers as Ra, and directed to consider yourself under close arrest."

"Arrest!" the girl exclaimed. Her wand jerked up. A film of green spread under the subaltern's dark skin, but there was no tremor in his voice. "You are to report to the Nal immediately," he continued, "and I am to take charge of your prisoner."

Prisoner! I didn't like the sound of that. I liked still less what I glimpsed over the shoulder of the man who had said it.

It was the hook-nosed, swarthy visage of Vanark I saw—expressionless save for the sneering triumph that leered out of his malign little eyes!

CHAPTER VI

Hugh Lambert's Narrative, continued:

NALINAH SPRANG OUT of the *lusan*, twisted to the Rata. "Vanark," she cried. "I saw in your cell—"

"Stop." He cut her off. "You forget that, an arrest order forbids communication between its subject and anyone but her judges. Surrender your *kitor* to me and obey the order to report to the Na!"

Nalinah stared at him, the luminance emanating from her excited little face fading to a grayish pallor. For a long moment she stood so, her lovely body tensed, Frantic appeal in her wide-pupiled eyes. Then she held out her wand to him, he took it; and she went past him, stumbling as if she were half-blinded by tears.

"Out!" the officer snapped. I shoved along the seat, emerged on a circular platform, some hundred yards in diameter, to which the end of the great spiral had broadened, here high above the city. At its further edge a half-dozen or so *lusans* were being serviced by Taphetnit under the watchful eyes of *coret*-armed guards. Between them and the three of us the wide expanse of darkly rubescent *lural* was untenanted, broken only by a small, six-sided penthouse at its center into which the flutter of Nalinah's robes was just disappearing.

"What are your orders, Rata?" the subaltern inquired.

"Fetch the prisoner along with me, Riskal." Vanark responded, his evil countenance an impassive mask. "He is to be brought before the Ratanit for questioning."

"Very well."

Vanark wheeled and stalked off toward the small structure into which Nalinah had gone. Riskal indicated by a gesture that I was to follow.

Vanark had not even glanced at me but an alarm bell was ringing within me, warning me of peril. I was now fully aware, from Nalinah's broken sentences, that it had not been simply because of my attack upon him that he had attempted to have me killed at the Gateway guardhouse. His purpose had been to cover up my substitution for the tramp who had vanished from Doc Stone's leather couch, apparently for no other reason than that I was living proof of his blunder.

Nalinah had saved me then, but I was in Vanark's power once more. I needed no other evidence than that he had accomplished this by somehow bringing about her arrest, to tell me that he did not intend me ever to come before the Mernian Council.

The girl had at least given me the choice of aiding the Mernians in their intended invasion of the Upper World. I had reckoned myself fairly safe as long as there was a possibility of my being of use to the Little Folk. Now, trotting after Vanark to the little hexagonal penthouse, I was tensely aware of immediate and deadly peril.

I glanced wildly around, searching for some means of escape. Other than Vanark and the officer, no one was near enough to make me out clearly, let alone interfere with me, but I saw at once the idea was hopeless. I might by some miracle overcome the two Surahnit, but a *lusan* would overtake me at once if I made for the ramp by which the platform was reached. There was no other visible exit, no way I could go except over the edge, to plunge headlong down to the ground, a half mile below.

Even if the Other, Leeahlee, permitted me to act, there was nothing I could do. Nothing at all.

REACHING THE penthouse, Vanark touched the wand he called a *kitor* to its *lural* wall. It slitted vertically, opened out. Within, an absolutely bare ceilingless chamber was disclosed. Startlingly though it took up the entire interior and only seconds before I had seen Nalinah enter it, she was not there.

The Rata went into the room. Wondering, what had become of Nalinah, I imitated him. I felt relieved as the subaltern joined us. Vanark had told him that they were taking me to the Ratanit. He would not have permitted the youth to come along if he had other plans. Perhaps my apprehension was reasonless.

The chamber wall shut—leaped upward. A familiar, whistling roar assailed my ears. The mystery of Nalinah's disappearance was solved. We had entered an elevator like the one in the cliff at the Eastern boundary of Mernia, were descending to Tashna's street level. The girl had preceded us, that was all.

Fast enough in all conscience, the speed of this drop was not nearly as stupendous as the first. It did not daze me as that had, did not rob me of my senses. I could see my companions, could see Riskal start suddenly and twist to the Rata—surprise, inquiry, written large on his swarthy, sensitive young face.

"Yes," Vanark answered that look, a thin smile licking his sadistic mouth. "We are now below the ground level. We descend to a secret passage beneath the city, known only to the Ratanit. You—"

A pile driver blow against the soles of my feet jarred the breath out of me. The chamber wall was no longer rushing upward. Vanark's gesture created an aperture in it, and we went out into a passageway.

Its roof just cleared our heads. It was just wide enough to permit us to proceed single file, Vanark ahead, Riskal behind me. The darkly glistening walls were glass-smooth, as though the same terrific heat that had shaped Mernia's rocks had been applied to pierce the foundations of Tashna.

I was oppressed by a sense of immense weight piled above me, by an illogical notion that any instant these walls would narrow and crush me. The whisper of our padded footfalls hissed away from us, pent in by the interminable burrow. The tunnel's sides ribboned past us far more swiftly than we could possibly be walking.

It was as if the floor were moving with us, utterly without sound or vibration, yet when I looked down I could descry no appreciable separation between it and the side walls, no visible motion of the rock beneath us.

There *was* no motion. We were being swept forward as I had seen surfboards swept, forward on the breast of a wave that was not water but a form rushing at breathless speed toward Waikiki beach. But here there was no wave, no change in the smooth surface of our footing, unless that change were so minute that its measurement was in the realm of the microscopic.

It occurred to me that the *lusan* might have been propelled in the same manner. I wondered… My startled speculations were interrupted by the abrupt appearance of a fork in the tunnel ahead. Vanark took its left-hand branch.

Riskal called out to him. "Are you not going wrong, Rata? Is not the other the direction of the Council House?"

"Follow," the man ahead responded. His voice resounded, hollow in the tunnel's sightless reaches, seeming never to die out. I was again afraid…

THE PASSAGE bent sharply. Vanark did not turn with it. He went straight at the solid rock ahead of him, went straight *into it*. For an instant his form shimmered within the stone, then it was gone.

The tunnel floor hurtled me straight ahead, my frantic efforts to stop or turn unavailing. I struck the wall.

There was no impact. I blanked out into a vertiginous darkness. It was not around me but within me; within every cell, every atom, of my being—and as suddenly was gone.

Falling forward, I twisted to a choked half cry, half scream behind me. I saw the other side of the wall; Riskal flinging out of it, out of its very substance, as though he were being formed from it. There was on his face the same shock, the same mixture of amazement and retching nausea as must have been on my own.

The subaltern reeled, straightened. Stark terror struck his countenance livid!

He was pinned to the wall by the brilliant, white glare of sunlight! His arm lifted. By a visibly tremendous effort it reached the horizontal. His contorted lips formed the words, *"Gor Surah!"* its syllables only a shadow of sound. Then he was blurring, agony shrieking from every melting line of his body.

The hands with which I had held myself to my knees shoved against the floor, pivoted me from that dreadful treachery. From Vanark's upraised grasp, the *kitor* blazed the lethal rays that were utterly destroying the subaltern who had obeyed and trusted him, the officer on whose presence I had relied for my safety!

How right I had been to be afraid!

The scene photographed itself on my brain. Vanark was half a dozen feet from me. Behind and to either side of him was a clutter of wires, bus-bars, fantastic metallic fabrications, apparatus whose purpose and nature I could not even guess at. The room, its very walls and ceiling, exuded an atmosphere of murky stealth, of buried secrecy. A screen, like that in the *lusan,* except for greater size, occupied the rearmost wall.

Before that screen stood the "tramp" who had strangely vanished from Stone's surgery.

I started to throw myself to my feet, aware that there was no possibility of escape from the murderous Mernian, aware that he could transfix and obliterate me with the *kitor's* deadly beam before I could reach him, but determined to attempt the impossible. I started to rise but froze rigid, paralyzed by the sound of my own name, cried out by the tramp.

"Mr. Lambert. Have they got you, too?"

Staring at him across the murk of that lair, only my bulging eyes alive, it dawned on me that he was *not* the tramp. He was Jeremiah Fenton, the farmer whose tale of a chess game mysteriously ended I had listened to.

He was Elijah Fenton's twin!

Vanark's scheme was clear now, in all its ingenuity. While Nalinah and I had been delayed in the *fortlik* field, he had somehow gotten hold of Fenton. He had beaten us to Tashna and provided for the girl's arrest. Murdering the guard, the only other Surahnit who could bear witness against him, he would destroy me next and then present the farmer as the emissary he had sent to spy on the Upper World.

There was no doubt that the deception would succeed. The resemblance between Fenton and the tramp was no accidental coincidence. The emissary was—had been—Elijah, Jeremiah Fenton's twin.

"Hughlambert!" Vanark's voice pulled my eyes to his saturnine countenance. "This is your end." The *kitor* swung around. Its blaze struck deep into my brain. I saw nothing but that white glare, felt nothing but the excruciating torture of those brilliant darts…

Radiogram from files of Transcontinental Western Airlines:

Flight 4 Eastbound Aug. 31/34 9:13 P.M. Commercial 25wds Paid
    Dr. Courtney Stone
    Albany N Y
    Arrive Albany airport Saturday a.m. special plane from Newark stop Please arrange transportation and accommodation Camp Wanooka stop Is there any good news lost lamb.
                        Ann Dicksister

Continuation of statement of Edith Horne, R.N.:

THE MARK ON Jethro Parker's chest faded. Until it was entirely gone from the skin under his black mat of hair, I did not move.

I could not have moved if I wanted to. I was held rigid within a tight shell of dread, all the more fearsome because I did not know, did not understand, what it was I had to dread. I might still be standing like that, if there had not been a sudden rush of light footfalls in the hall outside the room and a boyish voice crying, "Miss Horne! Miss Horne!" I turned in time to see a butterfly net come across the door opening, and Percy White appear behind it. The undersized youngster peered at me through the thick lenses without which he was blind as a bat.

"Anything wrong, Miss Home?" he panted. "I heard you scream and then I heard the window smash, and I came running from the woods."

"No, Perce." I managed to smile. "There isn't anything wrong. I—I tripped and cried out, and my elbow went through the window. I'm sorry I startled you."

"Aw gee!" The excitement died out of his face. "And I was just sneaking up on a Gold-banded Skipper. The books say they don't come as far North as this, but I'm sure this was one. It was perched on top of a goldenrod and—"

"Maybe it's still there, Percy. Better run and see."

"Do you think so? Golly!" He scampered away, the killing-box hung by a strap from his neck thumping against the wall as he went.

The interruption brought me back to normal. It hadn't happened, I told myself. I hadn't seen Parker pluck an invisible something from his chest and throw it through the window.

But the window *was* broken. There was no getting around that. And there was no reasonable explanation of how it came to be so. Or if there were, only Jethro Parker could give it to me.

I recalled what I knew about scopolamine, how though one under its influence retains no conscious recollection of what occurs to him, his subconscious memory will respond to questioning more truthfully than the waking one could.

I closed the door, and drew a chair up to the bedside. I took the farmer's gnarled, work-worn hand in mine. It closed on my fingers, confidingly, and I was abruptly ashamed of what I had done to him, of what I was about to do. But I had to know what had happened here in this room.

"Don't wake up," I said, clearly, distinctly. "Don't wake up, Jethro, but listen to me and answer me. Do you hear me, Jethro?"

"Yes." Deep-toned, husky, the voice that came from him was unfamiliar.

"What made you scream, Jethro?"

"Heavy—on my chest." It was as if someone else, some utter stranger, were speaking to me *through* him. "Lips, wet lips, mumbling my skin. Sucking." His stubbled, gaunt countenance was relaxed. "Woke me because I was—not really—asleep."

"What did you do?"

"Grabbed him. He fought—little hands fought me."

I was cold, quivering cold. "Paws, you mean." I could not help the interruption. "Paws, Jethro," I begged him to say.

"No. Hands. Baby hands. But no baby. Too—strong. No—baby. I jumped up—tore him away. Threw him…"

"What was it?" It was my own voice that was unfamiliar now, thin, edged with shrillness. "What was it you saw?"

"Saw nothing. Felt. Only felt."

"What was it you felt? Jethro! What was it you felt?"

Intonationless, mechanical, the weird, hoarse tones answered me. "Man. Little man. Wee man of Wanooka. Come back—out of the lake—like Injun Joe—told me they would—told me—long ago…"

The voice faded. Jethro Parker tossed restlessly in his sleep, turned over. The whisper that came from his lips was more nearly his own voice. It breathed, "No, mother. I won't go round with Injun Joe—no more."

I asked no more questions. I sat there, my eyes on the sleeping man, not seeing him. I was thinking of what Shean Morphy had cried out, last night in his drink-madness. "The leprechauns are all about. The Wee Folk!" I was thinking of the wraiths I had seen, or thought I had seen, creeping through the woods.

But more than all else I was thinking of the red blotch that had been, that morning, on Charlie Dorsey's sun-bronzed chest. The redness that had faded, before I was through bathing him, from his skin and from my thoughts.

Continuation of Hugh Lambert's narrative:

I COULD see nothing but the white, dazzling blaze of the *kitor*. I could feel nothing but its terrific heat. But I could hear out of the heart of that glare, Vanark's voice.

"Your end, Hughlambert." And then again, but more slowly, somehow puzzled. "I'm rid of you." Puzzled and uncertain.

I, too, was puzzled. That white brilliance stabbed my eyes though their lids were tight shut against it, yet otherwise I was merely hot. Sweat bathed me, crawling between the *sibral* that still clad me and my skin. I was parched. But I had endured scarcely less discomfort on the unshaded salt-sands of Death Valley one mid-August day. Surely,—if I were melting—

The light was gone!

My eyelids flew open. I saw great fuzzy rings; green, orange; continually expanding from a scarlet, center vivid against throbbing blackness. I was blinded, dazed, but I was still whole. Still alive!

Somewhere within the phantasmagoria into which I stared there was movement.

"Watch it!" Fenton screamed. "He's going to shoot!"

I leaped at that adumbration of movement, came against a body. My hand caught a skinny wrist; slipped over clenched fingers; caught cold metal, the flaring barrel of a *coret;* twisted it sideward. Sight beginning to return showed me the dim outline of a head. My free hand lashed to the throat just beneath it. Gripped!

Vanark wrenched at his *coret,* trying to get it loose. He lurched against me, fighting my hold. Despair, terror, must have doubled his strength, for he forced me back. Rage doubled mine, I braced a leg behind me, held him...

My foot slipped in the wetness on the floor—wetness that once had been, a youthful subaltern of the guard. I went down. My holds wrenched loose and I was on my knees. Seeing more clearly now, I saw Vanark reel backward, catch himself, slice his weapon down to pointblank aim.

His evil countenance, aflame with hate, seared itself on my

brain. Triumph flared in his malevolent eyes. The *kitor* had failed, they said, but the *coret* would not fail.

The red-glowing tube ended its arc, in line with my head. Its scarlet beam shot out—harmlessly past me.

In the ultimate instant, a form had catapulted from above onto Vanark's shoulders! It had pounded him to the floor, and the two were battling, Vanark and the other who had saved me.

He was a Surahnit! This much I saw as I came to my feet, eager to help, but more than that I could not make out as the combatants whirled over and over, clawing furiously at one another, silent save for the furious small sounds they made despite themselves; the tiny snarling sounds.

There was a dull thud before I could spring in, the impact of bone against the massive *lural* support of some machine my rescuer's skull had struck. It stunned him, momentarily at least. Vanark tore free, leaped erect. He still clung to the *coret*. It flailed down to annihilate his opponent.

I shouted incoherently. My thigh muscles exploded, hurled me at the enraged Rata in a low flying tackle. Seeing and reacting instantaneously, Vanark sprang sidewise to avoid me. Not quite far enough. My reaching arms missed him but my shoulder struck his thigh, sent him sprawling into the gray, solid-seeming stone.

Wrath robbing me of reason, I surged up, plunged in pursuit. Blue light flashed across the wall's surface in the instant before I crashed into it. *Crashed!* It bruised, battered me, as solid now as it had seemed. An impenetrable barrier!

Pinned to it by the momentum of my leap, my breath jolted out of my lungs, I was aware of a blue shimmer flowing over that wall, an electric vibrancy it had not before possessed. Something had transformed it, in the eye blink of time between when Vanark had reeled out through it and when I reached it, to impenetrable rock.

"Antil!" The exclamation, behind me, throbbed with the mellowness of a golden-stringed harp. "Antil. You—you are not—"

"Dead." Other tones, shaken, gasping, but oddly-insouciant with it all, responded. "Not even hurt—much."

"Jeehoshaphat!" Fenton's voice was harsh, crude, in contrast to those others. "Jeerusalem. What—how—"

Fenton was a stride away from where I had last seen him; amazement was written large on his big-boned countenance. Behind him to one side of the great screen, was Leeahlee.

Her slim white hand clung to a silvery switch handle in the wall as if she had just thrown it, but her lissome body was twisted away from it and her gray eyes were wide with anxiety.

"You come through the wall." The farmer's accents were a dull monotone his astonishment flattening all expression out of them as a typhoon's onset flattens the Indian Ocean. "They come through the ceiling. But there ain't no doors in wall *nor* ceiling."

It was the Surahnit at whom Leeahlee stared, her soul in her eyes. He was dragging himself up by the *lural* machine-base that had almost done for him. Now he was on his feet, facing Leeahlee.

"Good girl," he gasped. "You've sealed this chamber against Vanark. He dares not reveal its existence to have it blasted to dust and us with it. We are safe here."

"Safe, Antil," Leeahlee responded. "From Vanark. He cannot reach us to harm us as long as we keep the chamber sealed. But as long as we keep it sealed neither can we leave it. Quick death by Vanark's *coret* outside, slow, death by thirst and starvation within, either way we are doomed."

"Doomed," Jeremiah Fenton breathed, echoing her.

ANTIL WAS swarthy as the Surahnit I had seen, sharp-featured as they, but he was subtly different from the other men of Mernia's dominant race.

"We are safe for the moment, Leeahlee," he said. "Let us be content with that."

His difference from the others of his race did not lie alone in that he was clad in the chastely white, close-fitting garment of the Taphetnit, its wing slits sewn together. He was straight and slender as a sturdy birch and there was a shining quality of youth about him. He was poised lightly on the balls of his feet, the pose of his fine head jaunty, confident.

He faced Leeahlee, the hint of a smile on his thin, wistful lips, a hint of sadness edging his profile.

The girl said something more. I was aware that she spoke, but I did not hear what she said. A sudden realization had flashed on me.

Not long ago I had seen another profile, older, the ebony hair topping it graying at the temples, but otherwise a replica of this one. That face existed no longer, self-blasted into extinction by its own *coret*. That face was Colonel Skoolteh's. Antil's could be only the face of the son the subaltern of long ago had watched vanish in the arms of a Taphet.

Nothing could be more certain. Antil was the Surahnit who dwelt in Calinore. He was the leader of the brewing revolt of the Taphetnit, and he was here, in the Listeners' Post, as a spy on his own race against whom that revolt was brewing.

"Maybe Vanark won't dare report your presence," I said. "But Nalinah will. She saw you in the room with Leeahlee and she tried to tell Vanark about it."

Antil swung to me. "We were not quick enough, then, in having you cut off the search-ray?" His smile was gone, his expression bleak, his eyes thoughtful.

"Evidently not. Look here, mister. You tried to kill a defense-less woman, but I owe you something for saving my life. That's why I am telling you this. Vanark wouldn't let Nalinah talk, but by this time she must have told her story to Nal Surah, whoever he is, and the Nal must already be after you. If you have anyway of escaping you'd better get busy."

"No," Antil answered, speaking softly. "Nalinah has not told her story to the Nal. He is too busy to give her audience. We were watching—but see for yourself." He bounded lithely across the room, touched a switch alongside the one Leeahlee had thrown to isolate this chamber.

His slender, vibrant frame was silhouetted, not against the screen to which an instant ago it had leaped, but against a far-flung vista of six-sided, squat buildings that ran smoothly toward us, fanning out and sliding past the frame of the huge paneless window out of which we seemed to look. So realistic was the illusion that the wall had vanished, that before I could catch myself I made an involuntary forward movement to grab Antil's arm lest he fall out.

"Gee Whittakers!" the farmer ejaculated. "We're moving! Fast!"

I felt it, too—that sensation of swift, vibrationless gliding through Tashna's alien streets. "Shhh," I hissed. "They'll hear—"

"They cannot hear us," Antil interrupted, "but if we wish we can hear them." There was an audible click, and there was in my ears the murmur of a vast crowd.

It was low at first, but it grew momentarily louder as we neared its sources; grew louder still until it was the roar of the sea on a lonely beach, until it was the growl of a hurricane sweeping the jungle. The buildings lining a last street slid past the sides of the screen, and ended. Motion ended, too.

Tashna's great Plaza lay before us. Their roar now tremendous about us; an uncountable throng of Surahnit ringed the concourse's central space where a squadron of the L.S.G were drawn up in rigid, ruler-straight ranks. This squared, emerald phalanx faced the topless pillar at the Plaza's hub.

They were stiffly at attention, those green-dressed Mernian soldiers, and statuesque, but each chiseled face was marked by awe, by a veneration almost transcending piety.

I heard Fenton murmur, half to himself, half aloud, "They look like they was in church." That was true. The light on those dark countenances was that which glorifies the visages of the congregation in some cathedral at the moment the Host is unveiled.

In my dream, and when I had seen it from the spiraling *lusan* ramp whose distant trestle was a sharp-lined tracery against Mernia's brooding sky, the crystal pillar had been alive with a roil of spectrum-tinted vapors. Its variegated hues had deepened now, so that the shaft blazed with the red and purple and orange of a sunrise over the Sahara and was a nearly unendurable splendor.

They were not still, those hues, but flowed upward unendingly within the very substance of the immense column, streaming out of a wide, flat plinth from which the pillar soared. On this platform Surahnit men and women, perhaps a dozen, stood facing the soldiers. They were in two groups, silent, expectant, and across the platform in the gap dividing them lay a carpet of ruby light.

"Antil," Leeahlee murmured. "There is one missing among the Ratanit. Who?"

The scene leaped forward. We seemed to be at the very edge of the dais, seemed to be within arm's reach of its occupants.

Each held a *kitor* and each was clothed in an iridescent robe like that which Nalinah had worn, the only difference between the men's and the women's that the former were shorter kirtled. I leaned forward, scanning the dusky, vulturine faces.

Vanark was there, clad like the others. His lids were drooped, veiling what must have been a very hell of frustration and rage in his beady eyes. Vanark had gotten there somehow. But—but Nalinah had not.

She did not fit among them, I thought. Other than Vanark, these Ratanit were ancient, their masklike countenances seamed and sere. Among them her fragile laughing beauty would be out of place as a blossom-mantled apple tree in a dead orchard. But her absence was ominous. What had happened to her? Where was she?

I glared at the vari-hued pillar behind the Ratanit, as much of it as was now visible, as if it could give me the answer.

ABRUPTLY THE column's base flashed wholly scarlet, so

that it seemed one with the riband of light that streamed across the platform, and in that instant there welled out of the shaft a single, deep-toned bell stroke.

The crowd-roar surged upward in volume, a Niagara of appalling sound...

And cut off! The sudden silence was like a thunderclap.

Leeahlee's breath, catching in her throat, made a littler whimper. Out of the corner of my eye I saw that she had come close to Antil, the tiny oval of her face pallid and strained, and that his arm was protectingly about her.

"Look, Mr. Lambert!" Fenton's horny clutch gripped my elbow. "Look there!"

His forefinger jabbed at the pediment of Tashna's great shaft, backgrounding the waiting Ratanit. Within the crimson depths there was a swirl of shadow, shapeless, textured like the phantom of a dream.

They were turning, those upon the platform, to the pillar. The silence was brittle now, like a bubble of glass strained to the shattering point. The tension of the great crowd I could not see caught me up, an electric tremor almost unendurable.

The shadow within the pillar was at its surface; was breaking through. The silence splintered into a gasp from twenty thousand throats.

A man stood before the scarlet flame of the pylon, where the scarlet light-ribbon joined it!

"*Gor Surah!*" crashed out of the screen. "*Gor, Nal Surah!*"

Statement of Edith Horne, R.N., continued:

I DON'T know where the rest of that last day of August went to. I lived it through mechanically. I didn't think any more about what Jethro Parker had done or said. I didn't think about Charlie Dorsey. I tried not to think at all. I was simply waiting for Dr. Stone to return to camp.

It was not until long after sunset that I heard the squeal of his brakes at the camp gate. Even then I waited, inside the infirmary. I heard his car door slam. After a little I heard the gravel crunch under his feet. He was coming slowly, wearier than I had ever known him to be.

I opened the door for him before he knocked, and only then realized that I had been sitting in the dark, that I had not turned on the light because I was afraid of what I might see.

Queerly enough Doctor Stone said nothing about its being dark. He stumbled across the little office room that makes a sort of entrance foyer to the infirmary. The smell of formaldehyde came in with him I saw him only as a dark bulk in the darkness, but I heard his long, slow breathing. The chair at the desk creaked as he settled into it.

I fumbled for the switch tumbler beside the door, pushed it up. The darkness vanished. Dr. Stone was looking at me and his face was the gray of weathered wood. His Vandyke was a trim black triangle on his chin, but there were deep lines radiating from the corners of his eyes, and his cheeks seemed to have sunk in. He looked old.

"You're very tired, doctor," I said, moving to him. "Let me take your hat and help you off with your coat. I'll make some tea for you on my little electric stove and you'll feel better after you've had some." I had been waiting years, it seemed, to talk to him, and I could not. Not in the condition he was in.

"Edith," he said, not making a move. "Adath Jenks died today."

I stopped, puzzled. "Adath Jenks?"

"The first of the two cases of this strange coma that was brought to the hospital. He died sometime today, we don't know just when because he's been so nearly dead for a week. I've just come from the post mortem in the morgue. I performed the necroscopy myself, the first time in years."

That accounted for the odor of formaldehyde that clung to him "Well?" I asked. "What did you find?"

"It is not an encephalitis. The brain and the nervous system were perfectly normal. It is not a glandular malfunction. There is no aberration of the endocrines. It is not a disorder of the digestive system or of the respiratory tract. There is scar tissue in the left lobe of the lung, healed traces of an arrested pulmonary tuberculosis the man never knew he had, but otherwise these organs show no lesions of any kind."

He stopped there. He'd forgotten something. Or had he forgotten it? "The circulatory system?" I could not get my voice above a whisper. "The heart and arteries and veins?"

The surgeon's fingers closed on a paper on which his hand had happened to fall, crushed it. "What makes you ask that?" he demanded, his eyes abruptly veiled.

"You did find something wrong with them!" I exclaimed. "What?"

"No. Not with the heart or arteries or veins. With the capillaries in the superficial tissues of the cadaver's chest. I noticed a vague discoloration there, incised, found—found—"

"What? In God's name *what?*" I knew. As if I had been there I knew what its probing scalpel had laid bare in Adath Jenks chest.

"THE CAPILLARIES, the network of hair-like blood vessels, were hypertrophied, enlarged, and their walls split. As if—as if the mouth of a suction pump had been applied there for a long time, drawing out blood plasma."

"Sucking it out, doctor?"

"Yes."

"But how is it that this was not suspected? How is it that with all the trained watchers in the hospital a progressive anemia was not detected?"

"There was no anemia. I had the blood drained from the corpse, its quantity measured. There was no deficiency."

Was I wrong? "Then in spite of appearances no blood was really drained from Jenks. Perhaps it was a blow on the chest."

"Have you ever seen a bruise in which the capillaries were enlarged? No, Edith, it was not a blow that caused the condition. Blood had been sucked from Adath Jenks, all the blood he had—and other blood was substituted for it!"

It was my hand that reached for the desk now, clung to it for support. "That—that sounds utterly insane. How could there have been a complete transfusion before the farmer was admitted without some evidence of it? Or afterward, in the ward, without the knowledge of the attendants?"

"I don't know. I don't know! But it happened, somehow, while Jenks was lying there in the ward, never a moment alone."

"What—what makes you so sure?"

"Just this. When the farmer was admitted we thought a transfusion might be indicated and typed his blood. It was Type II, agglutinated by I and III, agglutinating III and IV. I took a sample of the blood drawn from his corpse to my own laboratory, typed it myself. And—and—"

"It was not the same?"

"It was not the same. Edith! It now agglutinates the corpuscles of Type IV and none of the sera of the other standard types agglutinates it!"

I understood now why the surgeon's face was filmed with gray. I understood why deep within his keen eyes a glimmer of horror crawled. My own face must also have been colorless, gray.

"But—but that was what the blood of the tramp was like," I whispered, "who vanished from your surgery."

"Yes, Edith. The blood of the tramp, and the blood of—Hugh Lambert."

We stared at each other, stared into each other's eyes. For a long moment there was a pregnant, significant silence. Then Doctor Stone was talking again.

"I went back to the hospital and I took a sample of the blood of the other patient, Job Grant, and I returned to my laboratory and tested that. I checked and rechecked, and I am certain that my results are correct.

"Unheard of as it may be, the blood of Job Grant is a mixture of two types. One is Type IV. The other is—"

"The same as Jenks' and Lambert's and the tramp's." I don't know how I contrived to speak, with the fingers of hysteria closing on my throat. "Of course. It is changing. When it has all changed Job Grant will die. When they are through with him, when the little invisible men are through sucking Gant's blood, he will die."

"The little, invisible—" The doctor came up out of his chair then. "Edith! What are you talking about?"

He listened to me. His look never left my face as I told him of the nightmare through which I had lived that day, and because of the strength that look gave me, I could tell him about it in a low, even tone that never once broke.

While I talked I heard the rustle of a sleepy breeze through the needle-laden boughs of the pine trees, the shrill piping of the crickets and the quiet *lap, lap* of the waters of Lake Wanooka. It was so quiet, there in the lap of the ancient hills. So peaceful.

Somewhere far off I heard Dickie Doring's gay laugh ring out. From an almost immeasurable distance came the long, melancholy hoot of a locomotive rushing through the autumn night. That would be the Twentieth Century, I thought, even as I went on with my breathless tale, rushing toward New York with its load of human happiness and human griefs and human hopes.

CHAPTER VII

Continuation of Hugh Lambert's narrative:

I GAZED AT the Master of Mernia, brought so near to me by the magic of that screen that it seemed I need but to take a step forward to touch him; and Homeric laughter rumbled in my breast.

He stood there in the pulsing heart of that living, crimson flame. The *kitors* of the Ratanit were flung toward him in salute, and I knew that every left arm in the vast assemblage lay outstretched in humble salutation to their Nal, their Overlord.

He stood there in the pulsing heart of that living, crimson flame.

This was their Emperor. This was their god, or if not god, then his vicar in the subterranean cavern that is their world. This—creature!

The ruby light that bathed him could not conceal the yeasty gray-whiteness of his skin, pallid and flabby as the substance of a slug. The intricate adornment of his jeweled robe, his spired headgear from which blazed, limned in diamonds and topazes and rubies, the design of the sun and its circling planets, could not lend to his grossly corpulent form the least trace of majesty. The brooding scowl drawn upon his pendulous-chinned, quivering-cheeked countenance, with its small mouth and its fat-drowned, tiny eyes, invested it with no force whatever and no dignity.

He was just a fat man, slightly vulgar in the display of his trappings, slightly comic in the divinity he assumed.

"So that's your Nal Surah," I gibed. "That's the great man you fear and worship."

"Wait." I think it was Antil who said that. "Wait, Hula."

The scene was retreating. I saw the soldiers again, their arms dropping to their sides after that salute. I saw the crowd ringing the Plaza, motionless now, rapt, breathless with attention.

He was holding them. The fat man was holding them by what magic of tradition, by what necromancy of personality, I had not yet fathomed.

There was, of course, the dramatic entrance he had made out of the tremendous pylon that once more dominated the panorama; lifting to some unguessable height against the drab sky in whose middle distance the ramifications of the *lusan* high-way's spiral strode Tashna's encircling chasm. But that *was* a trick, and they were too intelligent, these Surahnit, to believe that it was anything but a trick.

Unless (and there was basis for this reservation in certain—may I call them superstitions?—of my own people) the Mernians *wished* to believe that it was not a trick but a miracle.

"Surahnit!"

The voice of Nal Surah was not loud. Hearing it as I knew I was, from the very edge of the Plaza that was a full two hundred feet from the pylon whence he spoke, its every syllable was distinct as though it were spoken in my ear.

"Heritors of the Ancient Truths," he went on, "I have called you together, this leisure evening hour, from your well earned leisure, to witness a ceremony of which there has been no need for seventeen *sloonit*."

He paused briefly. "The Taphetnit—debased race that bows not to the suzerainty of the Ratanit who rule the destiny of the Mernian Folk—have forgotten the lesson that was dealt them when last I blessed from this holy spot the warriors of Tashna. Once more they threaten the Folk Weal, once more defy the edicts of the Law.

"Nay, more. Lost to all sense of honor, ungrateful for the mercy with which we forebore the extinction that they richly merited when they rebelled against us, they violated the generous treaty we extended to them even in the very moment they subscribed to it. False and traitorous to the last atom of their hideous beings, they concealed from us the existence of the babe of a proscribed Surahnit in their midst, and despicably have nurtured him to this very day. Not content to wallow in the night of ignorance that blackens their city of Calinore, they plot now against the Surahnit, against Tashna, seeking to drag you down to their own bestial level."

A MURMUR ran through the throng, a low and ominous growl. Nal Surah's tone began to deepen, to rise in volume. A

practiced orator, he was playing upon the emotions of his listeners as a skilled organist plays upon his console, and they were
responding to him as the pipes respond to the touch on the
organ's keys.

"We have been patient with the Taphetnit. Through the long
ages we have held our wrath in check, believing that some time
they would grow to know the enlightenment to which we of
the Surahnit have attained.

"And what is our reward? What, I ask you?"

There was a pause. It lengthened. There was the beginning
of a stir in the crowd, checked at the very instant of its inception
by the Nal's pealing cry: "Surahnit!"

"The wheel of our fate has turned almost full circle," Nal
Surah went on. "Yet a little, only a little, and the Folk return to
that Elysium from which in ages past we were banished for our
sins. Yet only a little and this drab sky that arches over us shall
be replaced by another sky ablaze with the colors whose memory
has been kept alive for us by this Shaft of the Eternal Truth
before which I stand. The moment of our delivery from exile
is at hand and nothing can defeat it."

There was a light on the faces of the people, the light of a
dawning hope in their eyes. Nal Surah dropped to a whisper, a
hiss of penetrating sound.

"Nothing? Aye. *They* can alter our destiny if we permit it.
They—the barbarians of Calinore, with their sly schemes; their
insidious treacheries, their open rebellion." That voice was rising
in a slow crescendo of fury. "They—our mortal enemies would
cheerfully destroy themselves if by so doing they can drag us
down to destruction. Shall we permit it?"

"No!" the answer blared. "No!"

"You answer no, and I say to you, no! I say to you, they must
be destroyed. There must be left not a single Taphet, not a single
feather of that base and ignoble race in all the land of Mernia.
Surahnit! Calinore must be destroyed!"

"Calinore must be destroyed!" He had lashed them to fury

*The slender, delicatey formed body was
contorted, now, in agony....*

at last. They roared, as in a distant time, in a distant place
another mob once roared: *"Carthago delenda est!"*

No, Nal Surah was no longer ridiculous. He was still a fat
man, standing there on the pylon, his triple chins quivering on

his bosom, his naked face utterly expressionless, but he was not ridiculous.

I should have remembered that it is the internal quality of a man that places in his hands the reins of power over a people and not his appearance. I should have recalled a certain strutting, square-jawed, pompous shouter, a certain individual whose clipped mustache is a black dribble from his pinched nostrils, and a certain round-faced, brush-mustached, suavely smiling leader whose word is life or death to a hundred and fifty million humans.

Nal Surah did not raise his hand. He made no gesture that I could detect. But suddenly the shouting crowd was silent; and he was speaking again, quietly, to the squadron of soldiers drawn up in rigid ranks before him.

"You have heard the voice of the Folk, men of the L.S.G. You have heard, not my command, nor that of the Ratanit, but the command of the Folk. Go now and obey it. Go now and assure the fulfillment of our destiny. Go! *Destroy Calinore!*"

"We're in for it now." It was Antil who spoke. I had forgotten his presence, forgotten that I was not a Surahnit, watching my fellows being dedicated to a holy crusade. "You accused me of trying to kill Ra Nalinah, awhile ago. I did not try to kill her, but I did plan to take her hostage, hoping in that way to forestall what you have just seen."

"You would not have stopped it," I answered him. "Nothing can stop that man, once he has determined on a course of action."

"We can still try," he responded. "Hula, you and I can still try to save our peoples. I can still try to save the Taphetnit and you—"

He paused. He was leaning forward again to the screen, eagerly.

"And I?"

"And you," Antil finished his sentence, his tone far-away, "can try to save your human kind. For, Hula my friend, if the

Taphetnit are destroyed then there is no longer any hope for the Upper World. No hope at all."

"WHAT DO you mean?" I exclaimed. "What connection is there between your Taphetnit and my human kind? What have we to do with anything that's going on here?"

Antil looked at me queerly. "Would you want to know, my friend?"

"Yes. Yes, of course." I grasped the youth's arm. "Tell me!"

"Tell him, Antil," Leeahlee breathed. "Tell him what it is the Taphetnit struggle against."

"No!" A strange quiver was running through the Surahnit, I felt it under my grip, I heard it in his voice. He was watching the imaged proceedings on the Plaza with a queer tensity, the L.S.G. squadron filing before the platform while the Nal gestured over their heads in some outré ritual of blessing. "No. I'll show him," he said.

The Plaza flicked the screen. I was gazing at another scene, a huge cave; its walls smooth, darkly shining; a gallery running along one of them, fifty feet above a floor cluttered with machinery. I recognized it, the cavern within the great Eastern Wall of Mernia, where I had seen dead humans.

They were no longer dead, those humans. They were upon their feet, dozens upon dozens of them, towering above the tiny Surahnit who had been tending them. Humans, did I call them? They had human form, but they were living cadavers, animate corpses of men and women who had been long-drowned, their bodies gross and lumpy and putty-gray, their countenances vacuous, their eyes not glazed, not blind, but seeing not what was before them, but the memory of that which it is eternally forbidden to know.

"You heard the Nal, Hula," Antil murmured in my ear. "Do you know now what it is he named the destiny of the Folk?"

And then, half dazed with sickness and horror, I was gazing at the Plaza again. In those few moments there had been an abrupt change out there. The crowd was a sea of upturned faces.

The soldiers were wheeling eastward, their hands tugging at the *corets* in their belts, jerking the splay-muzzled weapons from their holsters. The Nal, the Ratanit, were swinging toward the East. From somewhere a long-drawn siren note wailed an alarm.

"Yes, Antil," I groaned, "I know now. They mean to invade the Upper World. Those—those Things, are going out before them, to lead them; and it is only the Taphetnit who stay that dreadful invasion. But why?"

He did not answer. He was crouched, his whole soul concentrated on the scene in the screen. It was not at the Plaza he was looking. His eyes were staring into the eastern sky.

Undertoning the howling siren I was aware of a distant swish, like that of a hurricane's forerunning wind through palm fronds. But there were no palms in Mernia, no trees…

"Antil," Leeahlee throbbed. "Antil! What is it? What is that sound?"

I don't know if he answered or not. Still sick with what I had seen in the cavern, I was watching a peculiar pearly iridescence glimmer along the distant horizon like the first glint of dawn on the edge of a watery plain. A cloud lifted out of that faraway mystery, its whiteness a sparkle with the million variegated hues of diamond-shattered sunlight. It scudded toward Tashna on the breast of the typhoon's whirring whistle that now blanketed the siren's warning wail.

And there was sound aplenty in the city's Central Plaza. The trample of panic-stricken feet as the crowd burst apart and rushed to seek shelter where no shelter could be found from a storm above. Shrill cries of terror. Hoarse, crisp shouts of the L.S.G subalterns, and the rasp of leather as their underlings knelt in the open space, *corets* lifted and ready. Other shouts from the Watchers in the crow's nest on the trestle of the *lusan* ramp. Quavering cries from the senile Ratanit stuttering to the edges of their dais; waving their *kitors*.

Corets and *kitors* against a storm cloud! Had panic robbed them of their reason?

But it was no cloud. Nearer now with incredible speed, the threat in the sky was resolved into thousands of flashing white forms, thousands of great multicolored wings. No wind, but the beat of those wings, made that whistling, ominous roar. No storm, but a horde of Taphetnit, drove swift upon terrified Tashna.

"Hold your fire!" a command cracked from the Plaza. "Hold your fire till they are overhead."

It was Vanark who had barked that order. Straddle-legged in the scarlet glow from which Nal Surah had vanished as mysteriously as he had appeared, the Rata appeared far more fit for that station of honor than he whose right it was to occupy it. The open space was empty now save for the grimly kneeling soldiers and the aged but indomitable Ratanit lining the platform. *Corets* and *kitors* upraised and ready, they awaited the Taphetnit.

That swift, jeweled flock came on, a handful of opals flung across the sullen sky by some unseen giant. High, high they flew, but each glorious figure was distinct, tiny, doll-small.

"Fairies!" Jeremiah Fenton exclaimed. "Jinganeddy, they're fairies—"

"Unarmed," Leeahlee breathed. "Antil! Your Taphetnit have no weapons at all. What can they hope—"

"Watch!" The Surahnit youth's injunction fell flatly from his gray lips. "Watch Leeahlee."

THEY HAD almost reached the city. They were, indeed, directly above its encircling chasm. A white and splendid manbird was dropping headlong out of the covey, a whistling, wing-folded arrow of light.

A scarlet flash spat upward from the trestle beneath, and a blazing ember tumbled downwards toward the unseen gulf, trailing a black and greasy smoke.

"Oh," the girl moaned. "Oh…"

"Damn them!" It was I who cursed, the syllables wrung from me.

"Now!" Antil exclaimed. *"Now* my children."

As if they heard, the flock split. Opening in two darting arcs still tremendously high above Tashna, they embraced the city in a glittering ring.

And then the whole vast, splendid circle plummeted downward!

Swift, it seemed to me, as light they dove; but swifter the lurid rays from the Watchers' *corets* flashed to meet them.

As if some inverted bonfire in the sky rained downward its steamers of sparks the flaming victims of the Surahnit weapons fell, but past them swooped the Taphetnit who were as yet untouched, past them, down and down, and down.

Scores spun, living torches aflame, down past the airy arcs of the bridges, but hundreds alighted on those arches, hundreds clung to the lacy spiral, a buzzing swarm, and suddenly there were no longer any red flashes from the crow's nests whence the Nal's Watchers had spied upon the city.

"Get them!" Vanark shouted from the base of the soaring pylon at Tashna's hub. "Destroy them."

The Plaza vomited a crimson fountain of death, the air was lurid with lethal spray. Along the topmost curves of the trestled spiral the fiery destruction ran like larvae scorched from tree limbs by a gardener's blow torch, countless winged ones flared briefly and dropped from the girders where they had clustered.

"Your *kitors,* Ratanit!"

A white hell burst forth, a hell of sun-bright flame from wands of the ancient ones. I could not see the denuded girders through that blinding blaze. The screen blinked blank—blinked alive again!

We were beneath the canopy of the *kitors'* dazzling beams, beneath the interlacing curtain of the *corets'* crimson spray. At our feet gaped the black and awful maw of Tashna's bottomless moat and into it poured a continual, terrible hail of charred and shapeless lumps that once had been gloriously pinioned beings soaring the ambient air.

A rain drizzled into that chasm too, a rain of yellow and viscid droplets.

From above us, but from beneath the brilliant death-cloud out of which sifted that drip of horror, there came a wide spread excited twittering.

"Jeerusalem the golden!" my one human companion husked. "They're still sticking."

Yes, they were still sticking, those devoted Taphetnit! They were still clinging to the lower girders of the spans that arched the abyss, to the lower verticals of the viaduct's supports, where they were barely shielded from the angling aim of the Surahn-it weapons by the city's intervening buildings. They were clinging there and they were busy at some frenzied activity whose nature I did not at once make out.

Nor did Leeahlee. "What are they doing, Antil? What have they risked so much to do?"

"Watch." Grief in his tone, and pride. "Watch, Leeahlee. Ah, there it is! The first—"

That which whizzed down past us and vanished into the abyss was not a corpse. It was a long rod of *lural*, a girder.

"They're tearing the bridges apart!" I exclaimed hoarsely. "With their bare hands!"

Once that first member of the structure came free, the others were easier. Rapidly, now, the web disintegrated, melting swiftly almost as that horde who had dared hell itself to destroy the radiating plexus of high-carried roads that gave Tashna access to the rest of Mernia. And then the girdered arcs were gone and a pitiful remnant of Taphetnit were fluttering away out of that inferno, their task accomplished.

THE SCREEN went blank on an unspanned chasm, on a city isolated by a raid consummated with incredible courage against high insuperable odds.

"There will be no attack on Calinore this night," Antil's voice was fiat now, unresonant, and all the jauntiness was gone out of him as he turned away. "But the cost was more terrible than

I had counted it, and it yet remains to be seen whether we have gained anything at all."

"What was it you expected to gain?" I asked.

"Time, Hula, time for you to help me plan how we can defeat the Surahnit, and time for us to work out that plan."

"Wait a minute." I pulled the edge of my hand across my forehead behind which mingled in chaos that which I had just witnessed and the terrible scene in the Gateway Cavern. "For us—You haven't been in communication with Calinore since you saved me from Vanark. Did you know about me—before that?"

"Yes. A little. I knew that Vanark had lost track of the emissary he sent forth to the Upper World and that he had found him again and was returning with him. I knew that when the Ratanit had examined the emissary they would be possessed of the information they needed for their invasion of the lands above, and that it was most essential to prevent that."

"Then the trap in the *fortlik* field was for me, and not for Nalinah."

"No. That was for the Ra, to capture her and hold her as hostage, as I said. When the trap was sprung I was above here, in Vanark's cell in the Listeners Post, and had been there almost since you entered Mernia." Antil was scanning the floor as he answered me. He was looking for something, and I wondered what. "Since you began the descent within the Gateway Wall, in fact. It was I who controlled your attack on Vanark, I who made you speak and act as you did in the guardhouse there."

"While I lay bound in a corner of the cell," Leeahlee put in, "hating you, Antil, for the spy you are and the traitor that I thought you."

He straightened and looked around at her. "Do you still hate me as a traitor, Leeahlee?" he asked softly.

Her eyes would have told me the answer if her words had not. "No. Not since you told of your life among the Taphetnit, of your dreams for them and their dreams for Mernia. Not since

I listened with you to Hula's talk with Ra Nalinah and learned what wrong it is the Nal is determined to perpetrate."

I thought I understood. "This strife between Taphetnit and Surahnit is over the latter's desire to conquer the Upper World?"

"It has been so for more years than you can count." Antil was searching again, more actively now, peering under the various pieces of apparatus that cluttered the floor, getting on hands and knees to do so. "The Winged Ones have known through the ages that the Mernians only real happiness lies in Mernia. The Dark Ones—" He stopped suddenly, dived under a sloping cabinet. "Here it is!" He squirmed out, held up Nalinah's *kitor*. "I saw it drop from Vanark's hand and I knew it must be some-where here. This, Hula, is in part proof of the Taphetnit's hold-ings."

"What do you mean?"

"This orb"—he pointed to the central ball—"can blaze with a light that is not of Mernia but somehow was brought with them by the Ancients who first sought refuge here. That light, Hula, as you have seen, will utterly destroy a Mernian, yet full in its blaze you were not harmed. Why do you think this was?"

"I haven't the least idea."

"Because it is the light of your Sun. Because in its spectrum there are vibrations that to you are life, to us agony and death. Similar we are, Hula, humans and Mernians, because we stem from a common root, but because for aeons we have dwelt amidst vibration at opposite ends of the scale of that form of energy that is matter, the very essence of our beings have become different. We cannot live at all in your daylight. In your night we can exist a *roha* or two, and then must flee or we die."

"Wait. That sounds almost reasonable, but the evidence is against you. Neither I nor Fenton have felt any discomfort here."

"Because the wave lengths of our spectrum, beginning at the violet end of yours, and going beyond it are not as deadly to you as to us are the red and infrared with which your very at-mosphere is saturated, and which here are unknown."

I recalled how before my eyes had become accustomed to the colors of this cavern everything had appeared to me a different shade of violet or purple. "But how is it then that the Surahnit dare even think of living in our world?"

"They have learned how to change themselves. They—"

"Antil!" Leeahlee had adjusted something very like a set of earphones to her pretty head. "Antil! I've tuned to Vanark's thoughts. He is hastening to the Nal. In his rage at what the Taphetnit have done he has cast discretion to the winds and he is determined to tell of this chamber, of your presence here. He is concocting some explanation for its existence that he hopes will save him from the Nal's wrath, but he is determined to chance even that, for his revenge on you and Hula."

"That's swell." I grinned, without humor. "That's lovely. We can make a lot of plans now, Antil, but they won't do us much good. The Surahnit can't get out of Tashna till they repair the bridges, but we can't even get out of this room. You didn't think of that, my friend."

"No?" Antil's calmness seemed to me the quiet of a strong man's despair. "Did I not think of that, Hula?"

"What's it all about?" Jeremiah Fenton's voice was plaintive. "Won't somebody please tell me what this is all about? Fairies and gnomes, and people going through walls like they wasn't there, I don't believe it. It just ain't so."

Account of Courtney Stone, M.D., resumed:

IF ANYONE beside Edith Horne had told me her story. I would have dismissed it as so much nonsense, but I knew too well how level-headed she was; how keenly observant. If any woman can be said to possess scientific objectivity she has it.

I could not, therefore, dismiss her narrative as pure hysteria, much as I was tempted to do so. I was compelled to analyze the things she had seen in the same manner as I should have had I observed them myself.

I realized, however, that I was at the moment in no fit state to do so. I had allowed myself to be quite too much upset by the discoveries I had made during the afternoon of circumstances which however peculiar must have some logical explanation. Before I can think normally I must get *myself* back to normal.

"How about that tea you offered me?" I asked, and I think I managed a smile. "Fix it for me while I examine our patients. After we've drunk it we'll talk things over."

She answered my smile with a wistful one of her own. "You don't believe me, doctor," she murmured.

"Nonsense, child," I snorted. "Of course I believe you. Get busy, now. I'll bet you can't boil water without burning it."

She bristled at that. "Doctor Stone! If I can't cook up a better meal than your Mrs. Small, with my eyes closed, I'll eat my hat. Just for that I'm going to make some buttered cinnamon toast that will melt in your mouth."

"Go ahead." I chuckled. "I dare you." I suddenly realized that I had eaten neither lunch nor dinner, and was famished. "I can go about six slices." I slid off my coat and went out.

Jethro Parker was sleeping normally, I noticed a couple of boards fastened across the broken window. The twisted nails showed that no matter how good a nurse Edith was, she was no better a carpenter than any other of her sex. Evidently she had not told any of the men in the camp about the accident, probably because she did not wish to be questioned about its details.

My hand on the doorknob of the next room, I hesitated. It seemed to me that I had heard movement on the other side of the panel, a faint scrape as of sheets rubbing together. Could the Dorsey boy be coming out of his coma?

A night-light floated in a bowl of oil, the dim luminance of its tiny flame filling the room.

Something seemed to flit from the bed as I entered. It must have been the shadow of the night light, flickering with my disturbance of the air, though when I glanced at it, it burned again straight and unwavering.

I realized the extent of Edith's perturbation when I found that the blanket had folded down from the youngster's chest and that his pajama coat had flapped open. It was the first time I had known her to be even by that much neglectful of her duties as a nurse. As I adjusted the covers I looked for a discoloration, but in that unsatisfactory illumination, there was none apparent.

His pulse, well-nigh imperceptible, was no stronger than it had been on my previous examination. I stood looking down at him. He was a handsome child. Against the whiteness of the pillow his absolutely motionless head was like some bas-relief cameo of a sleeping Adonis, except for the down of adolescence fuzzing his pale, almost transparent cheeks.

I SIGHED, feeling old and useless. Here was this splendid lad drifting slowly into death, and with all my training, all my skill, there was nothing I could do to save him.

I was strangely uneasy. I had a distinct sensation that there was someone else in the room, watching me, waiting for me to leave it. So strong it was that I turned abruptly to catch the intruder unaware. There was, of course, no one there.

My nerves were certainly shot. I toyed with the idea of taking a bromide tablet from the tube in my kit, put the thought from me. What I needed was some food to fill my stomach, some tea to warm me. I went softly out.

The tea was ready for me in the infirmary office, and the toast, as delicious as Edith had promised. I insisted on her having some, against her protest that she could not eat, and refused to talk till we were through.

I wiped the crumbs from my lips with a paper napkin she had produced from somewhere, leaned back in my chair.

"Now my dear," I said, "we can think clearly. I've taught you how to give a case history, noting only the essential facts but not omitting any of these. Suppose you apply that method to the events of this afternoon, giving them to me item by item as they happened, objectively, leaving out your reactions and your interpretations."

"Yes, doctor," she replied meekly, her eyes on my face. "I'll do that. Item one." She checked it on a finger. "Jethro Parker screamed. I found him on his feet, acting as if he held something small and alive in his hands. I could see nothing there. He made a throwing motion and, item two, the window smashed."

"Did you see the glass, at the moment it broke?"

"No. I heard it. I was looking at Jethro."

"Go on."

"All right. Item three: I questioned Parker under the influence of the scopolamine. He said that he had been awakened by a weight on his chest, had felt something sucking there, had fought it, tearing it from his breast. He insisted that it was a 'little man.' Item four: There was a red mark on his chest that faded very quickly. I—I think that is all."

"No," I said quietly, "that is not all. You've forgotten to mention the fact that just before Jethro Parker's cries startled you, you were looking at swirls of ground vapor in the woods and seeing them as little men creeping up to attack you. And you've forgotten Shean Morphy's delirium last night, his ravings about the leprechauns that were all about."

Edith looked puzzled. "But what has Shean's d.t.'s got to do with the case?"

"Everything. The scientific method, my girl, demands an evaluation of the circumstances of an observation as well as of the observation itself. Of the observer. Note please, that you have been in a highly emotional condition for the last day or two, due to Hugh's mysterious disappearance. Note further, that rather distressing scene with Morphy could not but have upset you further, and that your illusions about the wraiths in the woods undoubtedly were suggested by his superstitious mouthings. You were beyond doubt conditioned to accept without proper evaluation any further outré suggestions that might be presented to you when the incident we are discussing occurred, initiated by the farmer's startling outcry.

"But now let us examine what you saw and heard as you would ordinarily examine similar circumstances, rejecting any supernatural explanation as long as a realistic one can be offered. You have no objection?"

"Objection! It's what I want most, a reasonable explanation."

"THEN HERE it is. Parker's sleep, under the influence of the drug we have administered to him, must necessarily have been a light one, and therefore his subconscious more than ordinarily active. The weight of the blankets on his chest induced a nightmare, a real experience to his subconscious. Even when out of bed he was not actually awake but acting somnambulistically; It was his subconscious self that replied to your questioning, and it honestly described to you circumstances which to it were real, but which were merely a dream-fantasy.

"It was no fantasy that something broke the window."

"No. But you did not see it break. This structure is not any too sturdily built. Parker is a heavy man and his jumping around must have shaken the house considerably. There was something on the sill, something you have forgotten about. It toppled over and went through the glass."

"The red mark—"

"He told you he tore at his chest when he first awakened. He irritated his skin. And that's all there is to your terror. There's your realistic explanation of all that has so terrified you. A nightmare, a flimsy house shaking. There are no invisible little men to be afraid of, are there, my dear?"

"No. I suppose not. I suppose I have been a silly fool." She smiled wearily. "Thank you, Doctor Stone. I'm not afraid any more." She sighed, and then she said; "There's one thing more I wish you would explain. The mark on Charley's—"

"The mark on Dorsey's skin may have been due to your rubbing it more vigorously than you realized, or—" I paused.

"Or what?" the nurse asked softly.

"Or it may be a hitherto unnoticed symptom of the disease that afflicts him." I fell into a brown study. "Let me see," I mused. "An intermittent flush, on the sinistral side of the dorsal integument—That is just about where I found Jenks capillaries hypertrophied—Can the infection be localized there? But the change in the blood structure—unheard of—"

"Look, doctor." The girl leaned forward, her, eyes bright now, her cheeks flushed. "My knowledge of medicine is that of an infant's compared to yours, but I have an idea. You won't laugh at me if it's silly?"

"No. I won't laugh at you."

"Then—then isn't it possible that that's just what the disease is, a progressive change in the blood structure? Isn't it possible that some people may have a greater resistance to it than others; that Hugh and the—the tramp—may both have had it without going into the coma?"

My palm smacked the desk top. *"You've got it!* By the great horn spoon, girl, you've got it. Lambert had the disease without knowing anything about it, and recovered with no ill effects except the alteration in his blood type. His splendid condition would account for that. The tramp had it, and also recovered, but was left with his mentality undermined and his physical appearance grotesquely changed. That means the malady is curable. If there is a natural resistance to it, we can induce it artificially. There's hope for the boy in there. There's hope for Grant!"

"Hope for them! Wonderful! How—"

"There must be antibodies in the blood of these who have recovered from the infection, that injected into its victims will cure them. Why didn't I think of it before? By gad, Edith, this will make me famous! All we've got to do is find Hugh or the tramp, and—and—"

She voiced the thought that had halted my exuberance. "How? How are we to find Hugh? How are we to find the—"

The telephone rang, cutting across her voice.

"Damn!" I blurted. "That must be for me. I left this number with Mrs. Small, but it's after midnight and—Hello!" I had the receiver to my ear.

"All right," I answered the voice in the phone. "I'll be there in twenty minutes." I hung up, pushed to my feet.

"Mrs. Small, all right. She got a telegram this evening, didn't bother calling me about it. Just now Ann Doring 'phoned from the airport. She's just landed and she wants me to bring her up here."

Edith jumped up. *"Ann!* Don't bring her here, Doctor! Don't let her come here. She's too glorious, too beautiful, for the little men to—to—"

And I thought I had found one female with as scientific mind!

Continuation of Hugh Lambert's Narrative:

"VANARK HAS reached the throne room." Leeahlee's quiet voice flowed into that underground chamber, reading aloud the Rata's thoughts on which she eaves-dropped. "He is not being permitted to enter as yet. A guard is telling Vanark that the Nal cannot be disturbed, that he is planning the reconstruction of the bridges, that he is ordering every Surahnit in Tashna to the gulf to take part in the work. All other services are suspended, even the watching, if there are any Watchers left. Even the Listeners. Vanark's brain is a shriek of rage at the news that his beloved Listeners' Post is being denuded of its workers. He—"

"Ah," Antil sighed. "I hoped for that." He was crossing to the screen. "Now if Seela has but obeyed his instructions."

"Vanark is wild with impatience," the girl droned on. "Now he is calming. He is considering whether there might not be a way to destroy you here without betraying himself. He recalls the blast projector, mounted on a *lusan* for the attack on Calinore and waiting on the terminal stage. If only it has not been damaged, he thinks, he will use it on the Listeners' Post, destroy the Post but destroy you, too. Taphetnit sabotage will be blamed. He is hastening out."

The screen was alive again. I glimpsed the destroyed trestle over the chasm, the abyss lips already crowded with Surahnit. Antil manipulated something and only a glowering murk was mirrored for me, the murk of Mernia's strange sky, directly overhead.

Leeahlee's voice never hesitated. "Vanark is out in the streets. He is being buffeted by the crowds hastening to the outer boundaries of Tashna in obedience to Nal Surah's command. He is going counter to their stream and he is getting through only by the display of his *kitor*. His rage is mounting again. He is about to turn on its light, to melt a way for himself. No he dares not. Even his position as Rata will not save him from punishment for such wanton killing. He comes within view of the terminal stage and he sees the blast—"

A white fleck appeared at the center of the imaged sky dome. Breath gusted from between Antil's lips.

"—the blast projector. It is undamaged and Vanark is jubilant because of that and because there is no one on the terminal stage. The elevator must be working. His luck must hold. His luck… He thinks fleetingly of Nalinah. If he succeeds in destroying the Listeners' Post he will not be able to produce against her the forged records purporting to show her seditious thoughts, her plotting with Hughlambert and the Taphetnit against the Folk Weal. No matter. The Nal…"

There was not one but four white dots at the screen's center. Not dots. Winged mannikins! Plummeting—straight at me, it appeared, but I was looking upward—plummeting *down* like planes in a vertical power dive. So fast that only because I was exactly in a line with that stupendous drop could I see them. From any other angle they must seem only a white blurred line—if there were any in Tashna who looked in this direction at all. My veins tingled watching that magnificent dive, and in the room from which I watched there was no sound but my breathing, the breathing of Fenton and Antil, and Leeahlee's monotone.

"The Nal will release Nalinah from arrest, the case against her not proved, but he will be suspicious of her and her influence with him will be gone. That will leave only Vanark with his full confidence. Vanark will be the real ruler of Mernia. This is better. This street has emptied. Around this corner is the elevator entrance. Dismay squeezes Vanark's brain. Rage flares into it. Wreckage lies across the lift door, blocking it."

The Taphetnit were plain now, dropping. What a tremendous height it must be where they had hovered out of sight while their fellows destroyed the bridges, hovered invisible till the time for their thunderbolt descent, that still they were dropping!

"Vanark tears at the wreckage but his strength cannot move it. Is there anyone to help? The street is deserted. No! Six youths, dashing into view, rushing, belated. 'Come here! Come here you!… The Nal's order? Cannot you see that I am a Rata and need your help? Clear that door. Clear it!'

"The girders move. The door is clear. But Vanark knows they will report this incident when the destruction of the Listeners Post is investigated. No they won't. They will report nothing, ever. The blast of the *kitor* caught them full, all of them at once. The door opens. The lift—is here—is working. Antil! Vanark is shooting up to the blast projector. Hurry! *Hurry!*"

"All right, Leeahlee." Swift stabs of Antil's hands had blanked the screen, had stopped the blue shimmer over the chambers walls and ceiling. And the ceiling. Down through it seethed four white-robed forms. The room was suddenly a shimmer of sparkling wings.

"*Seela!*" Antil's greeting was a shout of joy. Then he was twittering, and in the quick flurry of his birdlike notes there was sharp command. "Take them all, brethren. Quickly!"

"*Hurry,* Antil!" Leeahlee was tearing the phones from her head, her face a mask of terror. "Hurry!"

A Taphet leaped at me, his countenance like a god's. I was in his arms and I was being lifted, feather-light.

An instant of gray oblivion, an instant of gleaming metal; the cell where twice I had seen Leeahlee; then the swift rush of open air downward past me and the beat, beat of strong wings in my ears. All happened in a flash, so that not till then was I quite aware that I was being borne upward in the arms of a man-bird, that either side of us were Leeahlee and Fenton, similarly carried, and Antil in the arms of the one he had called Seela, clinging still to the *kitor*.

We leaped upward as though catapulted from a spring. Lucky, I thought, that the roof of that cell had been opened, and then I thought, "But of course Antil cleared it to admit the Taphetnit. It was part of his plan."

The honeycomb of the Listeners' Post dropped from beneath us. Beneath us spread the honeycomb that is Tashna.

And then there was a blast beneath us, the ground spurting blue fire, spurting the shreds of the Listeners' Post into the air. Two hundred yards above that holocaust we were, but the heat of it surged up to us, and it threw us in a single second to twice the height we had attained in ten.

When the shreds had settled there was a crater in the floor of Tashna into which fifty *lusans* might have been driven, a pitted shellhole where the Listeners Post had been. But we for whom the blast had been intended were high, so high that the city was a child's toy there below us, and we were leveling in flight toward the horizon over which the frowning fortress wall of Calinore was already lifting.

The last glimpse I had of Tashna and its people was of Vanark's mannikin figure on the *lusan* terminal stage. Beside some giant device whose outlines I could not discern, that tiny form jiggled in impotent rage.

I would have given much to have had the listening disks of his thought-tapping contrivance clamped to my ears in that moment. As it was, I could only imagine his emotions, realizing that if only he had not melted to nothingness those six Surahn-it lads, if only he had not set off the projector's futile blast, he would have brought us down, victims to the lancing, scarlet rays of the L.S.G.'s *corets*.

A RIDE such as no human ever had before! Cradled in powerful but gentle arms, hearing the beat, beat, beat of the Taphet's wings, and then we were slanting down on a long line to wall-bound Calinore, and it was over.

There is a white and shining temple in Calinore, where the glowing Taphetnit worship a god very like the God of abiding love a man once preached in Galilee. In that temple there is an altar clothed by the flames of myriad candles* so that it shines like star-dust in the dim, cathedral quiet.

It was to this temple that Antil brought us, Leeahlee and Fenton and me, at once upon our landing. After he had knelt awhile, giving thanks for his delivery, I asked the youth about the candled altar.

"It is the Shrine of Remembrance," he said. "When a Taphet dies we light a white candle there in token of our grief at his passing."

"A *white* candle. What about those two green tapers, half burned down? What about those scores of green ones that are just being lit?"

"Those," replied the youth, "those are for the two Surahnit we were compelled to kill in our attempt to capture Ra Nalinah as a hostage and for the others who died in our attack on Tashna."

After that I was not at all surprised to learn that there is no Law in Calinore, but that each of its people acts to his neighbors as he would wish them to act toward him. The doors of every dwelling here stand always open, shelter and food free to any one who chooses to enter. They must be careful of their

---

* Note: These altar lights are different from our candles in their chemistry, although like them in appearance. Notably, they do not consume oxygen in their burning, this life supporting gas being so limited in the cavern. H.L.

resources as the Surahnit are, because they too are subject to the close economy of Mernia, but there is none but his own conscience to limit a Taphet's greed.

These are the people whose destruction Nal Surah has proclaimed. These are the people who man their fortress walls even as I write, waiting for that destruction to come upon them. They man their Wall, but they have no weapons with which to defend it, for they are a people of peace.

CHAPTER VIII

Hugh Lambert's narrative continued:

I COULD CONTINUE for page after page recounting the marvels of Calinore and the wonderful people who dwell here. But I must get on with my tale. The time I have to write it grows very short, and Death may stay my hand.

After his act of devotion in the temple, Antil took us to the mansion of shining white that was his home and Seela's. There at once we met in a council of war.

I wanted to ask more about the troop of Dead-alive Antil had shown me on the screen, but there was no time. "Our scouts bring word that the Surahnit are repairing their bridges with incredible rapidity." Seela plunged at once to the heart of things. "Before this night is over they will be flocking across them to the attack."

There was about this Taphet the same *shining* quality I had noted in his foster son, but it was somehow more mellow, somehow more fragile. "To cope with their *corets* and *kitors*," he continued, "we have no weapons. We have only the Wall of Calinore, and that will not stand long against their blast projector. I have carried out your schemes faithfully, my son, but I cannot see what has been accomplished by your adventure into

Tashna and the raid that has put so many candles on the altar of remembrance."

"Accomplished nothing?" Antil's eyes strayed for a fleeing moment to Leeahlee, and by the way hers clung to them, I knew that to those two a transcendent something had come out of his expedition. "You are wrong, Father Seela. I am well satisfied. I have brought from Tashna two things that may save us."

"And what are those?"

"Hula, first and most important. Something tells me that if we are to be victorious it will depend on him.

"These two are both from the Upper World, father," Antil twittered. There was only that birdlike flutter to differentiate the language of the Taphetnit from that of the dark race of Tashna and I understood it quite as well. "The other one is similar to our cropped-winged brethren who have labored with the soil so long that their sluggish thoughts are of the earth, earthy. But I have read Hula's mind and it is like that of the Wise Ones of the Surahnit who have made it possible for them to hold our Taphetnit so long in subjection. You know that this had been our lack. Hula will remedy it. Also from Tashna I have brought that which will fill our next greatest need. A weapon, father. A *kitor*, the destroying sun-wand of the Ratanit."

"*One kitor*, Antil? I saw you carrying it, but what will one *kitor* avail against the host that will shortly descend on us?

"Very little. But with one to examine, Lura, the scientist, poor in knowledge as he is, may be able to learn its secret and fashion others. We'll have a chance—"

A whir at the open door interrupted him. A flash of white darted in through it. A white form hovered above the table, a diminutive Taphet. His small face, framed by blond curls and a beam, was the countenance of a della Robbia cherub carved from pure light; his naked little body a crystal Tanagra statuette. For an instant he poised there, suspended by a blur of wings vibrating so fast that they were invisible, then he darted to one side of Antil and alighted.

"A message from Lura," he piped. "He has solved the secret of the *kitor.*"

Antil whirled to Seela, "You hear, father? Lura has solved the *kitor's* secret, thus quickly, thus easily." He was fairly shaking with youthful excitement. "We shall have a surprise for Nal Surah's hordes when they swarm upon us. Before they are aware of their fate we shall destroy them with the light of that sun we have never seen. We shall—"

"Wait, son," the Taphet, grave and unsmiling, cut him off. "The messenger has more to say."

"He has? I know! Already Lura has found the way to make more of the orbs. Is that not it, youngster?"

The boy was flushed with his temporary importance. "No. He said to tell you that you are still possessed of only one *kitor.* He said to tell you there is not in all Mernia the elements needed to make another."

The animation went out of Antil. He dropped onto the cushioned divan from which he had sprung, and groaned.

"Any reply, Antil?" the boy demanded.

"No," Seela told him. "No reply." The Surahnit's face was buried in his hands. "You have done well. You may go!"

The cherub flashed out and away. "Only one *kitor,*" Antil muttered, "against so many. And I was sure, so sure, there would be a way to multiply its beams—"

"Wait!" I exclaimed, "To multiply its beams, you said, Antil! You said it was the light, the sunlight from the *kitor* that does the damage."

He looked up at me, a tremor of hope on his face. "Yes. You have an idea, Hula? You…"

"I think I have. It may work. It must work. Come on. Take me to Lura. It is something to try, at any rate."

THE PAST few hours have been ones of feverish, sweating

labor. Speeding to Lura's laboratory I had explained my scheme to Antil and Seela and by the time we reached it the great domed room was already filled with a crowd of Taphetnit ready to do anything I asked them.

All about me was the whir of the Taphetnits' *pintons,* the clangor of hammer on metal, the heat of forges. All about me was the twitter of the Winged Ones. Their only raw material is metal mined from somewhere in the cavern, remember, and so they are trained at least to its manipulation. But willing as they were, they were yet slow in coordinating themselves to fashioning anything but their traditional fabrications, and I had cause to bless Jeremiah Fenton's skill with tools. The farmer worked like a Trojan, not asking an unnecessary question.

There had been no time for that. We were working against Time, against Death.

I had cause, also, to bless Leeahlee for her quick-witted anticipation of my needs, her interpretation of them to the Taphetnit Antil and I could not reach with our voices. And then, at the end it was Leeahlee who found a way to polish the metal device we had made.

All the time we worked, there came in to us a low mutter of fear from the city outside. Scouts were arriving at decreasing intervals, telling of the speed with which Tashna's chasm was being bridged, telling of the army that was being formed to come against us.

Here is what we have done.

The roof of the temple of which I have written rises in a conelike spire whose truncated apex forms a platform high above the other buildings of Calinore and even above the level of the Wall.

At the center of this platform we have stepped a shaft to whose top we have fixed Nalinah's *kitor.*

In a circle around this shaft we have laid a single-railed track on which runs a two-wheeled trolley. Mounted on gimbals on this trolley is a sheet of metal polished till it makes a perfect mirror, and bent to a paraboloid form.

The *kitor's* sun orb is exactly at the focus of this parabola. There was a shield behind the ball to protect its user, and this I have removed.

Yes, it is a searchlight we have fashioned, a sort of searchlight that will concentrate the white rays of the *kitor* and project them as a tight beam out over the Wall and to the plain surrounding Calinore. I can direct this beam to any point of that plain, within certain limits, and I can only hope that its lethal qualities will not be diminished by the distance.

Fenton has been reading this account as fast as I write it. We two are alone up here. You see, we are the only ones who dare be so close to the *kitor* when it is turned on. The Taphetnit would melt like wax in its rays. We have erected a screen around the Wall, high enough to shadow from it the Winged Ones who crowd the rampart to defend it to the last if I fail. But anything they can do would be a futile, if magnificent, gesture and so the destiny of Mernia rests in my hands, and in Fenton's, two Earth-dwellers descended to fight in a civil war whose principles were as real to us as those of our own Civil War.

The destiny of Mernia and of the green, sunlit world that is not aware of Mernia's existence.

I shall have to stop writing in a moment. Antil has signaled from down below that the Surahnit have crossed the chasm and that their *lusans* have reached the points on the roads where Seela has destroyed the paths. They are debarking.

They are marching through the *fortlik* fields. I can see them, a great green cloud coming over the horizon. They will shortly be within reach of my searchlight beam. I must check this thing I have built in the few minutes I have left, and so I must stop writing.

Strange. I find that I am saying good-by in my mind to three women. Three, of all the women I have known.

Ann Doring, of course. And, not surprisingly, Nalinah, though she is an enemy.

I think it is the calm efficiency with which Leeahlee has helped me in these last feverish hours that has recalled the third girl to me.

She is—of all people—Edith Horne!

Extract from the diary of Ann Doring, Sept. 1, 1934:

HERE I am, back at Camp Wanooka, but how different everything is! Instead of the happy chatter of a half-hundred boisterous youngsters, a brooding quiet overlies it, an empty hush that seems underscored with fear.

Everyone seems to be trying to put a smiling face on an uneasy situation. Doctor Stone smiled, last night, when he tried to persuade me to go to a hotel in Albany, or to his home there, instead of to the camp. He kept smiling even when I blazed up at him, telling him that I was certain he was hiding from me the fact that Dickie was sick, and threatened to go to the authorities if he refused to take me to my brother. There is some advantage in being an actress; I am certain that he does not suspect the real reason for my hurried flight across the continent.

Edith Horne smiled when she met us at the gate. Like the doctor; she smiled with her lips, not with her eyes. She took me to her own infirmary, insisting that I must sleep with her instead of in the guest house. She wasn't fooled by my pretended anxiety over Dick. It was of Hugh Lambert we talked, lying beside each other in the dark.*

When Edith had finished, I peculiarly enough shared with her her inexplicable certainty that Hugh is alive somewhere,

---

* Editor's Note: Miss Doring here retells what little Miss Horne knew of the circumstances of Lambert's disappearance, a story already herein set forth and therefore omitted. The nurse did not of course reveal the real nature of Jethro Parker's illness nor did she say anything of the strange and disturbing events of the previous twenty-four hours.

and that somehow he will fight his way back to us. I shared something else with her, the knowledge that we are both desperately in love with him, although we neither of us had put *that* into words.

She is quite too grand a person for there to be any jealousy between us. On the contrary we were drawn together by our common distress, so that when sleep finally came to us, toward dawn, it found us the best of friends.

I am writing this in her room. Edith is tending to her patients and after she is through we shall go down to the mess hall for breakfast. The sun is streaming in through the window, and there is a bird on the sill, a brave little fellow with gray head, gray wings and yellow, black striped breast. His little throat swells as he peers impertinently in at me with his bright little black eyes, and he is telling me to "Cheer*up*, cheer*up*, cheer*up*." But I can't. I can't throw off the feeling that something dreadful has happened, something that I shall learn about when, with Edith, I go down the path between the empty bungalows.

I WAS right. Dick did not wake up this morning. They brought him to the infirmary a few minutes ago. I have just been looking at him. He seems only to be asleep, but he didn't answer when I called his name. His slow, even breathing didn't even quiver.

Can it be that the lie I told Doctor Stone last night has brought this on my little brother?

Silly to think so, I know, but...

Edith tells me there is only one way Dick can be saved. If Hugh returns in time. *If Hugh returns!*

Please, God, bring Hugh back.

Appendix to Hugh Lambert's Narrative, written by Jeremiah Fenton:

The last words Mr. Lambert said to me was, "Fenton! You keep on writing what's going on here, as long as you last. Maybe sometime, somehow, these papers will get to our people, and I'd like them to know how we fought for them, down here in this strange place." Then he took my hand and we said good-by.

Well, I'll try my best, though I know I'll make an awful bum job of it.

There we was, up on top of that church. I was feeling terrible after reading what Mr. Lambert had written, because now I knew how close my brother Elijah had been to me that night when the chess piece was moved, and what had become of him, of his body. It was like hearing that he had died over again, only it was worse.

I can't explain things like that in the grand way Mr. Lambert can, but I can feel them. Look. Even the lowest-down savages take care of the corpses of them they have loved. There's something in us that makes us feel a little better, no matter how deep our sorrow, to know where the bodies of those who have been near and dear to us are; to know that for a little time longer, at any rate, that much of them still exists. The nations recognized this need of ours after the World War, that's why each one has its grave of an Unknown Soldier so that everyone who lost someone in battle can feel that maybe, maybe, it is him that lies in that honored grave.

Well, I couldn't have that feeling. I knew now that Elijah's body didn't exist at all, anywhere. That it was gone, like no body was ever gone before. That this other part of me didn't exist any more, that it wasn't even dust, not even slime at the bottom of the Lake…

But that ain't telling my story. Like I said, there we was up top of the church, watching that green army coming toward Calinore. Mr. Lambert had tried out how far the light from the dingus he'd rigged up would reach, slanting it down so it just missed the top of the curtains we'd put up around the wall to keep it from hitting the Winged People we were trying to help. There was a kind of wave in the ground where the end of the beam would first hit, and there was another one further back beyond which it would go off into the air. It was only between those two folds that it would be any good, and we had to wait till the army reached it.

That waiting was the hardest thing I ever did.

They kept coming, maybe a couple of thousands of them. They came very slow, and either they didn't make any noise or they was too far off for us to hear them. But we could see them, spread out along the field, marching forward, slow and very sure.

THERE WAS something terrible about the sureness of them, and about the quiet. There wasn't any sound out there, and there wasn't any sound below us, in the City. The Taphetnit were hidden from us by the curtains on the wall, and they might not have been there for all the noise they made. The women and children were huddled inside the houses, so that when we looked down into Calinore we saw only empty streets with nothing and nobody at all moving. We were two humans all alone up there in the sky, watching that silent army coming, coming; slow as death and sure as death; and knowing that the fate of a race, that the fate of the world, depended on us alone.

I was standing by the pole to which we had fastened the thing they call a *kitor*, and my hand was on the kind of ring on its handle that we'd found out you moved a little to make the ball at its top shine. Mr. Lambert was back of me, at the reflector, ready to aim it.

The Surahnit came nearer and nearer. I started shaking with the buck ague. I wanted to yell something, anything to smash that awful silence.

"Steady," I heard Mr. Lambert's voice, quiet like. "Steady, Fenton. Calm and easy does it."

"Don't you worry about me," I said back, watching those green ranks come on. "I'm all right." I was, when I said it. It was like as if I had got some of his strength from his voice, some of the kind of strength that had made it possible for him to sit there and write page after page, when all the time he knew he might be dead before he could finish writing.

It can't be that he *is* dead now. It can't be that no one will ever again see the brown skin crinkle at the corners of his eyes and be warmed by his friendly grin.

The soldiers from Tashna kept coming on, coming on. Now I could make out two little figures out in front of them who were not in uniform, and behind those two leaders there were the others, rank after rank of them spread across the field and getting nearer and nearer.

I could hear the *thud, thud* of their marching feet now. Far away yet, but each thud a little bit louder than the one before. It put me in mind of the song we used to sing on Decoration Day:

> *He is trampling out the vintage where the grapes of wrath are stored.*
> *He hath loosed the fateful lightning of His terrible swift sword…*

Only this wasn't His host that trampled the grapes of wrath but the legion of His enemy, and the fateful lightning that would soon be loosed wasn't the thunderbolts of His anger but the terrible red darts of Antichrist's *corets*.

The two leaders went down into the hollow of a ground wave, and were hidden by the ridge that was our marker for where our light could first reach them. The front line of the soldiers from Tashna went down into that hollow, and the next, and the next, till we couldn't see any of the Surahnit any more.

For a minute it was an almighty peaceful scene I was looking at, but my hand was tight on the *kitor* ring and my palm was sweating.

"They'll get a surprise," Mr. Lambert said, "when they come up over the next crest. Get set, Fenton, but don't switch on the light till I say so." Then the line of rock—dark and shining-like, as if some black light was inside of it—was broken by two moving knobs. Two heads came up over the ridge, and then two bodies. I could see them plain.

One of the Surahnit Mr. Lambert and Antil had called Vanark. The other one was a Surahnit girl.

They came down the slope, right into the range of our searchlight of death. The first rank of the soldiers came over the crest behind them like the ground wave was breaking into a spume of green foam, but Mr. Lambert didn't say, "Turn it on."

He groaned instead, groaned a name. The name was "Nalinah."

VANARK TURNED around. The sound of his voice came clear across the rolling, dark field, though I could not make out what he said. I knew though, at once, that it was an order because the arms of all the soldiers moved like they was on a single string and their hands came up with the little rods of *corets* in them. I knew that they were coming within range of Calinore's Wall and that in another second the red rays would lash out to sweep the parapet clean of its defenders.

"Turn it on," Mr. Lambert said hoarsely. "Turn the *kitor* on."

My hand twisted the ring, and all of a sudden I could see nothing because of the blaze that blinded me and the heat that burned me. I closed my eyes, as we had planned, and dropped to the platform and crawled toward where I knew the reflector was.

My groping hand found the track we'd made for the reflector to move on. I pulled myself over it, got up to my knees, to my feet. The light didn't shine so strong through my lids any more and I opened them.

I was behind the reflector, like I'd figured; and I was alongside Mr. Lambert. His two hands were on the handles we'd fixed to the back of the metal that was like the top of an umbrella laying edgewise and he moving it.

I looked past the edge of the thing. My eye followed the blazing white beam it sent out over Calinore and over the Wall, and over the plain.

The beam slanted down over the Wall and across the plain. Its end moved slowly along the line of Surahnit soldiers. It was like a great white finger stroking a design of green chalk someone had drawn on the wavy rock out there, stroking the design and rubbing it out. For where the finger had passed there was no longer any military rank, there was no longer anything living. There was only a splash of wet yellow on the rock, some of which started dribbling in thick streamers down the slope.

A quarter of the left side of the line was already gone when I looked, and that dreadful finger of light was moving steadily to the right, but the soldiers of Tashna who remained were still coming on, marching as if nothing was happening, and from their *corets'* scarlet rays were streaking to the Wall of Calinore.

Screams from the Wall, screams of agony, killed the silence. Little bursts of flame spurted above the curtain that hid the Taphetnit there, and plumes of black, greasy smoke waved above the Wall. But the scythe of blazing death steadily mowed the Surahnit rank. Half of it was gone, and more than half; and in the next second the beam was going to hit Vanark and Nalinah. I remembered what Mr. Lambert had written about Nalinah and I felt cold fingers close on my throat.

THE WHITE light-finger jumped upward! It went over the head of those two and flashed downward to melt away the last of that oncoming rank of Surahnit. "I couldn't do it," Mr. Lambert groaned. "Heaven help me, I couldn't do it."

A second later the two Ratanit stood stock-still, because the blazing disk that was the tip of our death-beam lay on the ground right in front of them, and if they took another step they would walk into it. Then it started to creep toward them, slow as a cat creeping up on a bird. They stared at it for two beats of my heart. Then their nerve broke and they turned and ran back over the ridge.

There were no more Surahnit to be seen on the plain. There was only that dreadful yellow wetness. For a minute I was sick, looking at that, and then there was a great burst of twittering from the Wall, like cheers, and I was banging Mr. Lambert on the back.

"We got them licked," I was yelling; "We've—"

A cry from behind whirled me around to the Wall on the eastern side of Calinore, so I didn't hear the rest of what Mr. Lambert said. I saw that a Taphet was pulling open the curtain there and was yelling to us, waving his arm excited-like.

I looked over the curtain and out on the plain on that side to see what he was so excited about, and then I grabbed Mr. Lambert's arm. "Look!" I yelled. "Look there. They ain't licked yet. They're sneaking up and trying something else."

I pointed to the thing I had seen. It was coming over the top of a ridge like the one on the other side and just about as far away. It was a great big thing of shining metal, with a barrel sticking out of it so that it was as much like a big cannon as the *corets* were like pistols. There were about a dozen Surahnit pulling at it. Then it was on the gentle downward slope of the rock-wave, and the dozen soldiers were shoving back against it, braking it.

"That's a blast projector," Mr. Lambert exclaimed, "like the one with which Vanark wrecked the Listeners Post." He started pushing at the trolley on which the reflector was mounted, was wheeling it around behind the other side of the *kitor.* "They must have brought it up on a *lusan* from the Gateway. They've got an idea they can beat us with that, but we'll take care of them right now. Help me here, Fenton."

The Surahnit got the projector stopped, swarmed over it, working to slow it around in position to fire at the Wall. We had our reflector set first. Mr. Lambert grabbed the handles, slashed the beam across the ground out there. The light hit the green-uniformed men and blazed all about them.

Nothing happened.

They didn't melt. They didn't even stop working with the thing. They didn't pay any more attention to the blaze that had whiffed other beings just like them into a few drops of yellow liquid than I would have done if someone was flashing sunlight on me with a mirror!

Mr. Lambert made a kind of funny sound in his throat.

"What's happened?" I asked him. "Why don't it work any more?"

"I don't know," he said low-toned. "I haven't the least idea. I don't see how they could have figured out a way to combat its effect so quickly. And why are there only a few of them out there? Why, if they're no longer afraid of the light, aren't they coming over in force?"

"They are!" I popped back. "On this side." I'd looked back, and I'd seen the green wave coming over the first ridge again. "But that guy Vanark ain't leading them. I wonder—"

"He isn't?" Mr. Lambert exclaimed. "Maybe—" He was wheeling the reflector around once more. "Maybe…"

They were firing off their *corets* again when the white flash hit them. Then they weren't firing any longer. They weren't there!

"Something screwy," Mr. Lambert grunted. "These fellows aren't immune to it but the others are. Just the few of them. Watch them, Fenton, while I keep the main force back. Watch them and tell me what they're up to."

I DIDN'T have to tell him. A crash told him, the crash of the Wall falling in. A blue flame had flared across the plain from the blast projector. It had hit the great rampart, and the looming rock had exploded upward.

A great cloud of dust rose to the sky from where a gaping and terrible hole was torn in the Wall. Out of that cloud rained black stones, and white pieces of cloth, bits of flesh, and feathers, a many-colored snowfall of feathers.

"They've blown up the Wall, Mr. Lambert," I gasped when I could talk again. "They've killed Lord knows how many Taphetnit."

"Keep watching, Fenton," he answered, cool and steady. "Keep telling me what, they do. I don't dare turn around. Vanark is sending another wave of his L.S.G., over the ridge. They're going to get us, but I'll do for as many of them as I can before that happens."

"They're working with the blast projector. They—I think they're trying to swing it up so as to hit this tower. Now they've stopped. They couldn't do it. I guess it isn't made so as it can shoot up. They're lowering it again."

"Lord, Fenton," Mr. Lambert exclaimed, "those boys have guts. They keep coming over the ridge, keep trying to get across the zone I can reach with the beam. None of them has got past yet. That whole belt is running ankle-deep in the liquid I'm melting them down into. But still they come."

"The ones on this side just fired another blast." I went back to him. "It smashed a row of houses to smithereens. I wonder why they did that instead of blowing up some more of the Wall."

"Because it isn't the Taphetnit on the Wall that's bothering them. It's us, up here. Don't you get it, Fenton? They're clearing a way for their blasts to reach this temple, and then they'll blow it out from under us. Smart people, the Surahnit."

"We're done for, then—Lord! There goes another row of houses!"

"Yes, Fenton, they've beaten us, but they know they've been in a fight. If we have to go out, this is the best way to do it. Scrapping!"

"What about what they're going to do to the Upper World, Mr. Lambert? What about them dead humans in the Gateway Wall they're ready to send up where our people are, and the rest of them that's going to follow?"

"Don't think of it, Fenton. Don't dare to think of what it's going to mean to the human race when that blast projector blows this temple out from under us. Just fight. Just keep on fighting. We've done our best, and humanity is licked."

He sounded almost happy. He was flashing that terrible white sword of his up and down the field out there, melting the Surahnit soldiers down to a trickle of yellow liquid. I was watching the terrible blue flame of the blast projector smash nearer and nearer to us; and he sounded like he was having the time of his life.

Then he started singing.

The sons of the prophet are hardy and bold!

And his deep-chested baritone sounded above the screams of terrified Taphetnit and the thunder of exploded stones.

And quite unaccustomed to fear.

He was singing while he fought, while he wiped out score after score of the helpless Surahnit with his blazing shaft of death.

But of all the most reckless of life or of limb...

While another blinding flash burst from the projector and another slice of houses went smashing down to ruin.

... was Abdul the Bulbul Ameer.

"Oh, oh, one of them got through, Fenton! One of them's past where I can't catch him. He's *coreting* the Wall and I can't do anything about it."

I whipped around, shaking from the terror I was watching. I saw a green-uniformed young fellow, maybe he was about eighteen, running toward the wall, red flashes spitting from his outstretched hand, spitting at the Wall. And then I saw a flash of shining feathers dart up from the Wall, and out over the plain, three Taphetnit flying fast as flushed partridges. I saw one go down in a blaze, a second.

But the third one swooped down on the soldier, knocked the *coret* from his hand, and now he was flying up in the air again, carrying the boy.

HE WENT up a hundred feet, two hundred and then he dropped the screaming youth. I saw green-clad arms and legs jerking frantically in mid-air. I saw the youngster hit the rock, and I heard a squelching sound, as if a rotten pumpkin had smashed out there.

Behind me there was a crash! The blast projector had fired again. Mr. Lambert never turned a hair. He was bent over the reflector, and he was working it very steady. His jaw was sticking out, square and hard, but his hair was streaming back from his high brow, and his eyes were shining.

He was singing.

> *There are heroes in plenty and well known to fame*
> *In the ranks that are led by the Czar...*

Another crash behind me was like a peal of thunder, and the tower rocked under my feet, like this was the time it was going to come down. I spun around. Half the City lay in ruins, from where a great pile of rubble showed where the Wall had been to a hundred yards away from the base of the temple.

"They're close, Mr. Lambert. Another two shots and they'll have us."

> *But among the most reckless of fame or of name*
> *Was Ivan Skovinsky Skivar.*

That was all the answer I got. What Mr. Lambert sounded like was a man who had worried a long time, trying to find a way to stave off something terrible, and now it had happened and it was no use to worry any more about nothing.

> *He could swing the trapeze, play euchre or pool*
> *And perform on the Spanish guitar...*

"They're not coming any more, Fenton. Either I've got them all or they've given up hope. Here, help me slew this thing around. I'll try another shot at those artillerymen."

I jumped to help him. He went on with his song as we pushed at some contraption and the tower rocked with the detonation of another blast.

> *In fact quite the cream of the Muscovite team*

Was Ivan Skovinsky Skivar...

Just as we got the reflector around there was a tremendous swoosh of wings, and a crowd of the Taphetnit sailed straight up from the City. They went higher and higher.

"The yellow curs," I growled. "They know we're licked and they're running away."

"Never mind them, my frolicsome farmer." The light-beam was shooting out to that blast projector again, was playing on it, with no more result than before. "What I want to know is what magic those damned Surahnit have worked, to make those few sunuvaguns immune to sunlight. And why only that handful is immune."

Another bolt of blue lightning flashed from the projector. The street just below us blew up. The air was dark with dust, with falling stones.

"There's another one of them," I said, "just coming over the ridge. It's that guy Vanark." I could see him through the veil of dust, standing straddle-legged on that ridge. "He's laughing at us."

"Yeah, he's laughing at us, but he's not coming down to where I can reach him. He isn't immune. He's just gone around there to watch the next blast, the one that will finish us. So long, Fenton, it's all over. You better climb down with those papers and hide somewhere. Vanark seems to have some use for you; maybe he won't kill you." He held out his hand.

But I didn't shake it. A stone had come down out of the sky, plunk on one of the Surahnit out there. He went down, and another rock dropped, hit another soldier. They were coming down fast now, those stones, raining out of the sky, too fast for the cannon to be shot again.

"Look!" Mr. Lambert yelled.

He was pointing up into the sky. I looked where he pointed. Far, far, up against the muddy dome that was Mernia's sky, there was a little flash of white and the hail of rocks was streaming down from that.

"What—what—" I gasped.

"The Taphetnit, Fenton! The ones we called yellow. They've carried pieces of their ruined city up there and they're raining them down on the Surahnit we couldn't kill. They've saved the battle. They've saved us!"

I looked back to the projector. There wasn't any living being moving around it. It was covered by a pile of stones, and the pile was spreading out around it. I saw one green-sleeved arm twitch, and then that too was buried.

The white started drifting down. It was a fleecy cloud, and then it was a covey of Taphetnit, slanting fast toward the City. One great white figure flashed down ahead of the main body and I saw that it was Seeta. If ever I see one of God's Angels I know he will look just like that Taphet looked to me just then.

Mr. Lambert turned off the *kitor* light. I turned to him, and he didn't look as happy as I thought he should.

"They didn't get Vanark," he said. "The Rata ducked back over the ridge when the first stone fell, and got away." His hands closed slowly at his sides, into knuckled fists. "As long as that fellow's alive, we can still expect trouble."

He was right, but he didn't know how right he was.

CHAPTER IX

Account of Courtney Stone, M.D., continued:

THERE WAS NOTHING I could do for Dick Doring. How could there be, when I had been able to do nothing for Charles Dorsey, or for the two farmers in the hospital, one of whose bodies I had dissected the day before?

I knew now that there was only one hope of saving the boys and Job Grant. There was only one hope of stopping the slow spread of the mysterious disease from which they suffered. If I could find someone who had resisted the inroads of the disease, and make from his blood an antitoxic serum, I might be able to work out a successful treatment.

It would be entirely useless to start a search for the tramp. He must be miles away from Albany by now. Almost as futile to hope for Hugh Lambert's return. This was September first. He had been gone three days now, and there was no justification for Edith Horne's sturdy faith that he was still alive, that he would still return.

But I could not sit idly by and watch my patients die. I must try something. A possibility occurred to me, a million to one chance of my finding what I so desperately needed.

I had already decided that the focus of infection was in this Helderberg region. I knew of two cases of recovery from it, who were not aware even that they had been affected. There might be others. There might be one among the patients in the hospital, particularly in the surgical wards, or among the members of the staff.

If I ordered the blood of everyone in the institution typed, one among the two hundred might show up with the peculiar qualities of Lambert's and the tramp's. That was all I needed, just one.

Nurse Horne was like a quietly burning white flame moving about the infirmary. I called her out from Parker's room, and I told her my idea. I was no longer sure of myself, you see. I was no longer sure of anything.

There was something abnormal about the atmosphere of the camp, and I was abnormal as long as I was in it.

Edith smiled wanly when I got through talking.

"You can try it," she said. "It can't do any harm, and it will be something to do."

It was something to do. I went out to my car and I drove down to, Albany. They were waiting for me at the hospital. They knew how interested I was in the syndrome and they were waiting to tell me that three more patients suffering from it had been brought in during the night.

One was a woman, Hepzibah Foster, wife of the owner of a general store at Four Corners, on the highway that used to be called Waley Road. The other two were little children: a boy of four and a girl of five. I knew Jimmie Crane. Doctor Deutsch, our pediatrician, had presented him at a clinic as an outstanding example of what a course of treatment with vitamins could accomplish in curing rickets. He should have presented tiny Frances Hall as a control specimen. She was pigeon-breasted, bow-legged, emaciated. She came from the same sort of land-poor farmer family as Jimmie, but she had not had the benefit of modern scientific care.

It didn't make any difference now.

They were both deep in the coma of which I had seen too much in the past month, the sturdy, straight-boned lad and the twisted, pinch-faced little lass alike.

Unless I could find, somewhere in the hospital, an individual the serum of whose blood would agglutinate the corpuscles of Type IV and whose corpuscles would agglutinate the serum of no known type, those two infants were doomed.

The technicians looked askance at me when I gave the orders for a general typing, but they did not question me.

Perhaps there was something in my face that forbade any questioning.

Jeremiah Fenton's story, resumed:

SEELA WAS still about fifty yards above us. He stopped, sudden-like, hanging on his wings like a hawk would. He pointed off to the west and his head went back like he was hollering to the other Taphetnit above him. Four of them swooped off in that direction, and slid down, behind the ridge. Then Seela came on down to us.

"We have much to thank you two for," he said, low-toned, "but so many, many Mernians have gone from among us. I shall

declare a *fusran* [holy day] at once, so that all that are left in
Calinore may light white tapers and green upon the altar below."

"They're gone then, Seela?" Mr. Lambert asked. "The Surahnit?"

"A pitiful remnant are retreating. Curiously enough, they go
not towards Tashna but are making a great circle which will
take them to the Gateway Wall. All but one, after whom I have
sent my brethren."

"A wounded one? I didn't think any whom the light touched
escaped alive."

"Not wounded, Hula. She was coming toward Calinore,
staggering and weary, but whole."

"She! Who?"

"The Ra Nalinah, she whom Antil wished to take as hostage.
She is our prisoner now, but after what has happened this night
I have no illusion that she will avail us aught as a hostage. Our
only protection is this that you have devised"—he laid a hand
on the reflector—"and I misgive me that the Nal Surah and
the Surahnit scientists may not yet find a way to shield themselves from it."

"They did just that," I put in. "Those guys that were working
the blast projector didn't feel it no more than I would have."

Seela started to say something but Mr. Lambert butted in.

"What are they doing with her? Where are they going to
take her?"

The Taphet smiled, kind of sad.

"To my dwelling. I wish to question her and—"

"What are we waiting for?" We'd passed through a lot together but I never saw Mr. Lambert get so excited. "Let's go."

That Seela sure is strong. He scooped me up under one arm
and Mr. Lambert under the other and he took off from that
platform like he wasn't carrying no weight at all.

I wasn't scared this time. I went up in an airplane once at the

County Fair, and I was so tarnation frightened I swore I would never go up in one again. Flying with Seela was different.

I just looked down at that city below. Half of it was as beautiful as before, all shining white houses and big open circles where you could see grooves worn where the Taphetnit used to dance, and the other half of it was a terrible jumble of broken stones smeared with glistening red.

I wasn't scared, but I was awful sick, thinking of what that red was.

THERE WASN'T anyone in Seela's house when we got there except Leeahlee. She'd fixed up some kind of food and she made us eat it. It was kind of like corn mush except that it was orange color, and tasted a lot better, and we drunk wine with it that was better than Martha Parker's dandelion wine that she always sent around to Elijah and me in the fall.

Seela and I ate pretty hearty; but the two others kept looking out through the door. When we was about half through Antil came in. He was all ruffled up, and there was an angry weal across his cheek where it had got burned by a *coret* flash.

Leeahlee run to him; and she touched the mark on his cheek, and there was tears in her eyes. It wasn't much to make her take on so, but I guess women are the same all over the world and underneath it when the man they love gets hurt. In the middle of that fuss Mr. Lambert jumps up all of a sudden, his face lighting up.

I turned around to see who it was he was so glad was coming. There was two Taphetnit in the door-way, and between them was Nalinah, all sagged out.

Her dress was half torn from one shoulder, and her hair was all mussed up, but her little face was kind of smiling and peaceful, for all its being deathly tired. It put me in mind of someone that's been lost in the woods, and worried stiff, and now was on a path he knew would lead him home.

She kind of pulled away from the Taphetnit that were holding her and took a step into the house, and I knew she only saw Mr. Lambert. He came past me, taking big strides, and he took the hands she held out to him, and they stood there like that, looking into each other's eyes for a long minute. They made a grand looking couple, he tall and brown and strong; she little and frail and beautiful.

She kind of sighed, and then she said, "I had to come, Hula. I had to come to you."

"I know," he answered.

After a while he said, "Tell me about it, Nalinah." I can hear everything they said right now, in my ears, so can put it down just the way they said it.

"Vanark had reported to the Nal," Nalinah began, "that you had swayed me against the Folk Weal, and that I was plotting with you to defeat the invasion of the Upper World. That was why my arrest was ordered. Vanark lied, Hula, but waiting the long *roha* for a chance to defend myself, I thought over all we had spoken together and Vanark's lie became the truth. I saw that you were right and the Taphetnit were right, and that the weal of our Folk lies here in Mernia, just as the weal of yours lies among the green fields and the blue seas above."

"Yes, Nalinah," he murmured. "We each have our own sphere to which we are born and to which we are fitted."

"VANARK ACCUSED me before the Nal, while the bridges were being rebuilt, of being a traitor to the Folk. I denied that, for no traitor to them I am but more loyal than he who has lied and deceived the Ratanit and Nal Surah and is plotting to seize the Nalship for himself when once the invasion he has planned and urged shall be successful. I swore to my denial by the sun-shaft that rises from the Central Plaza of Tashna and the shaft turned white in token that I swore truly."

"You convinced the Nal and by some trick he turned the shaft white."

"Nay, Hula, the shaft is the heart and the brain of the Folk, and the shaft turned white. Therefore was the Nal convinced that I am no traitor, and I too was convinced that for their true

*He stood there in the pulsing heat of
that living crimson flame....*

happiness the Folk must remain in Mernia. But Vanark is very
shrewd. He proposed that I lead with him the attack on
Calinore, and I could not refuse. Could I, Hula?"

"No, Nalinah."

"So I led the attack beside Vanark, and though my heart bled for the gallant Surahnit as they died in your ray, yet was I also glad that Vanark and his host were being defeated, for that defeat, I thought, meant that the Folk would remain forever in Mernia, and too, I was so proud of you that you had found a way to defeat us.

"But Vanark, leaving orders for the attack to continue, took me far to one side of Calinore, chuckling with some secret mirth. From there he showed me the blast projector that had been dispatched on a *lusan* from the Gateway Wall, and he showed me that the Surahnit who served it were untouched by the white, destroying blaze of the Ray. I pretended joy at the sight, but within me I was desolate, till from the very sky began that rocky rain.

"Your Taphetnit smashed them, Hula, so that for a while you are safe. But only for a while. That is why I have come to you, openly a renegade now to the Nal and to Vanark, but not to the Folk; to warn you that you have won not a victory but only respite. They will be back, Hula and Seela and Antil!" Nalinah turned around to face us all; now for the first time showing she knew there was anyone there but Mr. Lambert. "The Surahnit will return to the attack in a day or less, and this time their hordes will be as little affected by your Ray as the twelve who lie out there. Vanark is not defeated yet!"

"Good Lord!" Mr. Lambert took a step back from her, another, and his face was white as a sheet. "You mean that he can make more of them immune to the *kitor's* light!"

"All of them, my Hula, given time. Unless before they come again you can devise a new defense against them, Calinore is doomed, and the Taphetnit, and your World Above is doomed to fall before the conquering hosts of Mernia."

"But—but—how can we figure out a new defense when we don't even know how they are protecting themselves against this one?"

"That last I can tell you, Hula, and with what I can tell you, perhaps you can meet this new threat. You are so very wise, so very wise."

"Tell me, Nalinah. Tell me all you know."

"I will tell you as much as I know, as much as I understand."

Well, Leeahlee got Nalinah to sit down, and Mr. Lambert sat down, and we all sat down, and we all sat around and listened while she told us about it. This is the part that's going to be hard for me to write down, because I didn't understand it any too well. But I'll try to make out as best as I can.

Account of Jeremiah Fenton, continued:

WHAT NALINAH told us was something like this. She began with very much the same thing Antil had told Mr. Lambert back there in that room under the Listeners' Post, when he was telling him why Vanark hadn't been able to kill him with the *kitor*.

The people down here, the Taphetnit, and the Surahnit both look a whole lot like humans, but the tiny building blocks their bodies is made up of (Mr. Lambert said the words she used meant the same as ions and protons and neutrons in English) are hitched together in a different sort of way, so that while they stay together all right in the kind of light there is in this cavern, they fall apart in the sunlight up above.

That was why they had never tried to capture the world before, because they could only live up there for a little while in the night, and never at all in the day. But when last winter the skating party from the Four Corners Church got drowned, they got hold of the bodies and some scientist or other among them got a bright idea.

There was one of the drowned people that wasn't all dead when they got him inside the Gateway Wall and this scientist took a little blood out of him and injected it into the veins of a Surahnit, and then sent him up to the surface in a *sibral* suit. Well, it seems that this Surahnit could stand it up there longer than any of them had ever been able to before, and he even stood about five minutes of sunlight. He came down then, but a week (Nalinah said a *steen*) later he went up again, and this time he stood the sun for all of fifteen minutes.

That seemed to prove that a little bit of human blood in the veins of a Mernian would fix him after a while so that he could live on the surface, but when they tried again with blood from one of the other bodies, it didn't work. That set them back for a while, till somebody got the bright idea of taking blood from the first Surahnit and then putting it into the veins of another.

That worked better, although not as well as the first transfusion, but it gave them the clue to what they had to do. The blood they needed had to come from living humans.

Well, they worked and worked, and finally they worked out a scheme for making corpses they had hold of come alive. They tried it on one, and he did come alive, but the blood from him wasn't any good.

So that put them up against the proposition that they had to get the blood from humans that had never been dead. They sent the first Surahnit up again, and he sneaked into someone's house, and sucked out a little blood, putting some of his own in its place. When he came down they tried out the *kitor* ray on him, that was the same as sunlight, and he stood it perfectly well.

They gave another Surahnit the blood from him, and after awhile the second guy got so that he could stand a little sunlight. They sent the two of them up for more. These two found that the human that the blood had been sucked from was lying in bed, not moving, and they thought he was dead but they saw his pulse beating in his neck and then they knew he wasn't. They both sucked blood from him and went down again, and gave the blood to others.

The next time they went up the first human was gone, so they tried another one. But somehow they found out where the first one was, too. He was quite a distance away, in a place where there were a lot of beds in a row.

"The hospital," I bust out. "That first human was Adath Jenks, and the second must've been Job Grant. That sleep they're in is caused by these Surahnit sucking their blood out of them. Drinking the life out of them."

Mr. Lambert's eyes were like slits. "You're right, Fenton," he said. "But keep quiet, and let Nalinah finish."

WELL, THERE wasn't much more. It seems the Surahnit can't be seen by humans so they could keep right on drinking the life out of their victims even though they was both in the hospital. After Mr. Lambert got took down to Mernia they started on another victim, that was in a little house near the lake.

"The camp!" It was Mr. Lambert who did the exclaiming this time. "One of the boys. Which one?"

Nalinah shook her head. "I don't know. But his blood is stronger than those of the first two, and the process is going on faster. There were twelve of the L.S.G who were altogether fitted for life in the sun, and it was those twelve whom Vanark detailed to serve the blast projector.

"When he saw that this experiment was successful he gave orders for an acceleration of the stealing of human blood. Even while the battle was going on, four more victims were attacked by the living test tubes he is dispatching to carry human life down to Mernia. Just now the sun is bright in your Upper World, and the drinking of life is perforce halted but in the laboratory there in the East that life is being pumped into the veins of many other Surahnit. As soon as it is again dark above, which will be in ten of our *roha* all these will flock up through the waters to seek out more and more victims. Thus multiplying the immune ones as fast as he can, Vanark figures that in a *ranhaltin* [a day] a thousand or more Surahnit will be immune to your ray. Then he will lead them once more against Calinore, and there can be no doubt of the result. Calinore will be wiped out."

"No doubt at all," Mr. Lambert groaned, his brown fist closing on the edge of the table. "No doubt that Calinore will be wiped out and no doubt that a hundred humans will be lying at the point of death above there."

"Maybe they're the lucky ones," I said. "I don't like to think of what's going to happen when this bunch of Vanark's gets ready to take over Albany County, with their *corets* and their blast projectors. You've got to stop it, Mr. Lambert. You've got to find a way to stop it."

He gave me a look, then—and if I ever saw hell staring out of a man's eyes, it was in that minute.

"How can I, Fenton? There isn't a single thing in what she has told me that gives me the glimmer of an idea. It's all black, blacker than the pit of hell."

"Look!" I answered him. "You're a million times smarter than I am, but sometimes even a fool can get a notion. If they're drinking the blood of the humans, maybe if the blood was poisoned that would poison the Surahnit, and—"

"If we could get word to the people above and if we knew how to poison the Surahnit without killing the human beings first. No, Fenton, that won't—"

"Hula!" Nalinah broke in. "Perhaps there is something in what your friend says. While I was standing with Vanark, a messenger came from the Gateway. He reported that something ailed the drinkers from one of the humans. They could not bear the test-flash of the *kitor* upon them. It was as if instead of being blunted, the power of the white blaze was redoubled by the blood they had drunk. One hundredth of a *neks* [minutes] they were exposed to it, and they melted as if they had been in its light a full five *neks*."

Mr. Lambert shouted out loud.

"Now we're getting somewhere! Was there any difference between this human do you know, and the others?"

"It was a small one, a tiny child. But that cannot mean anything; for others had drunk from another child and the blood of that one was effective as all the rest. Vanark thought it strange; too, that the second child was described to him weak and weazened, its bones all awry, while the first was perfectly formed."

MR. LAMBERT screwed up his face, thinking hard. "The one whose blood works is rickety, huh, the other one isn't? Rickety. There's something—Wait! I've got it! Nalinah, I've got it. There aren't many rickety children now; they give them viosterol and cure them. And what's viosterol, but a solution of vitamin D in oil, of the vitamin that's manufactured in the body by what? By sunlight! *By sunlight*, Nalinah! That's why your Surahnit who've drunk that blood burn up when just a little more sunlight hits them. It's like taking too strong a dose of something—a little's medicine but a lot's poison. *That's* what we've got to do, pump a lot of viosterol into the veins of all the Life Drinkers' victims, a lot of the sunshine vitamin. Then it will be death they bring down to Mernia. They and the others with whom they'll share that blood will be sensitized to the sunlight instead of being immunized. That's what…"

He stopped, all of a sudden, and the light went out of his face. "But that's all nonsense. How am I going to inject viosterol into any human's blood when I'm down here, miles underground, and they're up there, and there's no way for me to get up there?"

Mr. Lambert started pacing up and down. Like a wild animal in a cage he was; like something shut up and going crazy. I knew how he felt, too. It must have been awful for him; knowing how he could save us all and knowing at the same time that there was no way to do it.

"There is a way." It was Seela who said that. He'd been listening silently, sitting way back in a corner, but now he pushed forward. "If you have the courage, Hula, there is a way of reaching the Gateway lock without being spied by the Surahnit. Yon are still clad in the *sibral* suit, Hula, and once through the lock you can ascend through the waters. Failure means death, Hula, and the chance of failure is very great. Have you the courage to try it, friend Hula?"

"Have I?" Mr. Lambert pushed down on the table with both his hands, shoving himself to his feet. "What are we waiting for?"

It was then that he asked me to finish writing out what was happening in Mernia, and said good-by to me. He said good-by to Antil and Leeahlee. To Nalinah, too, he said good-by, but we left those two alone together for that.

I don't know what more I can say. They've, been gone almost a whole *ranhaltin* now, Mr. Lambert and Seela and the two picked Taphetnit that went with them. None of them has come back and we haven't heard a word from them. We're waiting in Seela's house, the four of us and we aren't saying a word to each other. We're just waiting.

That little messenger boy just came in to say that scouts report that the Surahnit are massing again, east of here, between Calinore and the Gateway Wall. They have three blast projectors with them, all mounted on *lusans*. I guess it's all over.

The Taphetnit are flocking to the Wall, and I'm going up to the top of the tower to work the reflector. It won't do no good, but I might as well die fighting as not.

What was that song Mr. Lambert was singing?

> *In fact quite the cream of the Muscovite team*
> *Was Ivan Skovinsky Skivar.*

I hope I'll be singing it when the tower is blown out from under me and I tumble with it into the ruins of Calinore.

CHAPTER X

Interpolation by Arthur Leo Zagat, B.S., L.L.B., Compiler of these documents:

THE STORY OF Hugh Lambert's attempt to escape from Mernia and communicate with humanity is an epic that now has never been written. How I learned its details will appear later, but this is, as nearly as I can determine, what occurred.

Seela's plan was simplicity itself. He proposed to carry Lambert straight upward from Calinore to the very roof of the monstrous cavern. At that immense height they would be well out of sight of any Surahnit between the Taphetnit's city and the Gateway Wall, and could fly to it unmolested.

There was, he assured Lambert, a shelf of rock near the summit of the great façade that kept Lake Wanooka from engulfing Mernia, and here they could land. Thus far their route would be devoid of danger, but from this point on it would be encompassed with peril.

As the reader is already aware, a constant watch was maintained by the Surahnit to hold the Taphetnit bottled up in their besieged city of Calinore. Lambert knew how slim were his chances for escape—how almost impossible it would be for Seela's white robes to go unnoticed as he attempted to fly with his burden to the ledge where the lock separated Mernia from Earth. No, the last stages of the flight would have to be negotiated by climbing down some sort of rope from the sheer crags above. The Surahnit would be guarding that lock—perhaps with one man, perhaps with a whole squad of L.S.G., armed with the deadly *corets*.

Lambert squared his shoulders and gazed it the young Taphetnit's radiant, troubled face. "Come on," he said. "All we can do is try."

Seela nodded. "It means so—much…"

The rope that Hugh would need in the last final climb was made ready, and Lambert began to take leave of those he might never see again. There were a few precious moments alone with Nalinah, and then Hugh Lambert took Antil's hand and shook it warmly. Once more he joined Seela and the two Taphetnit who were to accompany them.

During that long first part of their flight through the strange Mernian sky, few words were uttered. Lambert was too filled with conflicting emotions to put them into words. His whole body was keyed up with a stinging tension that is sometimes mistakenly named fear—but there was real dread in his heart, too. Not for himself, but for all these he knew and loved upon the earth—all of those he was making this final, desperate attempt to save. If he failed, what would happen to them? No man could safely say.

Then another, more terrible dread assailed him—sharper because it was, in a sense, more personal. Suppose he was mad? Suppose everything that had occurred—this strange, unworld-ly Odyssey—since those nights, on the shores of the Lake, was a nightmare—a lunatic's fantastic dream.

Tormented, Lambert found comfort in words. He began to question Seela—asking about the origins of the Taphetnit and the Surahnit.

"We come from the upper world, Hula. But it was so long ago that there is no memory of it—nor any trace, except our memory of the sun which we worship in the column of light."

But even Seela's words seemed to have a strange ring—the half-poetry of their utterance seemed the lilting cadences of a madman's song. They did, at least, until Hugh Lambert began to remember the strange things he had seen in Mernia: the *fortlik* from which our corn might well have evolved, the *Eohippi*, the *Dicroreri*. He recalled the *kitor*, that bore a repre-sentation of the Solar System. He knew he was not mad.

"The tale was told me," Seela went on, his voice flowing as the air flowed past them in his tireless flight, "by a wise one of the Surahnit who was trying to persuade us to join them in their intention to return. He told me how our ancestors lived once on the warm surface of the earth, under a sky of blue light in which the air hung a great white ball, or a sky that sparkled with golden lights as the dark rock of the Eastern Wall sparkles. They lived in houses then, very like the present houses of Calinore save that they were fashioned from the substance of great plants that grew on the hills. They had crude *lusans,* and primitive *corets,* and many other such things."

He went on for a while describing a civilization that has been quite forgotten. And then the steaming climate began to change.

"The air grew steadily colder, and one day some Taphetnit flying far to the north returned with an affrighting tale of a great wall of frozen water that was moving slowly but surely down upon our land. Mile upon mile high it towered they said, and the crash of the masses falling from it was like thunder multiplied a hundred fold."

"The Glacier," Lambert exclaimed. "The Great Glacier!"

"Our ancient ones could not believe at first that this doom was marching down upon them, but month by month and year by year the ice came nearer, till at last there was no doubt that the towering hills whereon they dwelt must be engulfed.

"Some, more cautious than the rest, had searched far and found this great bubble within the mountain, and now they proposed that the people seek shelter therein till the frozen water should retreat. Others wished to move south and ever southward before its face, believing that it would cover the land forever. Long and strenuously the dispute was waged, but it was the first party that prevailed.

"And so all the Mernian folk entered this great cavern through a small cave mouth where now is the lock to which we fly, bringing with them as much of the appurtenances of their lives as they could and their tame beasts, and they plugged up the aperture through which they came. The only light here was that which flowed from a shining pillar rising far to the west from floor to very roof of the cavern, encircled by a bottomless chasm."

LAMBERT INTERRUPTED the recital. "That pillar must be of fused quartz. It must go clear up through the mountain to its surface and it leads daylight down into this cavern. I've seen rods of fused quartz carry light around corners, and—"

"Perhaps so," Seela broke in, "but the Surahnit worship it as the concrete representation of their deity. At any rate, it was about this shaft of light that the refugees first clustered and began their life anew.

"Years passed, uncountable years, and still the water lay frozen against the Gateway Wall. Those first ancient ones lived, and gave life to their progeny, and died, and their descendants lived and multiplied and died, and still were we prisoners here. Little by little, with each generation, there grew to be more light in the cavern, till after an unthinkable space the rocks, the beasts that had been brought from outside, and the very bodies of Surahnit and Taphetnit, shone with some strange luminance of their own."

Lambert could not resist offering an explanation of this phenomenon also. "The rock and everything else always was emitting that light. It is an etheric vibration, a radiant emanation that is just beyond the threshold of perception of the visual organs of those who dwell in the light of the sun. A gradual evolution took place in the Mernians, a change in their very atomic structure so long exposed to these emanations, till at last they were able to perceive it. Fenton and I can see it too, though the change in us was sudden, and I think I know why.

"We were reduced in size by a reduction of the distances between the neutrons and protons in each electron of our constitution. That change affected our retinas in a single moment the same way all those centuries of evolution affected yours, but we still retain enough of our human attributes to be immune to the devastating effect on you of the sun's actinic rays."

"You may be right, Hula," Seela sighed. "We Taphetnit are

not skilled in such lore and I shall not attempt to discuss it with you.

"As time wore on disputes arose between the two races so strangely dissimilar. The Surahnit found a way to bridge the chasm about the shining shaft and erected their city of Tashna upon the island plateau it bounded. We Taphetnit withdrew eastward and constructed our own Calinore. It would take too long to narrate all that occurred here through the ages, and I shall not attempt it.

"Came a day when those who were appointed to keep watch on the Gateway Wall and that which lay beyond it brought word that there was no longer ice on the outside. But the fierce joy that swept Mernia was quickly stemmed. The ice had melted, it was true, yet the great valley where we had roamed the hills was filled now with a waste of waters, and we were as surely prisoners as before, save that no longer had we any hope of release.

"The Taphetnit were resigned to this fate, but the Surahnit would not accept it. They devised the lock through which you were brought into Mernia, and the garments of *sibral* that would permit them to pass up through the waters and reach its surface. The first daring one who made the ascent never returned. But the Nal Surah of that time was not content, and he dispatched one after another of his subjects to the Upper World till at last it was discovered that only when a moonless darkness covered the hills could a Mernian exist there for some short space. Not by the waters but by some inscrutable change in the very elements of our beings were we now condemned forever to dwell in this cavern.

"So thoroughly, however, was the longing for the open ingrained in us, that we, Taphetnit as well as Surahnit, chanced the dangers of forays above for even the short space that it was safe for us to remain there. We found a race of gigantic beings there, who had sprung from somewhere to populate the hills out of which we had been driven. Most times they could not see us at all, but some among them, their children, a few of their adults, could glimpse us. How is it, Hula, that those who did see us never told the others about us?"

"They did," was the simple response. "They told of what they had seen, calling you Taphetnit 'fairies' and the Surahnit 'gnomes,' but those who had not the power to see you did not believe them. They were called dreamers, superstitious, or, more rudely, drunk or insane. But look here, Seela. The little people have been seen not only here in the Helderbergs but all over the world. From what you say, you Mernians could not have wandered far. Is it possible that very much the same thing as you have told me about happened elsewhere on Earth, that this old globe of ours is honeycombed everywhere by caverns lake this, in which dwell the small folk of a pre-Glacial civilization we archaeologists have never dreamed existed?"

One of the other Taphetnit called out to Seela, just at that moment, forestalling whatever answer he might have made. They had reached the eastern boundary of the cavern.

HUGH LAMBERT was somewhat dazed with the strange narrative, that his knowledge of Earth's geologic history told him had covered in a few short sentences the events of far more than fifty thousand years. That long it was since the Fourth Glacier loosened its grip on the Helderbergs—how much longer since it fastened it there no one could be certain.

The human knew now that two great streams of evolution, following their own bent for five hundred centuries, were at this very moment confluent, and that upon him, upon the events of the next few minutes, depended whether one should swamp and obliterate it, or whether they would part again and go on their separate courses for another five hundred centuries.

The thought, the burden of his responsibility, was too appalling to contemplate. He shut it from his mind. He had to get down to the ledge below. That was the next move. That was the only thing he would think about, the next move.

He waited quietly while Seela wound the end of the leather rope over his shoulders and around his chest in a sort of harness and fastened it with a slip knot that would hold against a downward pull till doomsday, but would yield to a jerk of his hand.

"Pull once on the rope and we'll stop lowering you," Seela said. "Pull twice and we'll swing you in towards the cliff."

The two Taphetnit stepped behind Lambert and grasped the cable in their powerful fingers. Seela and Lambert stood facing each other. Then Lambert stepped off.

Little by little, little by little, that ludicrously inadequate thread lengthened. With infinite slowness Lambert moved down past the dark-glowing precipice that was first inches, then feet, then a yard from him. He grasped the rope above his head with his fingers, and he stared at the slowly mounting wall.

Lambert's fingers were tight on the free end of the slipknot—and stayed there. Stayed there while the precipice slid steadily upward, stayed there till abruptly he saw the long ledge scarring the face of the cliff, saw the fire-curtained mouth of the tunnel, and came level with it.

His left hand pulled once on the rope above his head. The infinitely long descent checked.

A shadow darkened the sparkling curtain in front of him, and then a figure came through it, the figure of Talim. The youth stared at the man dangling in midair before him, his pupils widening.

Lambert pulled twice on the rope.

He started to pendulum in toward the ledge. Talim crouched, his webbed fingers darting to his belt, to the handle of a *coret*. The swing of the rope was too slow; before it could carry Lambert to the ledge that *coret* would be out, would be spitting its scarlet death.

Too slow! Hugh Lambert arched backward, threw that magnificent torso of his forward—and jerked the rope—and that freed him from the suspending cable!

The impetus of that desperate effort of his carried his heels to the very edge of the ledge, and spent itself. For a split second he swayed there, which way he would fall in the lap of the gods. Time stood still.

Something, the luck of the greatly daring, the prayer that winged itself from his tortured brain, some effort of which he was unconscious, sent him forward. A scream shrilled from Talim's throat and Lambert's fist knocked the *coret* spinning from the Surahnit's hand.

It struck the wall, stayed there. Lambert's hands were on Talim's throat squeezing. The youth's fists battered the human's chest but the blows were fly-flicks to Lambert's perception. Talim went to his knees.

Other figures burst out of the tunnel's month, soldiers of the L.S.G., their weapons fisted. They looked about them for a confused instant, glimpsed the struggling pair. Their *corets* jabbed point-blank on Hugh Lambert.[*]

Hugh Lambert's narrative, continued:

I HAD no time to dodge, had no place to dodge to if I could have. This was the end.

Well, I'd done my—Something white, a flash of iridescent colors, swept between me and the soldiers! The Taphet received the full force of both lancing rays.

The *corets* whipped back to bear on me. Seela and the third Taphet swooped in, darted desperately at the Surahnit. Their flailing, frantic fingers clutched the soldiers arms, their wrists, before the weapons could be fired again. But they *were* fired.

---

[*]   Editor's Note: It is remarkable that in the midst of the appalling experiences through which Hugh Lambert was passing, with death always imminent and the fate of a race dependent on his lonely struggle, he should have contrived to maintain as complete a record of events, as detailed a commentary upon them, as he did.

With the exception of the hiatus filled in by Jeremiah Fenton's story and my own interpolation, there is no break in the narrative I have transcribed by the aid of a magnifying glass from the bundle of bleached tiny leather sheets, charred at the edges and water-stained, that came into my possession in the spring of 1935. It is with a great deal of satisfaction therefore that I am enabled to head the closing scenes of the strange and stirring drama we have followed so long with the caption:

The Taphetnit spurted into flame, reeled backward. Their great pinions incandescent, they reeled back over the brink, plunged downward out of sight.

They did not go alone. They took with them in their blazing arms the two L.S.G. guards who had so nearly done for me. A plume of black and greasy smoke was all I could see of them, all I could see of those brave and gallant beings who had swooped downward out of perfect safety to come to my aid.

Perhaps they had sensed something wrong because the rope had been freed of my weight an instant too quickly. Perhaps, and knowing how great-souled they were I believe this to be the truth, it had always been part of their plan to follow me down and make certain I should win through to the lock un-hampered.

At any rate, their sacrifice ensured the success of my enter-prise. No other Surahnit came out of the tunnel mouth to in-terfere with me, and I knew that there would be no alarm spread below for a long time. That which would soon smash on the cavern floor would be a mass of black-charred carbon indistin-guishable in shape or form, and the watchers there would think that a quartet of fleeing Taphetnit had been rayed by their comrades here.

I had only Talim to contend with now. The youth was choked half-unconscious; was terrified.

I let go with one hand, snatched up his *coret*. "Tell me how to work the lock," I said, "if you don't want a dose of this."

He was, after all, a youngster, and the desire for life was strong within him. "I—I'll tell you," he gasped, terror bulging his eyes. "Don't shoot."

He kept his word. The method of manipulating the lock mechanism was simple, almost ridiculously simple. It could be done single-handed with some small effort, and so I was enabled to tie up Talim with his own belt, gag him with a piece torn from his own uniform, and leave him behind me, well hidden in a niche in the tunnel slide.

Only brief minutes later, I was shooting up through Lake Wanooka's unfathomable depths, the hood of the *sibral* drawn once more over my head. I was following the long straight path of the violet ray that made a ladder to the world I had long ago given up hope of ever seeing again.

I REACHED the surface into a gray dusk that brooded ominously over a shoreless sea. Panic gripped me for a poignant moment, terror that I was lost, that somehow I had come up out of some distant, unbounded ocean. Then. I recalled how the familiar beaches of Lake Wanooka had appeared to me when I had dwindled to the mannikin I now was, and curving about in the water, saw the boulder-strewn slope where that transformation had occurred. I was home! Home!

In an instant I was clambering over the rocks upon that shore making my painful way toward the lush jungle out of which I had run, terrified, from a two yard earthworm and an enormous spider.

Three-foot green spears that were blades of timothy threatened to impale me; I twisted an ankle in a deep depression that might have been the footprint of a field mouse. Outré and exotic my surroundings were, but they were on the surface of the earth. They were home! A great pulse of elation throbbed within me that almost drove from my mind recollection of what lay miles beneath me, of the desperate mission in which I was engaged.

Almost, but not quite. I remembered I must get to the camp somehow. I remembered that I must somehow find a human being to whom to give my message.

A fist-size stone—a pebble smaller than a marble, it would be, if I were my proper size—turned, under my foot and threw me to my knees. The fall jarred me to the very core, and I did not have the strength to get up.

Tired! Suddenly fatigue had swept down upon me, the fatigue of a day and a night through which, without rest, without sleep, almost without food, I had been harrowed by such experiences as no man had ever encountered, had agonized and fought and agonized and fought again. Tired! Man only can stand so much.

I shook my head, trying to clear it of weariness, trying to think. I dared not rest. I had no right to rest. I must get to the office. No, to the infirmary. Edith was there. Edith was a nurse and she would be quickest to understand my message. It wasn't far. It was only two hundred yards from this point on the shore.

Two hundred yards? To me, as I was now those two hundred yards were twelve hundred, were, almost a mile. I couldn't do it. I couldn't.

But I must. I must! I would rest a little, only a little, and then I would go on.

THE MISTS closed in on me again. A Taphet swooped out of the sullen sky. Not a Taphet, but a small winged thing that swerved and alighted on a bending stalk above me. Its brown wings, nine inches across, fluttered a moment and folded.

This was a creature of my world, of my time. It was no *Eohippus*, no *Dicrorerus*, but a butterfly. A Gold-banded Skipper. The recognition did something to me, gave me strength to stand erect.

The ground shook beneath me, and I whirled in sudden terror. A looming, giant moved toward me, his tremendous knees level with my head.

His Gargantuan body loomed high as he came on. A white, filmy cloud wavered over me and behind it his face was a great round moon; grotesquely masked by lenses like crystal dinner plates, through which bulging, gargoylesque eyeballs peered balefully.

That face was weirdly familiar. Of course! Once more I had forgotten my size. This was no giant! it was a human boy.

It was Percy White. The cloud was a net and he was stalking the butterfly.

I choked, unable to speak for an instant.

What luck! What glorious—

I was still unable to make a sound, but it was horror that clutched my throat now. Percy was looking down at me, straight down at me—*and he didn't see me!* He saw only the Skipper, directly over my head. I was invisible to him, invisible as the Little Men had been to me till the change in my blood.

Was my voice inaudible to him too? I shouted.

Just in that instant his net swept forward. It missed the butterfly. The Insect leaped into the air, darted away—and Percy darted after it! Before I could shout again he was hidden by white, stupendous columns of a line of birch-saplings that edged the woods here.

I sobbed with disappointment. With rage. Fury exploded a red flare within my skull. It burned away the fatigue. It burned away everything but my purpose to get to the infirmary against all odds. The jungle could not stop me now. Nothing could stop me. I plunged onward, panting and furious, battling the grass and the leaves; battling lashing tendrils of that incredibly magnified vegetation.

Time blurred. The jungle blurred. I was aware only of a gray haze through which I struggled interminably, of a haze that at first was gray and then darkened as I fought onward through the night.

Account of Courtney Stone, M.D., continued:

I timed my return to Camp Saturday night so as to arrive there at suppertime. Not because I wanted to eat with those who were there, but quite to the contrary, I didn't want to face them at once. I didn't want to face Ann Doring or Edith Horne and answer the question I knew would be in their eyes till I had pulled myself together.

I was a tired and despairing man, that night, as I coasted my car to the Camp gate so that its arrival would not be noticed, and stumbled through the darkness of the infirmary.

I was thankful that I had left instructions with Edith that

she was to insist on Miss Doring's going down to the mess hall with her for all meals. There was no point in remaining with the three patients continually; there would be no change in them, no sudden emergency, and unless Dick's sister was diverted a little from her anxiety she would collapse.

These artists are high-strung, hyperthyroidic for the most part. They cannot bear strains as well as people with ordinary, unemotional temperaments.

The infirmary was quiet, as a result, quiet and peaceful. I went into Edith's little office and let myself down heavily into the chair at her desk. I did not bother to turn on the light.

The result of the tests I had ordered had been negative. Perhaps somewhere in Albany or in the Helderbergs there was someone with blood of the nature I sought, but he was not in the hospital, either as patient or intern or nurse.

The tests had failed, and my last hope had failed. Job Grant had died during the day. Charlie Dorsey would die, and Dick Doring. Hepzibah Foster, little Fanny Hall, tiny Jimmie Crane, would linger for a while, sinking, sinking, life slowly draining from them till they too would lie white and inanimate corpses, on their hospital beds.

And the disease would go on spreading. Tomorrow morning there would be more of its victims in the hospital, tomorrow morning, and the day after and the day after. Eventually some way to stop its spread would be found, but meantime how many lives would it finally claim? How many?

My dreary thoughts were interrupted by a sound from the threshold of the door that I had forgotten to close.

IT WAS a strange small sound. A dead leaf blown from a tree, I thought, but it came again, seemingly nearer. And again. *Pit—pit—pit.* Across the floor towards me. Like tiny footfalls stumbling, slow and weary across the wooden floor. *Pit—pit— pit.* Like the footfalls of some little man, tired unto death.

I smiled at myself, realizing the notion had been suggested by Edith's quaint apprehensions of the evening before. If there was anything there, if I was not imagining that *pit—pit—pit,* it was some hurt bird, that had hopped blindly into the place.

The idea intrigued me, of a wounded bird coming to the infirmary for treatment. Well, I thought, if it's as smart as that it shall be taken care of. But I couldn't see it in the darkness. I switched on Edith's desk lamp. The yellow light filled the room.

There was nothing on the floor. Nothing at all. *Pit—pit…* the sounds came from where there was nothing to be seen, and stopped.

A prickling chill rippled my vertebral column. *I was not alone!* The room was empty, except for me, but I knew that I was not alone.

"Court! Courtney Stone!"

The voice, tiny, shrill, came from where the last *pit* had sounded; from the absolute vacancy at which I stared.

"Court! Can you hear me? Tell me if you can hear me. Say something if you can hear me."

"I—I hear you." My own voice was a croak.

"Thank God! Court! This is Hugh. Hugh Lambert."

"Hugh!" I whispered. "You're not—not dead?" I asked, whispering to the nothingness out of which that tenuous, high-pitched voice spoke to me. I, Courtney Stone, to whom the very word "ghost" always had been a cause for Homeric laughter.

"Not dead, Court. Changed. You can't see me, but thank God you can hear me. I haven't time to explain. They're coming. They're coming from the lake; and—"

"Who's coming?"

"The—" I lost the word, or did not understand it. But I understood the next. "The *Little Men!* I've got to tell you something before the Life-Drinkers get here, before they see me. Listen. Are you listening, Court?"

"The little men! What—I am listening, Hugh."

"You've got to do as I say, exactly as I say. Tonight, right away, inject as much viosterol, as much Vitamin D as they can stand, into the veins of all your coma patients. All of them, Court, at once, and into their veins, into their blood. Do you understand?"

"I understand, but—"

"They're coming, Court. They mustn't see me. They mustn't know." The *pit—pit—pit* was commencing again faster now, retreating towards the door, and the voice was retreating with it, fading. "Hurry, Court, inject Vitamin D at once or nothing can save humanity. Good-by, Court."

"Hugh," a pulsing cry throbbed in my ears. "Don't go, Hugh." I whirled to it, to Edith Horne in the doorway from the corridor. She must have come in the back way, been standing there and listening. "Don't go, Hugh," she sobbed, her hands outstretched and pleading to the empty floor, the empty outer door from which no voice, no *pit—pit* of tiny feet, responded.

"You heard?" I croaked, staring at her. "I didn't imagine it? You heard it, and I'm not insane?"

"I heard. It was Hugh. Hugh, doctor, come back from where he has been to tell us what to do. I knew he would come, when we needed him. We must do what Hugh said, doctor. He said to hurry, doctor. We must hurry."

"Vitamin D, he said," I gulped. "Viosterol. But that's utterly ridiculous. No warrant in physiology, in any branch of science, for thinking of that as a treatment for coma—"

"I'll call the hospital and you can give them the orders," she interrupted me. "To inject viosterol into all the patients they have there and send us a supply for our two by motorcycle." Coming into the room she stumbled. I saw the lax form slumped on the floor over which she had stumbled, Ann Doring on the floor in a dead faint. They had come to the door together, and Ann had fainted at the sound of that spectral voice.

The rattle of the telephone dial beside me brought me around to, it. I caught Edith's hand.

"Wait!" I exclaimed. "Walt a second. Let me think. It's an

outrageous proposition. It's contrary to all medical knowledge. It may kill the patients. My reputation—"

"Hang your reputation," she flared out. "Hugh said we were to do it. Hugh…"

Ann Doring moaned, on the floor.

"All right," I said weakly. "We'll do it."

Continuation of Hugh Lambert's narrative:

I SAW the two girls come in as I stood in the center of an immense expanse of wooden floor and shouted my message at Courtney Stone, towering above me. I saw them come in and I saw Ann drop in at the sound of my voice, and I saw a fierce joy flare into Edith's face.

But I could not speak to her because I had to get my message over to Court and I had only seconds in which to do it.

Jumping the six-foot step from the infirmary threshold to the rocky desert of the path that led to it, I heard Edith's booming words. "We must do what Hugh said," and then I was running across that stretch of rocks and into the covert of the jungle that crowded it close. I gained that concealment just in time.

Past me, out there in the open, trotted one, two, a score of the *sibral*-garmented Surahnit I had heard following me up from the lake, just as I had collided with the great vertical cliff of the infirmary wall and came out of the daze through which I had somehow fought to my goal.

So close, after all I had endured, had I been to failure. For if they had come upon me talking to Court they would have sent back word of it to Vanark, and the Rata would have suspected at once that I had discovered a way to checkmate him and devised a countermove.

I watched four of the Surahnit climb the infirmary threshold and vanish within. I watched the rest skirt the infirmary corner and disappear into a looming dark thicket I knew to be the thick hemlock edge bordering the road to Albany.

Almost at once they appeared again, heaving out between them a teardrop *lusan*.

They tugged and heaved it to the road, climbed into it, and were off.

Then my weariness struck an almost physical blow, and oblivion claimed me.

CHAPTER XI

Continuation of Hugh Lambert's narrative:

I WAS AWAKENED by a hand on my shoulder; shaking me. "Blazes," I muttered. "This is the first time I didn't hear the bugle blow. A nightmare I was having must have dogged me, Ed. Wait till I tell—"

My drowsy mutter choked off. My eyes had opened and I was peering at a sharp-featured vulturine countenance just visible in the misty luminance of before dawn.

"What ails you?" the Surahnit demanded. "Lying here asleep? Good thing I got off the clear road and came upon you, or—" He broke off, and then: "By the shaft of the eternal, you are not a Mernian! You are—"

My hands flashed up. My thumbs clamped on his windpipe, tightened. I felt flesh crawl greasily under their pressure. I felt gristle crumple.

After a while the *sibrat*-clothed body was flaccid, lifeless.

I thrust it from me, rose to my feet, pulling the head of my garment over my head to hide the face that had betrayed me. Through a leafy screen I saw a wraithlike procession of Surahnit gliding past. They were returning to the lake, to Mernia, satiated with the blood they had sucked from the Lord alone knew how many humans.

What sort of blood was it? They were carrying with them death in their veins, but was it their death and that of their kind, or death to the gallant Taphetnit and to my own people?

Had Courtney Stone done as I had bidden him?

Even if he had, would the viosterol act in the manner I hoped? Well, I would know in a week, a month. If I had failed some time soon the lake would vomit forth a shambling troop of dead-alive, and after them a horde of Surahnit, and this pleasant countryside would become a harried hell as those who had been exiled from it five hundred centuries ago retook it.

Meantime, for a little space at least, I should see the sun again and feel it upon me. I should talk again with my own kind, and hold a girl of my own human race in my arms.

"What's the matter, Edith?" a great voice said. "Can't you sleep, either?"

"Sleep? I'm too tired to sleep after last, night. And besides, I have a feeling that Hugh Lambert is somewhere near, very near."

Near. I was not more than sixty feet from her! I started out of the jungle, got to the pathway. I halted, seeing them, Edith Horne and Courtney Stone, standing gigantic in the gigantic doorway of the infirmary.

"I've just been in to see Ann," Court said. "She's quietly asleep. She'll suffer no ill effects from her faint."

Edith was wan, pale, tired-looking. She must have been working hard, too hard for her strength. I started to call out to her...

I caught myself just in time. There were more Surahnit coming, in through the camp gateway, coming toward me along the path. If they'd heard me!

"Look, doctor; see that swirl of ground mist there." Edith was pointing straight at me. "Doesn't it look almost like a little mannikin, standing there?"

"Why are you dallying here?" the foremost Surahnit said gruffly as he came up to me. "Get going." It was Hafna, the subaltern who had come so near *coretting* me at Vanark's command at the very moment of my reaching Mernia. "There is more of the mist on the path now," Edith was saying. "When the sun comes up it will vanish, like Hugh vanished, into nothingness."

She was looking straight at me and all she saw was a little drifting vapor that the sun would dry in an instant. That was all any human would ever see.

I turned and went down to the lake with Hafna, down to the lake, and into it, and down, down; down through those stupendous depths to Mernia.

To Mernia, and the Taphetnit. To Fenton and Antil and Leeahlee...

And Nalinah.

INDISTINGUISHABLE FROM the Surahnit because, clad in the *sibral*-suit and hooded by it, there was nothing to set me apart from them, it was easy to reach the lock and go through it, and out to the ledge from which I first viewed Mernia.

There, however; my troubles began. The procession marched along the lofty shelf in the direction Vanark had led me, and I guessed that they were proceeding to the great cave that had been set aside as a laboratory. Here, undoubtedly, they would be stripped of their clothing and subjected to the transfusions Nalinah had described. Here my masquerade would be discovered.

I must never reach that cave. How could I avoid it? The first of the openings in the cliff wall whose curtains of living-light has so astonished me suggested a stratagem. I began limping, muttered something about having injured my foot. This enabled me to drift gradually to the end of the line of returning Mernians, and to duck unnoticed into a cave whose irregular opening marked it as a natural hollow.

It was a mere niche in the face of the cliff, so shallow that there was scarcely room for me, but it sufficed. Another group of Life-Drinkers shuffled by, beyond the veil of darting sparks which concealed me, and then a long silence let me know that I need fear encountering no more of them.

So far, so good, but how was I to reach the cavern floor, how make my way to distant Calinore?

Well, I had gotten as far as I had, not by planning, but by proceeding step by step, meeting each emergency as it arose, not thinking, not knowing, what the next one might be. I had only two choices, to go right along the ledge or to the left. To the right was toward detection and death. I cautiously emerged from my hiding place and darted left.

I went past the exit from the lock, went past a great fold in the Cliff's parapet. The ledge started to slant upward, and the faint hope I had nursed that I might come to some less impossible way of descent, died.

I kept on because there was nothing else to do, squeezed past another bulge in the face of the precipice, where for a terrible moment I clung to safety only by toe and fingerholds, my heels projecting over those awful depths. The rocky shelf widened, just beyond there, and I went to my knees, trembling with belated fear, blind with a dizzy vertigo.

Arms went around me from behind, clamping my arms! I was helpless in a terrible grip! The whir of powerful pinions was in my ears and I felt myself lifted. A hand, stripped the *sibral* hood, from my head, and I heard a chorus of twitters all about me, a chorus of birdlike Taphetnit.

"It is he. It is Hula! He has returned to us."

I was in the arms of a Taphet. A covey of his fellows were about me and we were darting in a swift, steep slant for the obscurity of the cavern roof!

They were scouts sent out from Calinore to watch the movements of the Surahnit concentration here in the east. Seeing me making my perilous way along the ledge, they had suspected who I was. The wide place where vertigo had overcome me was a bulge in the cliff side that had somewhat screened them from observation below and they had taken advantage of that to pluck me from it.

I AM once more at the platform high over Calinore, and Jeremiah Fenton is beside me. I am still warm with the greeting with which Antil and Leeahlee received me. I am still tingling with recollection of the look in Nalinah's eyes when she saw me return, and a few whispered words that passed between us. But I am cold, too, with apprehension. I am quivering with the tenseness of hope and fear and dread.

In minutes now, in a few short minutes, I shall know whether that tremendous journey of mine has been in vain. The scouts have flown in with word that Vanark's legions are advancing, and now I can see them on the far eastern horizon. The dark line limning the desolate, barren desert of rock that is Mernia's soil has come suddenly alive.

They are coming now, a thousand Surahnit with human blood in their veins, a thousand Surahnit armed with the dreadful *corets* against which no human army will be able to stand if ever they are confronted with that dark green host, and they are dragging with them three blast-projectors whose blue flares can level Calipore to a chaos of jumbled rock in ten of the Mernian *neska* [minute].

"Come on, Mr. Lambert," Jeremiah Fenton says to me, quietly. "You better quit writing. Time for us to get busy."

IT IS over. That Surahnit host came steadily onward, a fearful green wave engulfing the brooding plain till it reached the landmarks I had picked out as bounding the farthest range of reflector-magnified beam of our captured *kitor*.

I snapped a command to Fenton and the white ray shot blazed out. It reached to meet those advancing squadrons and fingered their serried front line tentatively, as if the light itself were doubtful of its own power.

Those green-clad forms melted to nothingness!

Strangely, I felt no elation, no such burst of jubilation as surged up from the breathless city, surged up in a great roar of sound from the Taphetnit watching upon the Wall. I played that destroying spray of artificial sunlight up and down the gallant ranks. I watched them dribble and melt down and film the rock with a glistening yellow pool and knew the victory was mine, and the taste of it was as ashes.

The world above was safe from the ancient race that had planned to reconquer it, but I knew I should never see it again.

I was thinking, in that moment, of an auburn-haired, pert-faced girl who had stood in the dim grayness of before-dawn and pointed to a winding gravel path. I was hearing her voice tremendous in my ears.

"Look, doctor," she was saying, "see that swirl of ground mist there. Doesn't it look almost like a little mannikin?"

THERE REMAINED, after the light-beam flashed, a few Surahnit that it had not destroyed—fortunate Mernians who had been completely immunized before Court Stone had injected the viosterol into the veins of the Life-Drinkers victims. Luckily none of these had been near the blast-projectors and though they fought gallantly they were overwhelmed by the swarms of Taphetnit who darkened the sky as soon as I shut off the beam Jeremiah Fenton dubbed, "the flaming sword."

True to their gentle nature, the Winged Ones attempted to capture rather than kill their ancient enemies, and they brought in a number of prisoners. Among these was Vanark.

The dark faced Rata, still snarling and defiant despite his defeat, threatened Antil and the Taphetnit with a dreadful vengeance, but in the midst of his tirade a messenger arrived from the Nal Surah proposing a truce and a conference between the two Mernian races to formulate a treaty to govern their future relations in the cavern.

The Winged Ones honored me by insisting upon my acting as one of their representatives, with Antil and Lura and a half-dozen others of their own people. I knew that the rest of my life would be spent among them, and I accepted.

The conference was held at once. I shall never forget Antil's speech in answer to the Nal's request for the Taphetnit's terms.

"We have no terms," he said. "We grieve that there has been this strife between us, and we desire nothing more than that our two races shall dwell henceforth in peace and friendship within this cavern. Different in certain respects as we are, we are yet brethren and as brethren we should work together for the common happiness of all Mernia.

"Tashna is yours and Calinore is ours and in each city we shall continue to dwell as we have been accustomed. For the rest, we propose that an equal number of Taphetnit be admitted to the Ratanit, and that this council govern Mernia for the peace and happiness of all Mernia. That is all."

So it was agreed. We returned to Calinore a very happy delegation feeling that despite all its limitations the great cavern within the earth will henceforth be a very pleasant place in which to live.

WE GATHERED at last in the house that had been Seela's and now was Antil's, the group, small but oddly assorted, that had endured so much together. There were Antil and Leeahlee, Felton and myself, and Nalinah. So much had happened that I found it hard to realize it was only the end of the second *ranhaltin* since Vanark had brought me to this strange, subterranean world that henceforth would be my home.

The girls had prepared a meal of *fortlik* and the wine they called *zingbar*. We sat down at the table, but before we began to eat, Antil rose. He stood there, a shining, handsome youth still vibrant, still jaunty despite the weariness that must have crept sluggishly in his veins as it crept in mine.

"My friends," he commenced. "We have come to the end of an arduous journey and at last we have a little time to think of ourselves. You all know, I am sure, how very happy I am with the issue of our long struggle with the peace that was ratified this day and will reign henceforth in this beloved Mernia of mine. You all share the happiness with me, and I wish to share with you another more personal happiness."

His glowing eyes strayed along the table and found Lee-ahlee's gray ones, and I knew what it was he meant. "I have dwelt all my life in Calinore," he continued, "and though I grew to know the Taphetnit as my people, as my very dear people, yet was I lonely always for my own kind. I am lonely no longer, my friends. I shall never be lonely again. I—I—" he stuttered suddenly. His face broke into a boyish smile. "Friends—Lee-ahlee has promised to be my wife. Leeahlee—I can't believe it yet but she says it is so."

I jumped to my feet, raising a goblet of *zingbar* in my hand. "Drink! To Antil and Leeahlee and their happiness! Drink! And no heel taps."

When we had drunk that toast, I remained standing. "Friends," I said, and there was a quiver in my voice. "Friends, I too have something to say to you. Or rather, to say to one of you, before the others."

I half turned so that I was facing Nalinah, so that I was looking into the blue depths of her eyes. "Nalinah," I said, slowly, distinctly. "In a certain book that had lived for many centuries among us of the Upper World, that lives still and will forever, there is a tale of two people of stranger races who met, and loved. In that book it tells how one of these said to the other, I will go with thee and be thy spouse. Thy people will be my people, and thy race my race.

"Nalinah, my dear, I say that to you now. Will you go with me and be my bride?"

I saw a great joy, a great happiness, flare into the sweet face I had learned to love. And then I saw it fade beneath a film of gray. I saw the warm lips of old rose move in a wistful smile.

"Thank you, my Hula," I heard them say. "You offer me as great an honor as ever man can to maid. But have you thought, really thought of what it would mean were I to accept that which you tender? You have heard Antil, just now. The Taphetnit were my people, my very dear people, yet was I lonely always for my own kind. If you wed me and remain here always, always you will be lonely."

"Yes," I murmured. "Yes. But—" I threw my arms wide in a hopeless gesture. "But whether or not you take me, I must still remain here."

She smiled again, that tender, pathetic smile. "Hula. While you were gone in Tashna, I went to Vanark. What I said to him matters not, but he told me finally that which I wanted to know of him. Hula, you can return, and very simply too. All you need do is lie bathed in the sun's full bright rays for a single hour."

"Nalinah! Vanark hates me, and he hates you. What was it you told him, what was it you promised him in exchange for that secret?"

The tiny oval of her countenance was a pallid mask, and her eyes were glazed, expressionless. "Vanark does not hate me," she said in dead monotone. "Or rather that virulent hate of his was born of a love that once I spurned. I told him that now, seeing him weak and defeated, I had learned that I loved him. I—I was wedded to him, Hula, in that cell of his, just before you returned from Tashna."

EPILOGUE

Letter from Hugh Lambert, B.S., M.Sc., F.A.G.S., F.R.G.S., etc.:

Dear Zagat:

You have asked me to finish up the tale of that unbelievable adventure of mine.

Let me skip to the moment when Fenton and I awoke on the shore of Lake Wanooka.

We were stark naked, and our bodies were wet with the perspiration brought out on them by the sun, still pretty hot even though we were well into autumn.

I ached all over, every muscle, every sinew of me. I felt as though someone had been going over me with a padded bludgeon, pound-

ing me to insensibility. But I didn't mind that. I didn't mind anything. For as I looked about me, I saw grass and bushes. I saw the old lake glimmering in the bright, early morning sunlight, and I could see the opposite bank, the hill rising from it, the old familiar hill I had looked at all summer. I was lying on a pebbly beach, and a grasshopper that leaped on my thigh and leaped off was half the size of my little finger.

From somewhere came the distant, deep tolling of a bell. It came again, welling slowly and lazily through the morning hush.

"It's Sunday," Fenton said. "That's the bell of the Four Corners Methodist Church and it only rings on Sunday."

"Sunday," I repeated, staring at him. "But it can't be. It was Thursday night when this thing began, and I was down there only two—two ranhaltinit. Two—" Then the amazing truth struck me. "Good Lord!" I groaned. "I should have realized it from the war the day and night didn't match up when I made that visit here. Time runs differently up here and down below. Time in one place is entirely different from that in the other."

"Everything is different there and here," the farmer replied. "But me, I'm glad I'm back. I want to see some people, some humans. That's what I want now. But we can't go prospecting around, naked like this."

I replied, jumping up, "I don't care whether I'm seen nude or not. But if you're so blooming modest we'll duck through the woods to the guest house. There's always a couple of bathing suits lying around there that people leave from year to year."

We did exactly that. I left the sheets there with Fenton, on which I'd written what had happened, and stole up through the woods to the infirmary. I heard girls voices.

Then I stepped out into the pathway.

The two girls, standing in their bathrobes just outside the infirmary door, didn't see me at once. I looked at them, at the two of them, eating them with my eyes.

I thought of them as I had seen them last, giants coming into the infirmary office. I remembered the look on Edith's face, and I remembered Ann dropping in a faint.

I thought of how Edith had leaped at once to carry out the behest of my message, so tremendously important.

I looked at Ann, so glamorous, and so very beautiful.

I called to them. I called a name.

The name was "Edith!"

She looked up, and saw me. She came to me, came into the arms I held out to receive her.*

It was only two weeks since I had come back from that weird adventure of mine and already it seemed as though it had never happened, never could have happened. One night, however, the moon streaming in through the window of the little infirmary room woke me. I listened to Edith's quiet breathing. I stared at the tangled, snakelike shadows of stripped tree-limbs on the ceiling, and there was no sleep in me. Gradually, so imperceptibly that I did not notice when it began, a feeling that I had forgotten stole over me.

It was the lake. The lake was calling me again. Calling me down to its shore.

I slid stealthily out of bed, hardly knowing what I was doing. Barefoot as I was, I tiptoed out of the room, out of the infirmary door, down through the woods to the bank of the waters.

The moonlight laid a shimmering, silver film over the quiet waters. Yards from shore that film deepened in color became almost violet.

A black bubble broke the glimmering surface just there. A tiny form lifted out of the waves. Dripping arms rose to its head, stripped back a hood that covered it.

I saw an aureole of flaxen hair. I saw a tiny doll's face, oval and sharp-chinned and sad. I saw miniature arms extend to me, gemmed by flashing droplets.

---

*   Editor's note: Hugh Lambert here tells of the jubilation with which his return was received, and how after a while it was decided that the real story of what had happened should be kept secret for a time at least. Mr. Lambert then goes back to fill the blank I have already noted, between the end of Jeremiah Fenton's story and his own fight with Talirn on the ledge.

Jethro Parker never knew that he was not really a victim of the same disease from which the others suffered. His Martha was so grateful to Doctor Stone for the care the physician had lavished on her husband that she forbade Parker to even mention the matter of the vanished tramp again.

Edith Horne and Hugh Lambert were married in the Four Corners Church the following Sunday. Ann Doring acted as bridesmaid and Jeremiah Fenton as best man. The happy couple for some inexplicable reason, decided to spend their honeymoon at the Camp, now deserted. It is with an incident there that Hugh Lambert closes his letter to me.—A.L.Z.

The water was suddenly cold on my feet. I was wading out into the lake wading out toward that tiny, pathetic form.

"Good-by!" I don't know whether I heard that voice, tinkling like a silver bell, or whether I imagined it. "Good-by, my Hula!"

She was gone. Nalinah was gone. There was nothing out there but the rippling shimmer of moonlight upon the lake. There was nothing there at all.

ABOUT THE AUTHOR

ARTHUR LEO ZAGAT (1895–1949), like fellow writer Erle Stanley Gardner, was a lawyer who forsook his profession in favor of the uncertain life of a pulp magazine writer.

A veteran of the First World War who attended City College of New York and Bordeaux University, Zagat graduated from Fordham University Law School in 1929, with the intent of practicing law. But it was the beginning of the Great Depression, and so he turned instead to writing with his fellow lawyer, Nathaniel Schachner.

Their first collaboration, "The Tower of Evil," appeared in *Wonder Stories Quarterly*, Summer 1930. Ten others followed, all appearing in the top Science Fiction titles of the era, *Amazing Stores, Wonder Stories* and *Astounding Stories of Super-Science*. They also sold to *Weird Tales*. In 1934, Zagat struck out on his own, branching out to write for Popular Publications magazines, where he made a name for himself writing detective stories and contributing to Popular's trio of weird menace magazines, *Dime Mystery Stories, Horror Stories* and *Terror Tales*. Thus he became known as "The Horror Story Man." He was also prolific in *Detective Tales, Ace G-Man Stories* and *Strange Detective Mysteries*.

When he had more than one story in a magazine, Zagat used the pseudonym of Grendon Alzee—the last name a play on his initials. For Culture Publications' sole entry in the weird menace sub-genre, *Spicy Mystery Stories,* Zagat wrote as Morgan Lafay.

He is said to have written as Anton York, which was the name of the hero of Eando Binder's famous story about an immortal. Curiously, Arthur Leo Zagat was known to some of his colleagues as Leo, but to intimates as "Bob."

Few series emerged from his typewriter over a 20-year writing career comprising an estimated 500 published stories. His longest and

Arthur Leo Zagat

most famous, Doc Turner of Morris Street, ran for nearly a decade in the back pages of *The Spider.* It was one of the most popular backup series in any similar pulp magazine. Featuring the ministrations of kindly old inner-city pharmacist Andrew "Doc" Turner, it was inspired by Zagat's period of working at his father's pharmacy while attending Fordham.

Zagat's stories starring Steven "Tiger" Carlin appeared in Street & Smith's *Detective Story Magazine* in the early 1940s. Carlin was assisted by an elderly neighborhood druggist, Richard Frost.

Red Finger had a much shorter run, of course. But he was the closest to a pulp superhero that Zagat ever penned.

Zagat was also known for his fantasy serials written for *Argosy,* among them, "Drink We Deep," "Seven Out of Time" and the "Tomorrow" stories featuring a boy Tarzan named Dikar battling Japanese invaders in a future conquered America. He also appeared in *Blue Book.*

During World War II, Zagat served as Chairman of the Pulp Writers' Section of the Authors' Guild, a branch of the Authors' League of America, where his legal background proved invaluable. Zagat left to join the Office of War Information, dividing his time between his New York apartment and his desk in Washington, while continuing to turn out stories. After the war, he taught short-story writing at New York University and was heavily involved in tutoring returning soldiers in the art of fiction writing. He subsequently founded the Writers' Work Shop for Veterans.

A lifelong resident of the Bronx, Arthur Leo Zagat died of a heart attack on April 3, 1949, at the age of 53. Of himself, he once wrote: "I have had no adventures in far lands. I have worked in a drugstore. I have sold insurance from door to door. I have ridden in the subway and walked the city streets with eyes and ears open. I have read Mother Goose… I do not think of myself as an artist. I am a tradesman, a merchant of tales. It is the way I make my living, and I behave towards it as any man behaves towards his means of livelihood."

TARZAN AND THE JEWELS OF OPAR
BY ARGOSY'S GREATEST AUTHOR
EDGAR RICE BURROUGHS

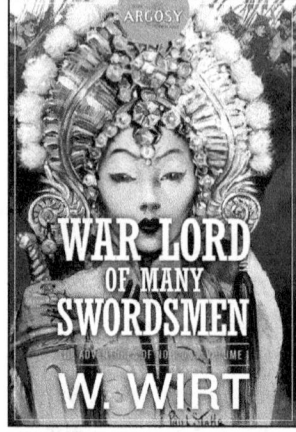

WAR LORD OF MANY SWORDSMEN
W. WIRT

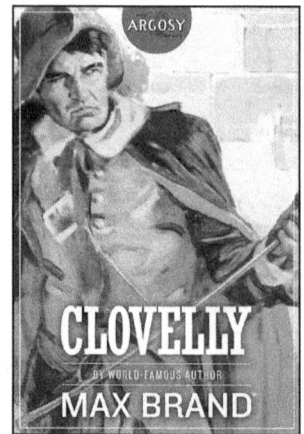

CLOVELLY
BY WORLD-FAMOUS AUTHOR
MAX BRAND

DRINK WE DEEP
THE SCIENCE FICTION CLASSIC
ARTHUR LEO ZAGAT

THE GUN-BRAND
BY NORTHWEST FICTION LEGEND
JAMES B. HENDRYX

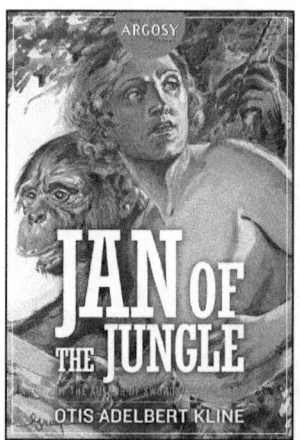

JAN OF THE JUNGLE
OTIS ADELBERT KLINE

THE BLUE FIRE PEARL
THE COMPLETE ADVENTURES OF SINGAPORE SAMMY VOLUME 1
GEORGE F. WORTS

THE MOON POOL & THE CONQUEST OF THE MOON POOL
BY THE INSPIRATION FOR H.P. LOVECRAFT
ABRAHAM MERRITT

MINIONS OF THE MOON
THE SCIENCE FICTION CLASSIC
WILLIAM GREY BEYER

ALIAS THE NIGHT WIND
BY THE CREATOR OF NICK CARTER
VARICK VANARDY

THE ARGOSY LIBRARY™

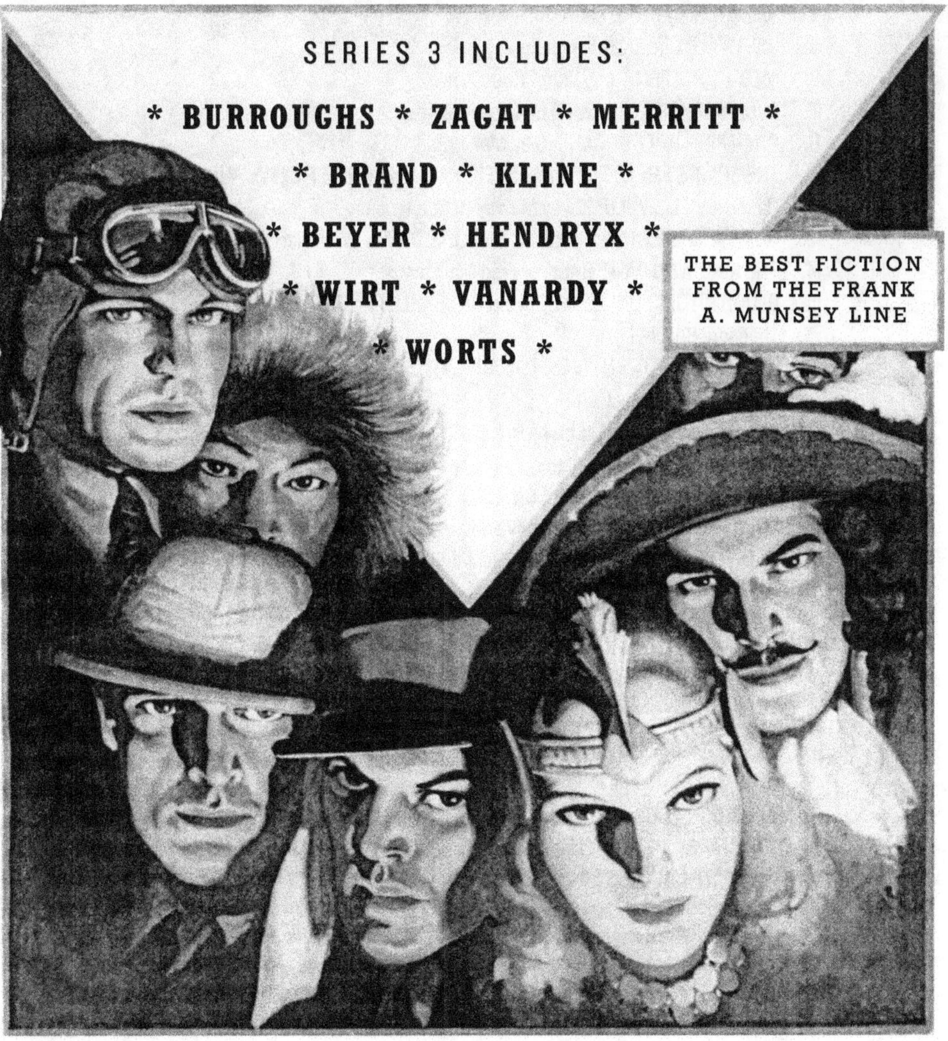

www.ingramcontent.com/pod-product-compliance
Lightning Source LLC
Chambersburg PA
CBHW071830020726
47502CB00004B/1297